CHRISTMAS AT THE LAKESIDE HOTEL

MELINDA HUBER

Christmas at the Lakeside Hotel

All rights reserved.

Copyright © 2023 Linda Huber

The right of Linda Huber to be identified as the Author of this Work has been asserted by her in accordance with the Copyright Designs and Patents Act 1988.

Apart from any use permitted under UK copyright law, this publication may only be reproduced, stored or transmitted, in any form, or by any means, with the prior permission in writing of the author. All characters appearing in this work are fictitious. Any resemblance to real persons, living or dead, is purely coincidental.

1

Friday, 30th November

Did she have everything? Carol Peterson squeezed a pair of tennis socks into the larger of her two suitcases and went back to the list on the chest of drawers. Her swimming gear would go in the Switzerland case, so the one she was taking to Australia was finished, and just as well, because you couldn't get another thing in there. Now for the smaller one, and blimey, packing for seven days in a Swiss spa hotel followed by four weeks in boiling hot sunshine in Perth meant she had to cram almost her entire wardrobe into these two cases. And that was before you even thought about Christmas presents for the grandchildren and the obligatory two tins of tomato soup, the kind the kids loved but was hard to get in Australia.

She slid her winter boots into a plastic bag and put them in the bottom of the small case – and now it was half full already. Maybe she should wear them on the flight? Oh, dear... Maureen's suggestion of the spa week first 'to make you even more beautiful for your family Christmas in Oz' was maybe a good idea, but the logistics were complicated. They were booked in for seven days of pre-Christmas indulgence in the Lakeside Hotel and Spa, which Maureen's sister had raved about last summer. Afterwards, Maureen would come home to London and Carol would continue her journey to Perth.

And how wonderful it would be to see Barry and Diane and the children again. Carol hugged herself, then sighed. It was such a long time since her last visit – Emma, her little granddaughter, would be four soon, and Carol had never seen baby Jonny in real life. He wasn't even a baby now; he was fifteen months old and she'd never cuddled him. It was tough when your family was so far away. Bursts of intensive visits plus Skype didn't make up for the lack of regular contact. Barry had wanted her to go with them when they emigrated five years ago, but it hadn't felt like the right time to Carol. Her life was here in London – or so she'd thought at the time. Now, with the reality of growing grandchildren she never got to hug, Carol wasn't so sure. If Barry asked her the same question again, and it was odds-on he would, what would she say this time? It was the million-dollar question, and really, there could only be one answer. She'd saved up six weeks' holidays and decimated her bank account for this trip, and when she came home at the end of it, she'd be confronted with another year and a half before she could afford to go again. Carol lifted the photo of Emma and Jonny, and pressed it to her heart. Eight more sleeps and she'd have them in her arms.

She wound a strap round the Australia case before organising the waiting piles of clothes into the Switzerland one, pressing her meds bag in at the top. Fingers crossed she wasn't going to need any of these. Had she packed the nasal spray? No, she hadn't – and oh, if only her ears behaved themselves this time. The six weeks after the last flight home from Australia had been filled with pain and antibiotics followed by more pain and more antibiotics. Talk about the ear infection from hell... Carol shivered. Imagine if she was sick for her whole lovely visit. Please, no, that mustn't happen.

'You'll be fine,' she said aloud, determinedly stamping down the insistent little whisper in her head. *You haven't been on a plane since. Supposing you're not fine?*

She zipped up the second case, thinking determinedly cheerful thoughts. She had saved every penny she could for this trip, and she was going to have a good time if it killed her. It *would* be fine. This time tomorrow, she'd be sitting in the dining room at the Lakeside Hotel, eating whatever they ate for dinner there. What *did* they eat in Switzerland? Schnitzel? Fondue? This was her first visit there and she was going to enjoy it.

A car horn tooted outside, and Carol grabbed the large case and bumped it downstairs.

Maureen was on the doorstep and the taxi was waiting by the gate. 'Ready? Good – I'll take your case, shall I? Make sure you lock up properly!'

Carol hid a smile. Typical Maureen. They'd known each other since their schooldays, when Mo's nickname had been Boss Cow. She hadn't mellowed much, either...

Grinning, Carol ran back up for the smaller case, grabbed her hand luggage, and carefully locked the house she wouldn't see again until next year. Heathrow and the evening flight to Zurich, here she came.

***

Tucking a few stray curls into a red woolly hat, Stacy Townsend left the flat at the top of the Lakeside Spa Hotel and clattered down four flights of wooden staircase to the ground floor, checking her gloves were in her jacket pocket as she went. Tomorrow was the first of December; not the time of year to go outside without full winter gear, or not when you lived in north-east Switzerland, anyway. Just ten minutes to go; she'd miss the action if she wasn't quick. This was going to be amazing – Rico, her fiancé and her job-partner too, as he was hotel manager at Lakeside and she was his assistant as well as head nurse in the spa, was going to switch on the brand-new Christmas lights display on the façade. Today was the start of the first ever Lakeside Christmas celebrations and it was going to be the most festive three weeks the old chalet had ever experienced, so heaven help them if this first part didn't go with a bang. Not literally, of course. A quick glance down from the living room balcony five minutes ago had revealed at least fifty people gathering in the darkness in front of the hotel, waiting for the spectacle of the lights, and no doubt waiting for the mulled wine and nibbles that were coming afterwards, too. Thankfully, the weather was doing its bit. No atmospheric snow, true, but the rain the weatherman was threatening them with hadn't arrived yet.

Stacy stuck her head into the hotel kitchen to make sure the mulled wine was on schedule.

'Ooh, that smells fabulous! What have you put in it?'

'Honey, cinnamon, oranges, cloves, and a few other things. And wine, of course. It's my own recipe. Try some.' Rob the chef handed her a spoon, and Stacy dipped it into the steaming cauldron on the stove and sipped.

'Yum. It certainly beats making it with the spice sachets you buy in the supermarket.'

As she expected, he rose to the bait. 'Did you think I'd – oh, very funny. It's five to five, Stace, you'd better get out there. I'll join you with the cauldron in ten minutes.'

Stacy fled, switching off the hallway lights as she went to join the gang on the driveway. The front of the hotel was in darkness now, and the waiting crowd fell silent in anticipation. A biting north wind was whistling across Lake Constance on the other side of the building, and Stacy zipped her jacket right up to her chin. Brr, she was looking forward to warming her hands as well as her insides with a nice mug of Rob's mulled wine. Two minutes to go now, and where was Rico?

He was talking to a reporter from the local paper, the remote control for the lights in one hand.

'Good, you're just in time,' he said, waving the remote at Stacy. 'The timer's set, so they should go on automatically, but I've brought this just in case!'

A car horn blared from the gate before the car it was attached to jerked to a halt at the end of the driveway, and Ralph, Rico's father, leapt out and raced through the crowd to join them.

'Thought I was going to miss the excitement,' he said, hugging Stacy and slapping Rico's shoulder.

Stacy could hardly believe her eyes. Last time she'd heard, Ralph was in his home in Lugano, several hundred kilometres to the south.

'I didn't know you were coming!' She turned to Rico. 'Did you?'

'No – and it's time for the countdown!' He stepped up on the wooden plant container by the door and yelled in Swiss German, 'Ready to count down! With me – ten, nine–'

Stacy joined in, her fingers and toes metaphorically crossed. '–four, three, two, one...'

A pause that felt like eternity hung in the air before lights blazed on the front of the hotel. A long 'Ooh!' came from the crowd, then clapping. Rico jumped down, a huge grin on his face.

Stacy grabbed his arm, hot tears in her eyes making the lights go blurry. Oh, how amazing – the hotel looked like something out of one of those lovely corny old Christmas movies. In place of summery red and pink geraniums in window boxes, they had moving cascades of silvery-white lights, with blue and silver snowflakes dotted irregularly here and there. A large-sized star shone out on each side of the roof, and little clusters of illuminated silver snowflakes were running down the slates from the middle of the top peak. Somehow, Lakeside was managing to look both festive and tasteful.

'Wow – you've done yourselves proud.' Ralph squeezed between them and put one arm around each of them. 'Right – where's this mulled wine I've been hearing about?'

Rico clapped his father's back. 'Right here! And it's great to see you!'

Stacy sipped her mulled wine and nibbled one of Rob's mini pesto pastries while people practically knocked each other over in the rush to tell them how fabulous the first set of Christmas lights on the façade of the Lakeside Hotel looked. This was the life. Everyone was here – hotel guests and employees, friends and some of the locals from Grimsbach too, as well as half the town council and two regional newspapers. Free advertising, just what they needed to kickstart the festive season. Until this year, the hotel had remained closed all December, but the new spa concept meant that people were queueing up for a long or short wellness break around Christmas. This would do their list of regular hotel guests all the good in the world.

Eventually, the promised rain arrived, and the party dispersed.

'I suppose I can bunk down with you?' said Ralph, as they followed the last of the guests inside.

''Course you can,' said Stacy. She linked arms with him as they waited for the lift. 'Our spare room is yours, you know that.' Which was fair enough, as Ralph had spent all his married life in the top-floor flat before gifting the hotel to Rico last Christmas. Now, after a year of hard work, they were running a very profitable business, in spite of the floods and dramas of the previous summer.

Stacy glanced at Ralph as the lift went up. The little smile playing round his mouth told her how pleased he was to be back in the hotel, but… he was thinner than last time she'd seen him, wasn't he? And those shadows under his eyes, what was causing them? He'd gone through a bad time after the death of Rico's mum three years ago, but semi-retirement and relocating to the south of Switzerland to be near his brother Guido and sister-in-law Julia had put the spring back in Ralph's step. He hadn't had baggy eyes like this for a long time. Definitely, it was something to find out about.

'Tell me all the news,' said Ralph, when they were sitting round the kitchen table eating the salmon steaks Stacy had defrosted in honour of Ralph's visit.

Rico leaned back, grinning at his father. 'We're pretty much booked out all December. Two women are arriving from England later tonight, then we'll be full until the changeover next weekend. We have a great Christmas programme planned for the guests, with everything from the Gala Dinner every Thursday to a weekly Christmas biscuit-making demo.'

'Not to mention my nursey talk on creating a New Year Healthy Eating Plan,' said Stacy, giggling.

Ralph roared with laughter. Stacy watched him, only partially convinced he was well. His behaviour seemed no different, but he did look drawn.

He leaned back in his chair, still chuckling. 'You'll go far, you two. I thought I'd stay until mid-week, if that's okay? I wanted to see your lights go on, and I may not manage north again this year. My car's on the way out, but the new one won't arrive until January, and when Guido and Julia come back, we'll have a load of Christmas stuff to do in Lugano.'

His eyes were bright at the prospect, and Stacy patted his arm. Guido and Julia had been on an extended visit to Berlin, where their son Michael lived with his daughter Salome. Two months was a long time; Ralph must have missed the company. Was that the reason for the change in him? He didn't seem ill.

'Sounds like a plan,' said Rico, and Stacy was touched to see how soft his eyes were as he looked at his father. 'But remember, trains exist too! We're hoping you'll come here for some of the Christmas hols as well. We close to guests on the twenty-second, so after that we'll be celebrating Christmas with family and friends. And we want to see more of you and the new car in January too, okay? I won't have much time for gadding around when I start my master's degree in February.'

'You're the boss,' said Ralph, and Stacy hugged herself. What a lovely family she was marrying into.

2

Friday, 30th November

Zurich Airport was all shiny floors and glass. Maureen bustled ahead, and Carol hurried after her, rubbing her left ear as she went. It had blocked almost as soon as they took off and was refusing to pop again, but at least it wasn't painful. And glory, did Maureen think the luggage would appear quicker if she got to baggage reclaim before everyone else did? Carol gave up her pursuit and trailed along in the middle of the crowd of chattering passengers – not that she could hear the people on her left. Pity she didn't have anything to drink, a couple of quick swallows might unblock this stupid ear. She caught up with Maureen at Passport Control, which thankfully wasn't busy, and grabbed the other woman's arm to stop her disappearing into the distance again. Baggage reclaim here they came... Their luggage started circling round on the carousel as soon as they arrived, and Carol grinned to herself. Timing was everything, wasn't it? This must be your famous Swiss efficiency at work.

Luggage piled on a trolley, they made their way downstairs to the train station beneath the airport. It was something over an hour in the train to Grimsbach and the hotel, and they had to change at Romanshorn, another little town by Lake Constance.

Maureen pulled out her mobile as the train left the airport. 'I've to text the hotel and let them know what train we're on. They said they'd have someone meet us at Grimsbach station.'

Carol was impressed. 'That's a good service. A lot of places would leave their guests to get a taxi.'

She stared into the night as the train sped eastwards. Switzerland was like anywhere else in the dark, large and small stations with stretches of blackness between them, and oh, this stupid ear. Carol rubbed the side of her head. It was such a lopsided feeling when one ear was behaving as if it was at the bottom of a large tank of water.

Romanshorn station was open to the elements on three sides, and Carol stepped off the train and bent her head against the ice-cold draught that was blasting along the platform. She wrestled her cases off one train and onto the other, thinking wryly that this journey was as good as a day at the gym. She was going to arrive at the hotel looking as if she'd run all the way from the airport. The second train was tiny, and stopped at several equally tiny places as it meandered along beside the lake. Carol fastened the top button on her jacket as the doors whooshed open yet again and three more well wrapped-up passengers boarded in the middle of an Arctic gust. Oh dear, she should be wearing something on her head. Her poor ears...

Grimsbach station was little bigger than a bus stop, and the wind cut right through Carol's jacket the moment she stepped out of the train. Heavens, going from this to the heat of Perth in the Australian summer was going to be a bit of a contrast. Sort of the reverse of coming out of the sauna and diving into an icy fjord, or something. Shivering, she pulled her cases to the end of the platform, where a young man was waiting beside a minibus.

'Lakeside Hotel?' he said, and seized Carol's larger case when she nodded. 'I'm Alex, Lakeside receptionist and general dogsbody. Good trip?'

His English was pretty much perfect, and Maureen immediately launched into a description of their journey. Carol relaxed into her seat in the minibus, glad that it was heated, and glad that the people at the hotel spoke such good English. A bracing week in wintry Switzerland would toughen her up nicely, then she'd be off to sunny Oz to relax. Christmas on the beach... Bring it on.

'Oh, look, Carol! Isn't it lovely?'

Maureen clutched her arm as they swung into the hotel grounds, and Carol jerked out of her daydream. The building was illuminated like something on a picture postcard, a traditional Swiss chalet set against a deep black backdrop that must be Lake Constance. Far-away lights on the other side were twinkling bravely, though the water was a black hole in the darkness. Surprise zipped through Carol – what a huge lake it must be. She'd see it properly tomorrow.

'All we need is snow to complete the picture!' Alex yanked the handbrake on and jumped out to deal with the luggage.

Carol followed Maureen into the warmth of the hotel, where a tall, undecorated Christmas tree was waiting to one side of a deep leather sofa, a crate of presumably decorations at its foot.

Alex nodded towards them. 'That's tomorrow's job. Let's get you ladies checked in and upstairs.'

Maureen wheeled the cases to the lift while Carol signed the form he produced and accepted two swipe cards for their room. She rubbed the side of her head again as they jerked up to the second floor. Her ear was buzzing now. Hopefully, it would pop soon and everything would be all right. You didn't feel right with one ear blocked, did you? Carol shivered again.

3

Saturday, 1st December, morning

Rico hauled the Christmas tree in its tub a couple of yards away from the sofa in the front hallway. They didn't want falling pine needles peppering sitting guests, and they didn't want any kids on the sofa to be tempted to start mountaineering up the tree, either. He stood back to admire his work.

'Nicely positioned,' said Alex, leaning over the reception desk and holding up his phone to take a photo.

Rico grinned. 'Are you doing the before and after pics? You can give me a hand with the decs while it's quiet.'

He heaved the crate of tree decorations Stacy had bought onto the coffee table, and opened a box of painted wooden figures – snowmen, Santas and the like. Where to start? He'd never decorated such a huge tree; the top was only centimetres from the ceiling.

Alex came over with a stepladder. 'Start at the top, and work down,' he said. 'When I was a kid, Mum sometimes helped put up the tree in her church, and that was their technique.'

He climbed onto the steps, and Rico handed up the box of figures. Denise, Alex's mum, had a hotel background too, but agoraphobia prevented her from working outside her home now. She was in a good phase at the moment, but still – Alex had a complicated life for a number of reasons.

Rico rummaged to see what else was in the crate. 'Doing anything nice at Christmas?'

Alex's sigh made the top of the tree shiver. 'Christmas dinner at Mum's, as usual, but it'll be just the two of us. Zoe's playing at a big concert on the twenty-fourth, another on the twenty-fifth and then the orchestra's off on tour on the twenty-seventh. For five months. New Year in Vienna, next up, Prague, and when they've done Europe, they're crossing the Atlantic. She can't wait.'

Rico winced. Alex and Zoe's long-distance relationship wouldn't have worked for him, but then, Alex didn't have much choice. Zoe was an amazingly talented violinist; her music was her passion and everything else, including poor Alex, came a long way behind. Rico blinked up at the other man, but Alex was grinning again.

'Of course, before Prague and Vienna and New York she has a very prestigious engagement right here at Lakeside. That final Gala Dinner's going to be something else!'

Rico handed up a couple of Rudolphs. Good for Alex. It was in his nature to look on the bright side, and it meant the younger man was able to juggle his life like this, with a girlfriend in Zurich, a job right up in the corner of Switzerland and a mother who often needed his support. Thankfully, Stacy and Denise got on well, so Stace was able to help out a bit too.

Rico hung a snowman on a low branch and inhaled deeply. You couldn't beat a real tree for that Christmassy smell. They were having real ones here and in the dining room, and smaller, artificial ones in the new snug bar and spa rooms. In all, he and Stacy would be decorating seven trees today, which possibly explained why Stace had opted for a second cup of coffee with Ralph instead of an early start in the hallway.

'Hello? Earth to Rico? Do you want more decs on this tree, or are we going for the minimalistic look?' Alex was empty-handed again.

Rico laughed, and passed up a box of silver stars.

'Hang on. I have to man the desk.' Alex handed the box back and jumped down, and Rico twisted round. Two elderly guests were standing at reception, a brochure clutched in the woman's hand.

Rico stepped up on the ladder. He was busy interspersing stars with the figures already hanging when another two guests, both fifty-something women, emerged from the lift clutching their spa baskets, one of them talking quickly in a south-of-England accent. Rico smiled down at them and was stretching round the tree with a star when the silent woman stumbled, crashing into the tree and grabbing the stepladder for support. Caught off balance, Rico leapt down and landed beside the talkative woman, who was now holding her friend up.

The talkative woman gave her friend a little shake. 'Heavens, Carol, what on earth happened? Are you all right?'

The other woman was rubbing her head with one hand. She nodded. 'I'm so sorry. I just – I felt dizzy for a second. I'm okay now. Are *you* all right?' She blinked at Rico.

'Never better, don't worry. Come and sit down.' He helped her to the sofa, where she fished in her bag for a tissue and blew her nose. Her face creased in pain, and Rico frowned. Something was up.

Alex hurried over with a glass of water. 'Here you are, Mrs Peterson. Shall I see if there's a nurse in the spa, Rico?'

Rico shook his head. 'Call Stacy. The spa's pretty full this morning; we shouldn't take Margrit away. No, we need to get you checked,' he added, as Carol protested. 'That was a big wobble.'

'Honestly, I'm fine. I don't want to make a fuss.' Carol looked upset as Alex stepped away to speak into his phone.

A minute or two later the lift doors pinged open and both Stacy and Ralph emerged. Stacy came straight over and sat down beside Carol. 'I'm Stacy, one of the nurses here. What's the problem?'

Rico watched as she took Carol's pulse, her eyes never leaving the woman's face, then felt her forehead. It was always fascinating, seeing Stace deal with people. Reassurance and comfort streamed out of her, and Carol and her friend relaxed visibly.

'I think it's just a sniffle,' said Carol. 'I do get dizzy sometimes.'

'Your temp seems normal. Let's get you into the medical room and see what your blood pressure's doing,' said Stacy.

Carol stood up, and the three women headed slowly into the spa. Alex was busy at reception now, and Rico went back to the tree. Ralph was staring after Stacy and her patient, his face thoughtful.

Rico slapped his back. 'Panic over. Come and help me with this?'

Ralph remained motionless for a moment before heaving a huge sigh. 'Sure. I was on my way to the sauna, but I can be all yours for half an hour.'

Rico handed his father a packet of tinsel, mulling over the hotel's medical staff. Stacy and Margrit were the only trained nurses, although the spa attendants all had Red Cross certificates as well as tub training. The doctor was in the village. Was that enough for a spa hotel?

***

'Ah – you do have a slight temp. Shall we see what a lie-down and a couple of paracetamol will do? Maybe you picked up a little cold on the plane yesterday.'

Stacy binned the thin plastic earpiece and put the thermometer back in the cupboard. By the look of Carol, it was more likely to be a horrible stonking cold than a little one, but there was no point worrying before the event.

'Oh dear. I hope it's not my ear again. No hot tub for me today – I'm so sorry, Maureen.'

Carol blinked at her friend. She was smiling, but her eyes were bleak and Stacy was glad she'd agreed to a rest. Poor soul, nobody enjoyed being on holiday and not feeling a hundred percent.

Maureen launched into a monologue about the flu she'd had last winter, and Stacy filled a glass with cold water and handed it to Carol with the pills. 'Maureen can try the tubs while you're resting, don't worry. Let's get you upstairs.'

She ushered the two women back into the spa, handed Maureen over to Sabine, the attendant on duty that morning, then took Carol's arm on the way back to the twin room the two women were sharing. What Carol needed now was a nap, and Maureen seemed to be one of those people who were constantly on the move and chatting.

Carol lay back on her bed, and Stacy pulled the curtains. 'I'll be back in an hour or two to see how you're doing,' she said firmly. 'You mentioned your ears downstairs. Have you had problems with them?'

Carol closed bleary eyes. 'I did in the past, but that was, um, years ago. I'm sure I'll be better after a rest.'

'Fingers crossed.' Stacy put a card beside Carol's phone on the table. 'My mobile number's there. If you need anything before I come back, just give me a call.'

Carol nodded. 'Please don't worry about me. The pills are helping already.'

'Have a good snooze!' Stacy gave Carol her most reassuring nursey smile, and closed the door quietly behind her. Now to see how Rico was getting on with the Christmas tree. She ran down to reception, where Rico was back up his ladder.

'Just the lights left,' he said, arranging them in a spiral around the branches.

Stacy plugged them in behind the sofa and clicked the switch. Immediately, tiny coloured lights twinkled all over the tree, and three guests waiting at reception clapped. Stacy gave them a mock curtsey. This was fun, making Christmas happen in their hotel. They'd put masses of ads in British magazines: *Spend Advent in Switzerland at the Lakeside Spa,* and *The Lakeside Spa Hotel in Snowy Switzerland – the perfect place for your Christmas break*, and it had worked. A high proportion of the guests over the next four weeks were from the UK, mostly middle-aged couples, though there were some younger ones coming in the third week too, and next Saturday they even had a couple of honeymooners. What they rarely had on the guest list now was children. Two had arrived with their parents yesterday afternoon, but apart from a three-year-old coming in the final week, they were the only ones staying in the whole Advent period. It was a pity; Christmas was such a special time for kids. Stacy spent a moment imagining what it would be like when she and Rico had their own little family to help decorate trees and bring the magic into Christmas. Oh, she couldn't wait... and unfortunately, having kids was still at the wishful thinking stage, wasn't it? With her busy in the hotel, and Rico starting his master's degree soon, they didn't have time for babies yet. Stacy sighed.

She followed Rico into the restaurant, where another tree was waiting to be decorated. This one was the centrepiece on the little dais at one end of the room.

'We'll put the throne for the *Samiclaus* up here at the Gala Dinner on Thursday,' said Rico, waving at the floor beside the tree. 'He can come in after the main course and I'll introduce him, then he can do his round of the tables while people are having dessert and coffee.'

Stacy laughed. Most of the guests wouldn't be familiar with the European tradition of St Nikolaus – or Samiclaus, in Switzerland – who distributed sweets and oranges on December 6th, after telling people off for their sins during the past year. 'They'll love it. And Hans'll be a brilliant Samiclaus.'

Hans was the sixty-something, pleasantly rounded owner of the Alpstein Hotel further along the lake bank, and he was always in demand to be Samiclaus because of his thick white beard. With a long red coat and bishop's hat, he was the best person Stacy could imagine for the part.

Now, she glanced at Rico. They were alone; Ralph had gone off for a heat in the sauna followed by a soak in the tub room. This was a good time to see if Rico had noticed anything.

'How does your dad seem to you? I thought he was looking a bit strained.'

Rico stood still. 'Is he? I hadn't noticed.' He frowned. 'But now you mention it, he does have bags under his eyes that weren't there before. Perhaps you should give him a check-up or something? You know what he's like – he won't listen to me.'

'I'll do my best.' Stacy pulled a face. 'Giving Ralph a check-up' was going to be considerably easier said than done. He was sensitive about his health, and he also tended to overindulge in the *vino rosso*, especially when he was feeling down. She'd need to plan her attack very carefully, or he'd refuse point-blank.

She stood back to admire the finished tree. 'Lovely. Let's put the Advent crown on the desk at reception now.'

The Advent crown was actually a row of four fat white candles side by side on a bed of pine tree and holly sprigs on a rectangular pottery plate that was almost invisible under the greenery. Stacy arranged it on one side of the desk. Tomorrow, the first Sunday in Advent, they would light the tallest candle, then next Sunday they'd light the second to accompany it, and so on. She stood back and admired the front hall – with the tree and the candles and the lovely Christmassy smell, the first Lakeside Christmas was beginning to come alive. And now she'd better check her first Christmas patient – and hopefully, her last.

4

Saturday, 1st December, afternoon

Carol was still dozing on top of her bed when a tapping noise came at the door, and for a moment she lay still. That would be Maureen back from the spa room. Bye-bye peace and quiet. Oh dear, she was being horrible, but peace and quiet was what she needed to chase off this cold or whatever it was, and Maureen was such a chatterbox. Her ear gave a sudden twinge, and a cold shiver rippled through Carol. This was exactly how it had started after the flight home from Australia, and it was scaring her silly now. A day or two feeling just slightly off, and then – bam! The infection that stuck around forever. She was *not* going to be ill here. End of. Ah, well, better sit up and listen to Maureen's account of the tubs.

She was gathering her strength when the noise came again before the door cracked open. Oh – it was Stacy. Carol swung her legs over and sat up. She did feel a bit better, actually. Good.

'Come in, I'm awake.'

'Sorry, I didn't mean to startle you. I used the master keycard. How are you feeling now?' Stacy sat down on Carol's bed and reached out to take her pulse.

'Almost normal. I thought you were Maureen coming back, so I didn't rush to open the door.'

Stacy felt her forehead. 'Pulse okay, and your temp seems fine too. You look pale, though – like a woman who needs a holiday! Maureen's still in a tub, and she's going for a massage afterwards, so she won't be back for a while.'

Plenty more peace and quiet to worry in, then. Carol held out her arm to have her blood pressure taken, then watched as the machine beeped down. Should she tell Stacy about that last infection? No, she'd cross everything she had that this was just a bit of a cold and she'd be fine after a good night's sleep.

'Your BP's normal now, thank goodness. You'll live. See me or the other nurse first if you're thinking about venturing into a tub tomorrow, though.'

'I will. I'll try not to knock your husband off his ladder next time, too!'

'Oh, we're not married yet – that's next year's bit of excitement. And no harm done, don't worry. Rico's lived in the hotel all his life, so he's used to guests rampaging around!'

Carol laughed. Chatting to Stacy was healing. If a trained nurse thought she'd be fine, it was odds-on she would be.

'Where are you getting married? I'm guessing your family's in England?'

'Yes, in Cheshire. We're having the civil ceremony here plus a party in the hotel, then the honeymoon, then a church blessing in Elton Abbey. Mum's delighted – she gets to choose two mother-of-the-bride outfits!'

'Good for her. I bet she misses you, though.' Like she missed Barry… A lump rose in Carol's throat. But this time next week, she'd be en route for Australia.

Stacy pulled a face. 'She does, and I can see you know the feeling too.'

Carol nodded dumbly, then put a hand on the younger woman's arm. 'Families are complicated, and the world isn't as small a place as we all like to think. It's a privilege if you have your nearest and dearest close by. I guess Rico's family is here? I saw in the brochure that this is a family-run hotel.'

'Yes. Rico's parents – that was his dad with us downstairs this morning – ran the place until a couple of years ago, when his mum died. We've taken over now, though Ralph's still very interested, of course.'

Ralph. How strange… Carol sat still, bittersweet memories flitting though her head. Ralph had been her David's middle name, and come to think of it, the two men were rather similar. Same kind face – and the eyes watching her this morning had been concerned.

Stacy packed up her blood pressure machine, and Carol stood up. 'I think I'll go down and have a look at those things for sale in your cabinet downstairs. I'd like to buy some nice smellies to take back to London, and some to go to Australia, too.'

'Do – we're very pleased with our spa shop!' Stacy looked round the room, then lifted the shop brochure from the table. 'You'll find everything here, too, and if you want a little basket of spa items put together specially, you can pick 'n' mix the products as you like and put in an order at reception.' She gave Carol a smile and a wave, and was gone.

Downstairs, Carol stood in front of the glass cabinet, comparing pictures in the brochure with the articles in real life. Little bottles of salts and different oils, soaps and hand creams, body lotions and things like face flannels and bath bombs – crumbs, she could easily spend a small fortune here. The problem was going to be transporting it all to the places she wanted it.

'Are you feeling better now? Need any help?'

Ralph Weber was by her elbow, and Carol squinted at him. She'd been right, he did have a kind face.

'I want some things to take home to London, and maybe a few to go to Australia with me first. It's the logistics I can't get my head round.'

He pouted, his head on one side. 'I'm guessing your winter woollies will be staying at Zurich while you're in Australia? You could leave the London things there too, and take some light sachets etcetera to Australia.'

Carol smiled. 'It's twenty-eight degrees where my son lives at the moment, no winter woollies needed there! And you're right, I'm leaving one case in a locker at the airport. The things I buy to take home can stay there too. What do you recommend?'

Ralph smiled. 'My sister-in-law likes the delphinium hand cream, and I'm sure it comes in smaller tubes than the ones here. I'll look out a sample for you. And if you want salts for Australia, Flavia can make up some sachets of those too, instead of the bottles.'

'Thank you. Your – Stacy has just been to see me. She was very reassuring.' Carol touched her ear. Her hearing was back to normal, but the ear wasn't quite right yet, was it? She pushed the anxious feeling away.

His face lit up. 'Stacy's a gem. We're so lucky to have her. I'll leave you to make your selection, and do ask someone – Alex or myself – if you want anything more.'

He gave her an oddly touching little bow, and moved away into the restaurant. Carol stared after him.

***

By mid-afternoon, Rico was finishing the last Christmas tree, the one in Kim the manicurist's nail parlour, and good job this was the last one – the box of decs was all but empty. He arranged a silver star on the top and stepped back, his phone buzzing in his pocket. Ah, this was Hans from the Alpstein; he'd be calling about the arrangements for his Samiclaus appearance on Thursday night.

Rico tapped connect, and the other man's guttural Swiss German boomed in his ear. 'Rico, I'm sorry.'

Dismay thudded into Rico's middle. Whatever was coming now, he probably wasn't going to like it. He abandoned the tree and headed through to the office behind reception. 'Let's have it, then.'

'My mother's broken her hip. We're driving down to Lausanne tomorrow, and I'm pretty sure we won't be back by Thursday.'

Rico flinched. Lausanne was on Lake Geneva in the diagonally opposite corner of Switzerland, well over three hours away by car. This wasn't what they needed, but poor Hans... 'Oh no, that's awful. How old is she, Hans?'

'Ninety-three. She's otherwise in not bad health, but any operation at that age is a biggie.'

'Give her our regards, and take care. Don't worry about Thursday. We'll find someone.'

Rico ended the call and sat staring into space. A Samiclaus was never easy to organise and at short notice… Hell. No one on the staff here would be able to take over. The waiters and bar staff were all on extra duties for the Gala Dinner, Alex was too young to be a convincing *Klaus*, and anyway, he was to be *Schmützli*, the dark-robed companion to the Samiclaus. Rico tapped his fingers on the desk, mentally working his way through the people connected in some way with the hotel. Herr Ammann from the town council was the right age, but he was a serious kind of bloke and there was nothing to say he'd enjoy dressing up and jollying his way round a restaurant for a couple of hours. Something like panic fluttered through Rico. The Gala Dinner was to be the highlight of this week, and not having a Samiclaus would ruin it.

Stacy stuck her head round the door. 'I've just seen your tree in Kim's room. Good work, except you had two snowmen right beside each other and too many stars around the bottom, too. I shifted a few bits. You weren't concentrating, were you?' She laughed down at him, then came in and touched his arm. 'Hey, what's up?'

Rico told her, his panic ebbing away as she pulled out the chair opposite. Stacy was a great problem-solver. That was the difference between them – he allowed things to eat away at him, while Stacy got on with finding a solution. She sat there, deep in thought, then beamed at him.

'Not a problem, Rico, love. You have the perfect Klaus right here in the hotel – all you need to do is persuade him to stay until Friday.'

Rico closed his eyes in relief. Why hadn't he thought of that? It wouldn't even be the first time his father had been a Samiclaus.

'Brilliant. Let's take him out for Kaffee und Kuchen, then tell – I mean ask – him. Then if you get the costume ready with him, it would be the ideal opportunity to ask discreetly about his health, too.'

'Two problems solved, then. I'm sure he'll be up for it. We'll have to buy him a beard, though.'

Rico tapped his phone to connect to his father. 'I think the investment will be worth it.'

***

Fortunately, Ralph had no objections to going for coffee and something gooey in the village that afternoon. Rico ushered him into Grimsbach's one posh coffee shop, and sat down opposite his father with Stacy beside him.

'Tiramisu Torte – this looks amazing.' Ralph sat back while the waitress brought over the plates, then lifted his cake fork. 'Okay, I can tell there's something going on. Spill.'

Rico gaped at Ralph on the other side of the table, then shot Stacy a quick look. He wasn't sure he shared her optimism that Ralph was going to be pleased about their proposition.

Stacy took the hint, and gave Ralph her best smile. 'You don't have anything special planned for Thursday and Friday, do you, Ralph?'

Ralph looked puzzled. 'No. Just checking what's been going on in Guido's business, and getting things ready for them coming back at the weekend. Why? You don't want to come to the Ticino, do you? There's such a lot happening here.'

Rico shook his head. 'Nope. And good. We have a massive favour to ask you.'

'Rico Weber! That sounds much too needy and negative!' Stacy wagged a finger at him, then turned to Ralph. 'We'd like to offer you a real opportunity to shine, and be remembered as something other than the ex-hotel manager.'

Rico had to concentrate to keep his face straight as Ralph's eyebrows almost hit the ceiling.

'Now you're scaring me. What do I have to do?'

Stacy took Ralph's hand over the table. 'Put on a red costume and a beard on Thursday night. You'll go down in the hotel annals as Lakeside's first ever Samiclaus. Hans can't make it.'

Ralph's pleasure was shining through as he rubbed his hands together. 'I would *love* to be your Samiclaus. Especially if I get to sample the Gala Dinner.'

Rico relaxed, feeling several kilos lighter. 'You can have two Gala Dinners if you help us out. Thanks, Dad.' Good, good, and surely there was nothing wrong with his father. Look at those bright eyes.

Stacy was tapping away on her phone. 'Okay, gents, while we're all here – next problem. According to the latest weather report, we're forecast no snow at all this week. Are we doing a "Winter Wonderland" trip for the guests tomorrow?'

Rico grimaced. The programme for the guests included a 'mystery tour' on the Sunday, and it sounded like this week's trip would be a long one.

He nodded at Stacy. 'We'd better, in case anyone feels hard done by about the lack of snow around here. If we show them right at the start that the stuff does exist, they can make up their own minds about going back to the mountains under their own steam later in the week. I'll announce it at dinner tonight when everyone's there.' That was the main difference between summer season guests and the Advent crowd. It was much easier to leave the summer people to organise their own entertainment.

'Where's the Winter Wonderland?' Ralph's face was one big question mark.

Rico scraped up his last few crumbs of cake. 'Davos. We can get twenty in the hotel minibus, and if more want to come, Alex can hire another from the garage. The snag is it means both Stacy and me being away from the hotel all day, as we can't send a big spa group with no nurse, and she can't drive the minibus yet.'

'I'll be bus driver, and you can stay at Lakeside, Rico.' Ralph was looking happier by the minute. 'Children, I have a feeling this is going to be a good week.'

5

Sunday, 2nd December, morning

Stacy took her seat at the front of the hotel minibus and nodded to Ralph. 'We're all here – let's go!'

It was an hour and a half's drive to Davos, where they were guaranteed snowy scenery and a cable car to take them up a proper mountain where they could admire the views – in sunshine today, thankfully. Eighteen guests had signed up, including Maureen and Carol, who was looking cheerful, if still rather washed out. Stacy twisted round in her seat as high-pitched giggles came from the back of the minibus. Simon and Sharon Cooper, aged eight and nine, were peering at something on an iPad, and Stacy gave them a wave before settling down for the trip. She'd had a word with the children's mum yesterday – both kids were clued up about Santa really being Mum and Dad, so none of the celebrations would be a problem. And come to think of it, they should organise something special for the three-year-old who would be here in the third week. The Samiclaus dinner was a one-off, and their normal Gala Dinner programme of fine food and festive surprise might not cut it for a tiny one. It was something to think about.

And they were off. Stacy beamed across at Ralph. This would her first time in Davos too. It would be fab to visit the place she'd only ever seen on TV.

The first part of the trip was on the motorway that ran along the border with Austria. Liechtenstein flashed past on their left as they went, and white-topped mountains in Austria loomed high further away. The Alpstein range on the other side was side-on here, and the peak of the Säntis had a sprinkling of snow. The guests were kept busy taking photos. After an hour they left the motorway, and the climb to Davos began. And – wow. Stacy took a deep breath. She'd seen winter scenery before, of course, but it gave her a kick every time. Snowy-white meadows with clusters of houses and chalets – it was picture-perfect Switzerland all over again.

Onwards and upwards they went. The road was snow-covered now too, but ploughed and gritted, and the minibus continued steadily. Driving through Klosters gave the guests plenty to speculate about – did anyone in the Royal Family still come here? Stacy listened to the buzz of chatter and oohs as the guests pointed out the luxurious hotels that Princess Diana might have stayed in, back in the day. Ralph winked at her, and Stacy smiled back. This was worth the early start. The outing was a huge success already, and they hadn't even reached Davos yet.

They arrived at eleven o'clock, and Stacy gaped from right to left as Ralph drove through the town. Heavens, this wasn't at all what she'd expected. Apartment buildings outnumbered quaint and traditional chalets by about ten to one, and the place was definitely slap-bang in the 21st century – in a 21st century winter, too. Freshly ploughed banks of whiteness lined the road, and the roofs all around had a thick and pristine covering. Wooded hills stretched up beyond the town, up and up to become mountains, the trees on the lower slopes sugar-coated with snow and glistening in the sunshine. It was like something you'd see on a calendar.

'I can't believe this snow!' said Maureen from the seat behind Stacy, her nose glued to the window.

Stacy turned round. Maureen's deep voice had been rumbling in the background for most of the trip, with only the odd comment from her friend. Poor Carol, it must be a little wearing listening to a running commentary all the time. Carol was sitting up looking around, though, and good, she looked better today.

Stacy raised her eyebrows at them. 'Okay, you two?'

As usual, it was Maureen who replied. 'Never been better. This is glorious.'

Carol shot her friend a rather cynical look, then turned her head slightly and winked the eye that Maureen couldn't see. Stacy grinned back. She and Carol had a similar sense of humour. And this was fun, background chatter, modern buildings or not. Ralph swung into the car park at the Jakobshorn cable car and turned the engine off. Time to do her job, now.

Stacy stood up at the front of the bus and clapped for attention, as everyone had immediately started talking. 'Okay, folks. There are plenty of restaurants, cafés and shops here in the village. Ralph and I will go up in the cable car now with anyone who wants to go to the top – it's a two-cable-car ride, and there's a restaurant and viewing platforms at the top, but you can't walk far. We'll leave you up there to do whatever you want and come down in your own time, and we'll all meet back here at four. The bus will be locked, so take your things with you – and have fun!'

The guests jumped down into the snow, exclaiming as the cold air hit their bus-warmed cheeks. The two children immediately ran to the side of the car park where there was some loose snow, and started throwing snowballs. Stacy laughed. Pity they didn't have snow back at Lakeside; this pair would have had a ball. She turned to speak to Ralph, then stopped. He was gazing at Carol and Maureen, who were listening to something another guest was saying, and – she'd never seen that expression on his face before. His mouth was turned down and he looked... lost, yes, that was it. Two seconds later he jerked out of his daydream and pulled on thick gloves.

Stacy shook herself, then called to the group. 'This way to the cable car – have you all got your woolly hats, etcetera? It'll be colder at the top. Everyone coming? Good choice!'

Ralph went off to buy tickets, and the party was ushered into the first cable car. It glided off up the mountain, Stacy standing by the window. Some people in here were skiers with their skis bound together and clutched to their fronts, and everyone was in a good mood; noisy chatter and laughter filled the car. Stacy turned to the window, the views bringing tears to her eyes. Wow. The air here was even clearer than when she'd been up the Säntis last spring, and range after range of mountains were spreading from right to left in front of her. Stacy shivered. How lovely Switzerland was, and how lucky she was to live here.

Ralph hugged her. 'Get Rico to take you to the mountains in January,' he said.

'I will. This is couldn't be better.' Or yes, it could, if Rico was here too. A lump rose in Stacy's throat. And if– She listened as little Simon and Sharon fired question after question at their parents. Life would be doubly perfect if she had her own family. One day.

They reached the middle station and trooped across to the second cable car before soaring upwards again, and a few minutes later they'd reached the summit, where the thin, bitingly cold air made Stacy's ears pop and her breath fog. She looked round for Carol, but the older woman was busy taking photos. No ear problems today, then. Good.

Ralph gathered everyone together. 'Restaurant over that way, and you'll find a few paths where you can have a little walk. We'll all make our own way down, and if anyone's late for the minibus they can sing Christmas carols all the way home!'

The guests laughed and drifted off in different directions, and Stacy took Ralph's arm. Should she ask what he'd been thinking about, down there in the car park? He'd looked like a lost soul… They joined a jostling crowd heading for the viewing platform, and she put the idea away. Some things were better talked about when it was quiet.

***

Carol jumped as Maureen grabbed her arm yet again. They were on one of the paths Ralph had pointed out, but neither of them was wearing what you'd call suitable footwear for an icy path, so it was more of a slide than a walk. But the views were worth it. Carol gazed out over peak beyond peak – she'd never imagined anything like this. Skiers were speeding down the slopes on her right, and further along she could see several ski lifts.

'This is exactly how I imagined "typical Switzerland",' she said to Maureen.

Maureen stamped her feet. 'Me too, but it's flipping cold out here. Let's go for lunch. I'm sure we'll get an equally good view from the restaurant – look at all the windows it has. I wonder if they'll have schnitzel with noodles, like in the song? Do you remember...'

Carol only half-listened as a story about a school trip they'd both been on started. Inside was actually a good idea. Her ears had popped in the second cable car, though her woolly hat was keeping them happy for the moment. But Mo was right; it was cold up here, and it was best to take no risks.

The restaurant was self-service, and Carol grabbed a table near the window while Maureen went for food. Most people here were in ski gear, and the sound of ski boots clacking on the floor was ringing round the room. Not exactly elegant dining, but wow, she was hungry enough to eat two dinners. She must be getting better. Or maybe it was just the Swiss fresh air. Maureen reappeared with two plates of *G'hacktes mit Hörnli*, or mince and macaroni. They had bowls of apple sauce on the side, and Carol was intrigued to see people spooning up the apple sauce along with the mince. Different country, different food traditions, how interesting.

Maureen was silent as they ate, and the thought that it was nice to have a break from the constant chatter slid into Carol's head before guilt flooded through her. She shouldn't be so ungrateful. Look at the way Mo had helped back when David died so unexpectedly. She was a kind soul, in spite of all the noise she generated around her, and as she'd been through the same thing a year or two beforehand, she'd been great at explaining some of the admin stuff you have to deal with after a death. Carol forked up her last few chunks of macaroni, feeling quite motherly about her friend. Maureen was lonely. Her problem was, not everyone liked wall-to-wall chatter, and of course that led poor Mo into a real vicious circle of loneliness and even more frantic chat and people vanishing into their own lives to escape it. Carol sat back in her chair, gazing out of the huge picture window to her left. Heaven help her, she knew what loneliness was. The past seven years without David had often been – challenging. TV dinners for one lost their charm very quickly.

The few moments of peace were short-lived. As soon as they'd reached the coffee stage, Maureen started on a long and complicated story about her mother's holiday in Inverness one snowy winter, and Carol's feeling of frustration swept back full force. Why couldn't Mo just sit quietly for a few minutes and enjoy the incredible scenery that was stretching out beside them? The Inverness story came to an end and another about January sales began, and something in Carol snapped. Her head was reeling now.

'Maureen – I'm sorry, but the heat in here and all this talk has given me a headache. I'm going for a quiet walk by myself. Shall we meet at the cable car station in half an hour, and go back to the village?'

'Oh – yes – of course.' Maureen gaped, her face flushing deep red, and Carol grabbed her things and left.

Heck. She'd been pretty abrupt there. But it was true about the headache, and no way did she want to have Maureen yakking in her ear the entire time she was trying to drink in the scenery. If she went to live in Australia, this might be the last time she'd see snowy mountains, and it would definitely be the last time she'd see these particular mountains, anyway. She should fix it all in her head to remember. Although – the thought of leaving everything she knew and living so far away was suddenly almost claustrophobic. Oh dear… how would she ever decide?

Carol started along a path to a viewing platform about two hundred yards away, and was soon overtaken by the Cooper family from the hotel. The children shot on ahead, closely followed by their father.

Mrs Cooper fell into step beside Carol. 'Spectacular, isn't it? The kids are in heaven. We've had to promise them another day in the mountains before we go home again. It's Carol, isn't it? I'm Elaine.'

Carol grinned as an excited shriek came from Sharon Cooper. 'Make the most of your holidays with them. You might not believe it now, but these holidays are some of the best times of your life.'

'Oh, I know. I love them to bits, but it's intensive at this age. Don't suppose it gets better when they're teenagers, does it?'

'Nope. But you'll cope.'

Another shriek came, and Elaine hurried on to keep the peace. Carol arrived at the platform and stood at one end. The skiers below her included families, and over to her right was what looked like a pair of grandparents with two young children. Carol watched them chat, then the grandmother hugged one child – impossible to say under all the clothes if it was a boy or a girl – and kissed the small face. Tears shot into Carol's eyes. She could do that too, every day, if she lived in Australia. She only had one child, and he and his children were half a world away. Fierce longing for her family swept through Carol, then her eyes strayed back to the scenery. She should definitely make the most of this.

They had mountains in Australia too, didn't they?

6

Sunday, 2nd December, afternoon

After two hours and a very nice lunch in the summit restaurant, Stacy was ready to go down again. The guests had all dispersed, and she and Ralph joined the queue for the cable car, which was much less busy as all the skiers they'd come up with would be skiing down. One last look at those slopes – would she ever learn to ski? She'd need about a month's holiday to do it, though, and this wasn't the best place, as a nursery slope was nowhere to be seen. In spite of that, plenty of very young children were zooming around, looking as if they'd been born with skis on. Help, one of these kids over there even had a dummy stuck in his mouth as he swooped his way across the snow to stop beside his family.

Stacy sighed. That was the age to learn, wasn't it? Maybe she could take lessons with her own kids, one day? That wouldn't be soon, though. They'd need to wait for kids until the hotel was hopefully more established and Rico had finished the master's degree he hadn't even started yet, so it was going to take forever. A slow-motion film of her life…

Back in the village, she and Ralph strolled along the main street in Davos looking at the mixture of ski outfitters and souvenir shops.

You could decimate your bank balance very quickly here, and Stacy made do with buying an old-fashioned postcard for Mum and Dad. She wrote it in the shop and posted it in the yellow post box on the main road so that it would have a Davos date stamp on it – Dad would appreciate that. They arrived back in the car park at ten to four to find a group of guests already there.

'Carol doesn't look well,' said Ralph in a low voice as they approached the waiting crowd.

Stacy glanced at him first. He'd sounded a bit odd again, and he was frowning darkly, too. But he was right. Carol was leaning on the bus, her eyes closed and one gloved hand clutching her jacket more firmly closed at her throat.

Stacy hurried over. 'Tired?'

'Yes. My ear popped coming down in the cable car, but it's blocked again now and it's quite painful, to be honest.' Her face was drawn, and even Maureen was looking worried.

Stacy winced. 'Paracetamol coming up. In you get and sit down in the warm. We'll be home in no time.' She ushered Carol onto the bus, pulled out the first aid box and handed over the pills. Hopefully, they'd do the trick again, but she'd keep an eye on Carol for a day or two.

'Will she be okay?' Ralph still sounded worried.

'I hope so.' Stacy sat down, frowning inwardly. Was Ralph's concern more than she'd expect for a hotel guest?

He was counting heads now, looking more his usual self, and Stacy shrugged mentally. She was imagining things.

Ralph came to the end of his head count. 'We're four down – the Cooper family.'

Stacy stared around the car park, but there was no sign of the family, and ten minutes later they were still missing. Ralph was tapping his feet beside her.

'We need to get going, or we'll be caught up in traffic going home. I'll run back to the cable car station and chivvy them along if they're there, and you check the main road and the shops.'

Stacy nodded, and hurried back the way she'd come. The street was thronged with tourists now, this seemed to be the time everyone came back from skiing. It was hard to see far in either direction, but – was that the Coopers along there, staring into a shop window as if they had all the time in the world?

It was. Stacy waved frantically, but the family was over two hundred yards away. No use yelling at this distance, either. Stacy ran as fast as she could, sliding in the snow and slush underfoot but miraculously not falling. She was nearly halfway there when Elaine Cooper shrieked and pulled at her husband's arm. They grabbed the hand of a child each and began to run towards Stacy, who slowed down, then stopped. She whipped out her phone and called Ralph.

'Found! See you at the bus.'

Elaine Cooper shot past her with Sharon. 'So sorry – we lost track of the time.'

Stacy trotted back in the family's wake, and arrived at the bus to find Ralph already at the wheel and everyone clicking on seatbelts. She dropped into her seat and rubbed her thighs. Running on snow was hard work; she'd be limping around like a hundred-and ten-year-old tomorrow.

***

Talk about a worst-case scenario. Her ear was throbbing, and now she had hot and cold shivers as well. Today had been much too much for her poorly ear. Carol lay in bed feeling hopeless and emotional, watching Maureen potter around in her nightie. Please, please, this pain had to stop, right now, and let her get on with her holiday. It wasn't this week she cared about, lovely as the hotel was – next week was the important part. Australia. And Barry and Diane, and little Emma and Jonny. She was aching to see then all, and oh, she felt so awful. Why had she ever come here? If she'd gone straight to Australia like she'd first planned, okay, she could still have been ill, but she'd have been with her family. If this went on, she might not be able to go. Hot tears of frustration spilled down Carol's cheeks.

'Poor you.' Maureen hung her blouse in the wardrobe, and flipped the kettle on. 'I'll make you a nice cuppa, shall I?'

Carol wiped her eyes and blew her nose gently. This was dreadful. Maureen was being kind, but they weren't good enough friends for Carol to feel comfortable being ill in such close proximity to the other woman. A room-share, okay, excursions, etcetera, fine – but not feeling like death warmed up while Maureen prattled non-stop in an attempt to jolly Carol out of her misery.

She accepted a steaming mug from Maureen and blew on the tea. But the first swallow set her throat on fire and she abandoned the mug for her water glass, forcing down another paracetamol. Sleep, Carol, and heal. If only she could wake up in the morning and find all this pain and temperature malarkey was gone.

She slept, but not for long. 02.10 was shining redly from the radio alarm when Carol next opened her eyes, her head thumping and her nightdress sticking to her. Maureen was snoring faintly in the other bed, and Carol propped herself up on one elbow, her head swimming. A drink, she needed a drink.

One swallow, and it was as if a knife was stabbing from the back of her throat all the way into her left ear. Carol couldn't stop the moan of pain.

'Wha – what is it?' A bedside lamp clicked on, and Maureen was peering over to her. 'Oh, Carol. What a state you're in. I'll get you fresh water.'

Carol lay back and closed her eyes. If only, only she was safe at home right now.

The bed lurched as Maureen sat down. 'Here. Try a few sips. Do you want a throat lozenge?'

Carol nodded, waving the glass of water away in favour of the throat sweet. More tears trickled down her face.

'I'm calling Stacy.' Maureen lifted her phone from the bedside table.

Carol tried to protest, but no sound came. She listened as Maureen passed on the details, and a few minutes later Stacy appeared in the room, wearing a black towelling bathrobe over red pyjamas and carrying a medical bag.

'Feeling worse? Let me look.'

Carol croaked out an answer as Stacy took her pulse and peered into her mouth, then opened a box of tablets from her bag.

'Extra-strong pain and fever-killers. Have two, then it'll be off to the doctor with you in the morning. No, they don't visit here unless you're in totally dire straits,' she added, as Maureen protested. 'Don't worry, Carol, I'll go with you, and he speaks excellent English. We'll soon have you right.'

Carol swallowed the pills and lay back, comforted. It was good to know that Stacy wasn't *too* concerned about her.

7

Monday, 3rd December, early morning

Rico tapped his fingers on the kitchen worktop while he waited for the toast to pop up. He grabbed the first two pieces when the toaster released them, swung round to the table and dropped one on his plate and the other on Stacy's.

'I don't know how you can do that,' she said, reaching for the butter. 'You must have asbestos fingers.'

He traced toasty fingers across the back of her neck, and she squealed. 'Behave – you're not a student yet! Where's the posh hotel manager I fell in love with?'

Rico dropped into a chair. 'Right here – and I know, it's Monday morning and we have a hotel to run. And first up, I want to know why you're drooping all over the table like that?'

Stacy jerked her head away from the hand she'd been leaning it on. 'I'm waiting for the caffeine to kick in. Typical bloke, you are. You snored all through me getting up to help Carol in the night. I'll need to organise an emergency doctor's appointment for her and her earache as soon as the surgery opens.'

'Up in the night? Stace, we're not a nursing home. Is it really our job to be there 24/7 for people with earache?'

She stared. 'In an emergency yes, I think it is. Don't be so cold-hearted, Rico. The woman's ill. I'll go to the doctor with her, too, because I don't think he'll have good news for her. It would be best if someone drove us there, then we wouldn't have to worry about parking.'

Shame flushed through Rico. The dark circles under Stacy's eyes were telling their own story. He frowned. 'You have the spa staff meeting on Monday mornings – can't Carol's friend go with her in a taxi?'

Stacy shook her head. 'Let's see when the appointment is. Margrit can take the meeting if necessary. And Carol seems a bit lost, Rico. I don't think she and Maureen are what you'd call close friends. This is all getting on top of her.'

Rico swallowed the sudden lump in his throat. This was why he loved Stacy; she cared about everyone she came into contact with. 'I'll drive you.' He lifted her hand and kissed it.

'Stop canoodling, you two.' Ralph appeared in the kitchen and went straight to the coffee machine, ruffling Stacy's hair on the way past.

Rico had never heard the word. 'Stop *what*?'

Ralph laughed. '*Schmusen*. You didn't think your old man could teach you words like that, did you?'

Rico glared. There wasn't a lot he could say to that without looking even more clueless than he did already. 'My vocabulary is perfectly adequate, thank you very much. In both languages.'

Ralph smirked. 'If you say so. Any jobs for me this morning?'

'You could keep an eye on the desk for half an hour while I take Stace and a guest to the doctor. Alex isn't in until twelve.'

Ralph froze, then sat down with his coffee and stirred in a generous spoonful of sugar before taking a large swallow and turning to Rico. 'You need another receptionist, Rico, part time at least. When you start your course, Stacy and Alex will struggle to man reception all day every day, even with Maria and Flavia doing the odd shift. I'll drive Stacy and her patient, and you can stay at the desk – you know better what needs to be done there.'

Rico happened to be looking at Stacy at the end of Ralph's speech. Heck, she was rubbing her face like an old woman. Knowing her, she'd lain awake worrying about Carol. What she needed was another hour or two's kip, and that was exactly what she wasn't going to get.

She sipped her coffee, squinting at Ralph now with a very odd expression on her face, and Rico frowned again. What was going on there? She sounded her usual self when she spoke, though.

'Sounds like a plan. You could pick up the Samiclaus outfit from the Alpstein, Ralph, while Carol and I are with the doctor, then this afternoon we can check it fits you. And I'll want you in the medical room for a BP check too, please. Family privilege.' She blew a kiss in Ralph's direction.

Rico sat back, looking from Ralph to Stacy and back. She still looked odd... There was something going on he didn't know about, and please God it was nothing to do with his father's health.

A slightly awkward silence hung in the air, then Ralph rose to put his mug in the dishwasher.

'I'll be in the fitness room if you need me. Let me know when you want to go, Stacy.' He almost ran from the kitchen.

Rico began to clear the table. 'Was I imagining things, or was there something a bit off there with Dad?'

'Off? What, exactly?'

'He's not ill, is he? Or...' Rico swallowed.

Stacy got up and rubbed his shoulder on the way past. 'Let me have a chat with Ralph this afternoon, and if there's anything to worry about, we can talk it through tonight.'

Rico pulled a face – but he could trust her, couldn't he? He grabbed her for a kiss, holding her tightly. 'Promise?'

'Promise.'

She gave him a rather absent kind of smile, and went to refill her coffee cup. Rico ran downstairs to start Monday morning, trying to ignore little voice niggling away in his head as he walked through reception to the office. *Something's going on, Rico...*

***

Carol squinted at the radio alarm. Quarter to eight. Maureen was in the shower, and Carol lay still, taking stock of her symptoms. Was she maybe a little better now? The headache was still there in the background, and her ear... she swallowed, and white-hot pain stabbed across her throat to her left ear. Double ouch. She swung her legs over the side of her bed and sat taking tiny sips of last night's water from the glass by her bed.

Maureen emerged from the en suite, swathed in a huge white towel. 'You're awake – good. How do you feel?'

'Much better,' whispered Carol determinedly, and Maureen rolled her eyes, lifting her phone.

'Stacy told me to call her when you were awake.'

Carol staggered across the room to the loo. At least she could be up and washed when Stacy arrived. She was sitting in her bathrobe trying to feel more alive when a knock came at the door.

'How's the pain?' Stacy came in and felt Carol's forehead.

Carol touched her ear. 'It's – oh! My God – what's that?' She held up her hand, two fingers covered in a creamy, blood-streaked discharge. 'Is it – oh! I can hardly hear at all in that ear now!' Her heart thundered – this wasn't good, and what it meant for Saturday's flight she could only imagine.

Stacy pulled a wad of gauze from her bag. 'I think your eardrum may have perforated. It happens sometimes, but try not to worry. It's not an emergency and it often heals without treatment. The important thing for now is that you don't get water in that ear, and for heaven's sake don't poke anything into it. I'll call the doctor and get you an appointment this morning.'

Carol pulled a face. 'I had problems with this ear after my last visit to Australia,' she whispered. 'I should have told you. I just wanted it all to go away.'

'That's understandable.' Stacy put a dressing on the ear and patted Carol's shoulder.

'Oh, I wish–' Carol couldn't hold the tears back.

Stacy gave her a brief hug. 'You wish you'd never come here. I know. But better having problems here than on a plane halfway to Australia. Imagine if you had to disembark in Singapore, or wherever. And this *is* fixable. Get dressed, have some breakfast and then come to reception. We'll soon get you sorted.'

Carol reached for her make-up bag. She could try to look halfway healthy, even if she didn't feel it.

Apart from Ralph standing behind the desk peering at a wad of papers in his hand, the front hallway was deserted when she went downstairs later, having toyed with a soft roll and jam in her room. Her appointment was at half ten, and they were leaving at quarter past.

Carol hesitated, and he glanced up, then hurried round to usher her over to the sofa.

'I've come to see Stacy,' she croaked.

'She'll be here in two minutes. Have a seat while you're waiting. I'm chauffeuring you both to the doctor, by the way.'

Carol sat. 'I'm so sorry. I'm being a nuisance.'

Ralph perched on the coffee table opposite. 'You're not – you can't help being ill. Try not to think about it.' He waved his handful of papers. 'I'm making an info leaflet to go with the twigs for St Barbara's Day tomorrow.'

Carol wasn't sure she'd heard right. 'Twigs for St Barbara's Day?' This must be a Swiss custom, and his distraction tactic was working. It was nice to think about something other than her ear and throat.

'Barbara was an early Christian martyr, and the fourth of December is her feast day. Apparently, she found a little twig from a cherry tree on her clothes when she was on the way to prison, and watered it with her tears until it bloomed. So on the fourth, we gather branches from fruit trees or flowering shrubs, and put them in water. If they're in flower by Christmas, we'll have good luck.'

His eyes twinkled at her, and Carol managed a shaky smile. 'I hope they bloom, then. I could do with some luck.'

'Don't worry.' Stacy appeared in the hallway. 'We'll soon have you right. I'll check in with Margrit, and we'll get going.'

'Don't worry,' said Ralph. 'I'll drop you off right outside the surgery.'

Carol opened her mouth to protest that she could walk a few steps, then shut it again as Stacy gave her a look.

'She's a fantastic nurse,' said Ralph, when Stacy had vanished into the spa. 'If you had to be ill on holiday, this is the place to do it.'

His eyes were shining at her, and Carol stared back. His arm moved, and for a second she thought he was going to pat her shoulder, then he let it drop, an oddly uncertain look on his face.

Stacy reappeared, and gripped Carol's elbow. 'Come on, Mrs. Let's get you sorted.'

Tears came into Carol's eyes. How kind they all were. And if only they didn't have to be. Or not to her, at least.

8

Monday, 3rd December, late morning

The waiting room at the doctor's was busy, and Stacy gave Carol what she hoped was a reassuring smile. The poor soul was sitting picking at her fingers and probably wishing she was a million miles away – almost literally. How far away *was* Australia, actually?

The practice was a busy one, with two receptionists manning the desk and three practice assistants rushing around organising blood tests, ECGs, the odd X-ray. Stacy settled down to wait, thinking about the hotel. Ralph was right, wasn't he? They needed more reception staff at Lakeside. You couldn't run a supposedly classy hotel if you didn't have enough staff, and right now they were only managing to be efficient because she and Rico were putting in all the hours God sent. It was only the third of December and she was bushed already – what would she be like by Christmas?

'They do a lot here, don't they?' said Carol, watching as a small boy emerged from a side room with a new, bright blue plaster on one wrist.

'It's a different system to the UK,' said Stacy. 'This is a GP practice, but they do things like X-ray and blood work here as well. A lot of specialists have their own practices too, and some do minor surgery in them.'

Carol wiped her hands on her trousers. 'Well, I hope I don't need surgery, minor or otherwise. Will you come in with me, Stacy?'

The receptionist called Carol's name, and Stacy followed the English woman into the consulting room. Dr Erisman listened as Carol told him what had happened, then examined the affected ear. Stacy saw his brow crease thoughtfully as he held the otoscope to Carol's ear, then his eyes met hers briefly as he pulled up a chair opposite them and sat down.

'You have an infection, and a large hole in your eardrum,' he said simply.

Carol's shoulders slumped. 'Stacy said that would be the problem – and that it should heal by itself,' she said, clasping her hands together so hard her knuckles turned white.

The doctor shook his head. 'Usually that is correct. But I'm afraid this hole is too large. You will need a small procedure.'

'An operation?'

Carol's hands shot towards her mouth, and Stacy's heart sank for the woman. What an awful prospect for someone who only wanted to spend Christmas in Australia with her son.

'Yes. You could have it done here this week, in the Ear, Nose and Throat hospital at St Gallen, or you can go back to England for it – but I wouldn't advise flying until the infection is gone. You could go overland, though.'

'How long would I be in hospital, if I have it done here?'

'You would be a day patient. The general anaesthetic for this is a short one.'

'And when could I fly to my family in Australia?'

Dr Erisman put his head to one side. 'Ten days to two weeks? It depends on the healing process.'

'I'd like it done here, as soon as possible, please. Would you be doing it?'

'A colleague at the *Klinik*. If you agree, I can refer you today. I'll phone when we have a date and time.'

'Thank you. I'd like it done as soon as possible, please.'

Stacy listened to the doctor's instructions about antibiotics and dressings, then ushered her patient back outside. Carol was determined to get this fixed ASAP, and who could blame her?

Ralph was waiting in the car outside the surgery, and the concern on his face when he leapt out to open the passenger seat door for Carol told Stacy volumes. Oh, gosh and golly, there *was* something going on here, but then it was natural that Ralph would move on after Edie's death, wasn't it? Three years plus wasn't exactly rushing into a new relationship, either. If that was what it was. Wishing with all her heart that she knew what Carol thought about it – if she'd even noticed Ralph, the state she was in – Stacy got into the back of the car, leaving Ralph to settle Carol, who was now almost tearful, into the front.

The car pulled away from the surgery with Carol sniffing into a tissue and Ralph clearing his throat. Stacy glanced to the north as they turned into the main road. There was the lake, grey-blue today, a cold, blustery wind sending white-topped little waves towards the bank. A watery sun was struggling through, but there was no warmth in it. Silence reigned in the car as they waited at the pedestrian crossing by the church, and Stacy searched around for something to say.

'Did you get your, um, ah, things from the Alpstein, Ralph?' she said, realising as soon as she began to speak that a more direct question could spoil the dinner event on Thursday for Carol, if she was well enough to go.

His voice was higher than usual. 'Yep. They look fine, but we'll see after lunch.'

The brief conversation brought them to the Lakeside gates, and again, Stacy had no time to help Carol, because Ralph was there before her, taking Carol's elbow as she rose from the passenger seat.

'Thank you so much, but I can manage, really. I think I'll go upstairs and have a rest before Maureen gets back from her shopping trip.' Carol treated them both to a big smile that didn't go anywhere near her eyes, and hurried through the front door.

Scowling, Ralph clicked the key to lock the car. 'Why didn't her friend come to the doctor's with her?'

Stacy took his arm. 'Probably Carol didn't let her. Maureen's one of those very chatty people. I think Carol finds that tiring, especially when she's feeling poorly.'

Ralph tutted. 'And they are sharing a room.'

Stacy turned to look at him. Had he checked that in the computer? 'Well, two single rooms would have been twice as expensive, and Carol's forking out for a trip to Australia, too.'

Ralph stopped her before they reached the front door. 'The attic floor rooms are all empty,' he said abruptly. 'We could give Carol one of those. Then she'd have her own space, and be nearer to – to you if she needed help again in the night.'

He *had* been in the computer. The attic rooms had originally been the quarters for the live-in summer staff, and were now slightly smaller hotel rooms which they'd decided not to use for the Christmas package. Stacy thought swiftly. Completely aside from Ralph's possible feelings for Carol, it was a good idea, especially if Carol ended up staying on past her booking.

'Good idea,' she said. And she would try to sort out what was happening with Ralph and Carol, too, but that might not be such a quick fix...

Ralph hurried on to usher Carol into the lift, and Stacy trailed across to reception. Gawd – what were her legs like? She wasn't 'getting older' already – was she? Because that was what her legs were thinking. It would be all that running around in Davos yesterday followed by five hours' sleep – and the Christmas jobs seemed never-ending. Next on the list was to find a vase large enough for tomorrow's Barbara twigs, which were going to be forsythia from the garden. The hallway coffee table would be the perfect place for them, and she'd prop the laminated card Ralph was making to explain the legend up beside the vase.

Rico came out of the office. 'That's all the table decs set out,' he said, indicating the pile of empty decorations boxes behind the desk.

'Well done. Help me put them away for now?' Stacy grabbed an armful of boxes and took them through to the storeroom in the small spa. The box of miscellaneous vases and jugs was in here somewhere... Yes, here it was. Ooh, and this vase would be perfect for the Barbara decoration – nice and high, and lovely old silver – or was it pewter?

'Pewter,' said Rico, dumping his boxes on top of hers. 'Mum used to put stuff in it at Christmas too. We had it in the flat by the balcony door.'

His eyes had gone suspiciously bright, and Stacy touched his arm. A quick change of plan was needed here. 'We'll do the same, shall we?

Look, this white vase will be great for the Barbara twigs in reception. It'll be a lovely contrast to the yellow flowers on the forsythia.'

Rico agreed, and Stacy took the two vases up to the flat to wash them out. It might be over three years since Rico's mum had died, but he still had fits of grieving for her – and perhaps he always would. Cancer was so cruel. Stacy couldn't imagine how she would feel if her own loveable, exasperating mum suddenly wasn't there any longer. She set the pewter vase in the corner of the living room, then ran downstairs again to put the white one in the office ready for the next day. Preparation was everything, wasn't it? And heavens, no wonder her stomach was growling; it was half past one now and she hadn't had elevenses, never mind lunch.

Ralph was leafing through the paper at the kitchen table when she went back upstairs to make herself a cheese sandwich. Lunch was frequently eaten on the run these days, though they tried to eat together at night.

He chuckled. 'It's been busy, hasn't it?'

Stacy sat down with her sandwich. 'Yup. Rico was a bit upset when I took out the pewter vase. He was remembering how Edie used to fill it at Christmas.'

Ralph patted her shoulder. 'I saw you'd put it in the living room. It's good to remember the old times, Stacy, and keep all the memories. As long as we don't let them choke us.'

'I'm sure he won't. It was seeing the vase again, I think, and you know… Christmas.'

'How's your patient?'

Stacy blinked at the sudden change of subject. 'I'll check her when I've eaten. I do hope the operation fixes things for her. Australia's a long way to fly with a wonky ear.'

Ralph grunted, and went back to his paper.

***

Carol lay on her bed, trying hard to swallow the lump of self-pity in her throat. What a mess she was in, but blubbing would get her nowhere and it might even make her ear worse. Here she was, persuaded by a friend she wasn't that close to that a holiday she hadn't really wanted would be good for her – and now her Australian trip was being shortened, at best. Worst case, she might not even be able to go. The only good thing was, Maureen had gone into town for the day, so she could drip self-pity in solitary comfort.

The sound of a couple laughing in the corridor on their way down to lunch prompted a fresh surge of tears for Carol to blink down. How she missed being one of a pair. David's heart attack seven years ago had come out of the blue; it had turned her life upside down, then Barry's move to Perth had turned it inside out. He'd been gutted when she hadn't gone with them, and he'd brought up the subject of her moving Down Under on her last visit, too. Well, now she was going to give it her serious consideration. If she ever got there, that was. She'd need to call Barry today and give them the news – the children would be disappointed. Carol lay still, imagining how different life would be if Barry and Diane still lived in London and the grandkids could run in and out as they wanted.

A different line of thought started. Moving to Oz was huge, and she was happy in London, wasn't she? Plenty to do, lots of friends… who were all couples. Ralph's face swam into her mind. He liked her;

she could tell. And there didn't seem to be a significant other in his life; but then, what did she know?

A tap on the door had her scrambling to her feet.

'Only me.' Stacy put her head into the room. 'The doc called and they've squeezed you in at the clinic on Wednesday morning. We'll sort out the details later, but what we'll do now is move you up to the top floor, where our flat is as well as some spare rooms. You'll need peace after your op. I'll come by with a trolley in half an hour – is that okay?'

Carol touched the dressing on her ear. 'Lovely. Thanks, Stacy.'

She sank down on the bed again when Stacy was gone. Well. This was as good a time as any to call Barry, before it was too late in Perth.

'Hey, Mum! How's Switzerland?'

And of course, she burst into tears. Carol struggled for self-control, and the small matter of a huge dressing on the ear she usually held the phone to didn't help. Eventually, she managed to splutter out her programme for the next week. Barry, being Barry, was calm and cheerful as ever.

'No worries, Mum – sounds like you're in the best place for getting speedy and efficient treatment. You'll be here by Christmas, even if you're a week late. And we might just have a surprise for you!'

Carol nearly dropped the phone. 'Another baby?' The thought of a third grandchild she'd hardly ever see was enough to start the tears again.

'No, nothing like that. I'm not saying a word more, but I promise you're going to love it. Concentrate on getting better now.'

A few minutes' chat, during which he refused point-blank to tell her anything more about the mysterious surprise, and the call ended.

Carol stared at her phone. Not another baby, but she was going to love it... Could it be – an even firmer invite to stay for good? Maybe a little flat near Barry? The chance of a job somewhere? And yes... she would love that.

Wouldn't she?

9

Monday, 3rd December, afternoon

Ralph came into the living room and stood with his arms outstretched. 'How do I look?'

Stacy was waiting with the sewing box. 'Like a Samiclaus. Wow.' Grinning broadly, she walked around him. He was wearing a long red cloak over a longer white linen shift with a red cord knotted round the waist. Gold braid lined the front opening of the cloak and was repeated along the hemline of the shift. On his head was a wig of long white hair topped with a red bishop's mitre, also with gold braid around the base and top.

He pulled at his neckline. 'Hurry up. I'm boiling with all this on.'

'I don't think we need to do anything – the shift's a bit big, but that doesn't matter. What will you wear on your feet?'

Ralph shrugged. 'Black shoes? It's not as if I'll be tramping through the snow to get here. And I'll not be wearing much underneath all this, I can tell you.'

Stacy put the sewing box back into the cupboard. 'Too much info, Ralph. But you're practically perfect. Now – the beard?'

'I've ordered one in St Gallen. I'll go up and collect it before Thursday.'

'Then I pronounce you sorted. Let's go down and do that BP check I promised you, then raid the kitchen. Rob's trying some new Christmas biscuits for the demo tomorrow.'

'Christmas *Guetzli*, yum. But, Stace – I don't need my blood pressure checked.' Ralph deposited his cloak over the back of the sofa, and pulled the shift over his head to emerge in his jeans and sweatshirt. 'I'm sure it'll be raised anyway, after wearing this lot.'

Stacy took hold of her courage with both hands. She wasn't going to let him fob her off; his health was way too important. 'You could be right. But we were worried about you when you arrived, you know. You seemed so down, and I don't like those bags under your eyes. Have you been overdoing things in Lugano?'

He raised both arms in a shrug. 'I've been looking after Guido's boat business, but there's not much to do there in winter. Some days I barely see a soul from morning until night. I'm tired, I guess. You can buy me some vitamin pills.'

Stacy got up, reassured. Vitamin pills, yes, tired, yes – but the sub-text was clear. Ralph was lonely. Was it only Guido and Julia's absence for the past several weeks? Ralph's face as he'd watched Carol emerge from the doctor's surgery slid into Stacy's mind. If she was right, and Ralph had feelings for Carol – well. How could that possibly *not* end without tears?

Ralph gave her a sideways look. 'Did you give Carol a room on this floor?'

'She's settling in as we speak. I'll go by later and see how she is, but the antibiotics should make a difference soon.' Stacy shot him a smile, but he changed the subject.

'Let's go down and try out these biscuits. You need more meat on your bones too, miss.'

After half hour spent in a very hot kitchen with Ralph and Rob the chef, Stacy emerged with a sugar rush and the conviction that aside from what was going on with Carol, there was nothing wrong with Ralph that living with other people wouldn't cure.

'I'm going for a walk to get rid of some of those calories,' he said, shrugging into the jacket he'd brought down with him. 'You?'

'I'm working, remember?' Stacy shot him a grin, and headed towards the lift. 'I'll visit my patient first, then see what Rico's doing.'

And tell him about the chat with Ralph, she added silently. She and Rico had got into problems a couple of times before when one of them hadn't told the other what was worrying them. It was important not to make that mistake again. Stacy screwed her face up. It would be all cards on the table today, and Rico wasn't going to like what she had to say.

Rico was at the computer in the office room behind reception when Stacy caught up with him later. He was silent as she told him about the chat with his father, keeping it to Ralph's health only for the moment.

He waited until she'd finished, then nodded slowly. 'Yes, I can buy it that Dad's been lonely without Guido and Julia. I guess even in Mediterranean-style Lugano, people don't get out and about in winter the same way they do in summer, and Dad's never been what you'd call an enthusiastic loner. So you don't think he's ill?'

Stacy slid her chair closer to his and put a hand on his knee. 'He wouldn't let me check him over, but I think he's just been too isolated. He's perked up quite a lot this week – the haunted look he arrived with has faded.'

Rico sniffed. 'Or maybe we've got used to it. Stace, he – I really want him to be well.'

He was thinking about his mother's short illness; Stacy could tell. Sympathy and frustration mixed with love and the wish to help rose in her gut. Rico fretted about things.

'I'm not worried about his health now, Rico, and by the time he heads south again, Guido and Julia will be back. So that problem's solved.'

This was true. Ralph lived in the same apartment block as his brother and sister-in-law, and the three spent a lot of their time together. Rico rose to his feet, and Stacy grasped her courage with both hands. He'd dive off to do something completely different if she didn't pin him down here. Somehow, Advent guests made for ten times the work summer guests did.

She twisted her hands together, scowling down at them. Go, Stace. He has to know this. 'Rico–'

One look at her face and he sank down again. 'Tell me. We promised no more secrets.'

'I know.' She stared into his eyes. 'I think your dad likes Carol,' she said simply.

Rico gaped at her for a few seconds then looked away, the growing frown between his eyes and the way his mouth was turning down showing clearly what he thought.

'He likes – you mean – *no*. I don't believe it.' He leaned back in his chair, rubbing one hand over his face. 'No, Stace, that can't be...'

Stacy said nothing. It had always been 'Mum and Dad' for Rico, hadn't it? And it must be weird, thinking about his father in that way. But Ralph was only sixty-two. There was nothing to say he'd want to spend the rest of his life alone with his memories, and Rico would have to accept that.

She stood up when he did, and hugged him. 'Rico, love, I told you because we don't want secrets. But it's up to Ralph what he does. And I could be wrong. I think we should leave well alone until Ralph comes to us with it – if he ever does.'

Rico leaned his head on hers and closed his eyes. 'I suppose. Oh, Stace, I don't want him to–'

He stopped, and Stacy's heart broke for him. He loved his dad, but this was catapulting his precious memories of his mother and their family life all together even further into the past. Poor Rico.

Stacy spent the rest of the afternoon helping Flavia reorganise the spa shop cabinet and gift wrap some orders for guests. By five o'clock she could barely see straight for fiddling around with bows and tinsel. Golly, she hadn't been this ready to drop for ages, and it was her turn to cook. Freezer here she came.

Alex was tidying the reception when she passed. 'Stacy, can I have a word?'

Stacy went to lean on the desk, and he grinned at her. 'You look like someone who needs an evening off!'

'Gee, thanks for the compliment. Nothing a blob in front of the telly with my feet up won't fix.' She hoped... 'What's up?'

'Zoe called this morning, and she's looking forward to playing her violin here at the Gala Dinner on the twentieth. Do you want her to play anything in particular?'

'Oh, popular carols and Christmas songs, I think. Maybe a couple that people can sing along to. Shall I make a list of suggestions?'

'That would be great. And...'

He fiddled with a pen, not meeting her eyes. Stacey waited. Help, what was coming now?

'Mum was wondering when you were coming to see her again? She wants to show you how much progress she's making with the CBT. It's making a difference.'

Help again. Stacy thought swiftly. She'd been the one who'd pushed Denise towards Cognitive Behavioural Therapy, so it was gratifying to know it was helping, and of course she would normally have visited a week ago, but...

'Tell her I'm really sorry, it's just I've been rushed off my feet. Or no, don't – I'll call her soon and tell her myself, and I'll make a point of going over this week sometime.'

Relief flashed over Alex's face. 'Thanks. Go on a good-weather day, and she might go out for a walk with you.'

'Really? That's fantastic progress!' It was, too, so why was he looking so down about it? 'Alex? What's up?'

He sniffed. 'It's nothing. I'm fine. Just – I can't get my head round Zoe going away on tour for so long.'

Stacy went round to the other side of the desk, thanking fate that no guests were about. She put an arm round Alex, hugging gently and feeling quite motherly, although he was only a couple of years younger than she was. Alex worshipped the ground Zoe walked on, but although she loved him, he was always going to take second place to her music. She was one of those rare talents, the star violinist in one of the most prestigious orchestras in Europe, and her music was the driving force in her life. Zoe wouldn't change, and maybe Alex would have to accommodate that.

'Alex, we'd hate to lose you, but have you considered going with her?'

He shook his head. 'There's Mum. And partners don't really go on tour with the musicians. I suppose that's why so many of them partner each other!' He was smiling, but his eyes were bleak.

Stacy hugged him again. 'Let's get your mum as well as we possibly can over the next few months, then when Zoe comes back from the tour, you can take stock again. Even a job in Zurich would give you a more normal life together.'

He nodded, and Stacy went on upstairs. At least she didn't have problems like that to grapple with. The love of her life was right here in the hotel, and steak and salad would have to do for his dinner. Stacy fished for the meat in the freezer and slid it into the microwave to defrost. She'd make some oven chips as well. Comfort food, exactly what they needed after a busy day.

Ralph appeared a few minutes later, and leaned in the kitchen doorway. 'How's your patient?'

Stacy looked round. He'd asked that before... 'She'll be fine. Antibiotics work quickly.'

His face creased in concern. 'Do you think she'll–'

The flat door banged as Rico came in, and Ralph broke off and called down the hall.

'Steak and chips, Rico!'

'Yum.' Rico went through to the living room, then reappeared half a minute later and came to hug Stacy. 'Mum's vase looks brilliant, doesn't it, Dad?'

Ralph agreed, but he didn't meet Stacy's gaze, and the shadow in his eyes was still there.

10

TUESDAY, 4TH NOVEMBER

Carol walked through the spa rooms, smiling at the people sitting up to their necks in various tubs of lovely warm water as she passed. If jealousy was the green-eyed monster, she'd be the colour of pea soup soon, but it was wonderful to be feeling so much better, even if she still needed an op. Thank heavens for antibiotics; she'd be totally scuppered without them. And thank you Stacy for making her go to the doctor so quickly, because if she hadn't, heaven only knew when she'd have made it to Australia. Now at least she could hope to be there by Christmas.

Stacy was tapping away at a laptop in the medical room at the far end of the tub area. 'Come for your dressing-change? How did you sleep?'

Carol sat down on the chair by a chrome trolley. 'Best night's sleep since I've been here.'

'You needed it.' Stacy peeled off the old dressing and peered at Carol's ear. 'Good, this has stopped weeping. We'll give it a quick clean, and new wadding.'

She worked as she spoke, and soon Carol was sitting with a freshly dressed ear.

Stacy reached for the hand sanitiser. 'What are you doing today?'

'I thought about getting my nails done, but then I wondered if they'd want to take it all off again for my op tomorrow. What do you think?'

Stacy pondered, her head to one side. 'I don't know. It's a short anaesthetic so they might not, but it would be a pity if they did. Why don't you make your nail appointment for Thursday, ready for the Gala Dinner?' She adjusted the tape holding the dressing on, and stepped back. 'Okay, you're done. Come and find me this evening and I'll repeat the process. And keep up the antibiotics!'

Carol wandered back to reception, where she made an appointment for a manicure on Thursday. Maureen was in the sauna, but it was a lovely day – she would go for a walk outside. Carol pressed the button for the lift and was still waiting when Ralph strode through from the stairwell, clad in a thick quilted jacket and gloves.

He stopped abruptly and waved a sackcloth bag at her. 'I'm off to cut the twigs for St Barbara's Day – want to join me?'

Carol blinked at him. Should she? But why not? 'I was just planning a walk, actually. I'll fetch my jacket.'

It was an unaccustomed feeling, getting ready to go for a walk with a man. Not that she had time to do any major reconstruction, mind you. Carol checked her reflection, stuck her tongue out at the dressing, grabbed her things and hurried downstairs again.

Ralph was in the office room behind reception. He came out when she appeared and handed her a still-warm laminated flyer with the story of St Barbara and her cherry tree twig, plus a couple of pictures.

'Lovely,' said Carol. 'I'm sure people will be interested. I'd never heard of her before.'

Ralph put the flyer on the desk. 'Had you heard of our Christmas biscuits?'

'No.' Carol walked with her good ear beside him as they left the hotel. 'I'm looking forward to the demonstration tonight. And I expect there's something special coming at the Gala Dinner on Thursday, too?'

He wagged a finger at her, smiling all the while. 'There is, but you won't hear about it from me. Are you a little glad you came to Lakeside after all?'

Carol considered. 'A little, though I'm gutted I won't get to Australia at the weekend.' She followed him across the decking outside and on to the garden behind the hotel. The ice-blue water of Lake Constance was only about fifty yards away in front of them, the opposite bank hazy in the distance.

Carol pulled her woolly hat right over the dressing on her poorly ear. 'Tell me what we're looking at – that's Germany over there, isn't it?'

'It is. We can cut our twigs and have a short walk along the lake path. From there, you'll see three countries, an island if it's clear enough, and a lake that stretches sideways as far as your eyes can see.'

Ralph's love of the place shone from his face as he led Carol down the garden to the forsythia bush, where he cut around ten 'twigs' – metre-long thin branches – and put them in his bag before slinging it over one shoulder and grinning at her. 'Done! This way to the lake path.'

Carol followed him past some high rhododendron bushes, then they stopped at a little jetty to the side of a grey stone boathouse. Ralph pointed across the lake. 'Germany. Straight across is Langenargen, and further to your left is Friedrichshafen, the Zeppelin town. There's a lovely Christmas market there, but not until next week. And to the right – see that little blob? That's the German island of Lindau, and beyond is the border with Austria. That peak there is the Pfänder, in Austria.'

The winter sun was shining on the other side of the lake, and Carol took her time looking up and down. Why on earth had Ralph left a place he clearly loved?

They strolled along the path, silent for a few minutes before Carol spoke. 'How long have you been away from the hotel?'

'Over a year. It went through a bad patch financially after my wife died three years ago, and I nearly sold it. Then Rico and Stacy came up with the spa idea and took over the management, and they haven't looked back. But part of my family has always been in Lugano, and my brother's there, so it feels like home too. And the weather's better!' He was smiling, but his eyes were dim.

Carol was touched. 'It's hard when you lose your partner. It's been seven years for me.'

He took her elbow and guided her further along the path. 'And your son is in Australia. Not so easy. Do you think he'll ever return to Europe?'

Carol shrugged. 'Who knows? He went for his job, but they love it there.'

'Yes, they have to make their own lives, our children, don't they?' He stared into the distance, his face suddenly bleak. 'I was lost when Edie died, but while Rico was a comfort, he wasn't really a help, if you see what I mean.'

'I do. It's the loneliness of losing your other half, isn't it?'

'Exactly.' His eyes were shining at her again. 'You remind me of her, you know. You have the same kind expression.'

Yikes. Carol bent and pretended to adjust her shoe. Anything to break away from those eyes. This was heading in a direction she'd had no idea of going in when she arrived at Lakeside, and it was a road she wasn't ready for. As for him, three years since his wife's death wasn't so very long. Had he recovered enough to be looking at her like that? And saying she reminded him of his wife – he'd meant it as a compliment, but was it? Heck. He was a nice man, and he definitely liked her, but this was happening at the wrong time, in the wrong place and possibly for the wrong reasons, too. She should take a step right back.

She straightened up and gave him a bright smile. 'Shall we go inside now? I don't want my ear to get cold.'

A question about the boathouse filled the time until they were inside, and Ralph went off to deal with his forsythia while Carol took the lift upstairs, wondering if she'd imagined the expression on his face. Could it be that she had brushed him off when all he'd wanted was to talk about his wife? No. That wasn't it; he'd looked at her like someone who wanted more than he had. So did she, actually, and oh, this was complicated. Ralph was a lovely bloke, and wouldn't she like to be one of a pair again? Yes, she decided, but for the right reasons. And preferably in London. Or dare she even think it, in Australia. She didn't know what she wanted... Or no, she did. She wanted to be with her family.

The sooner she was on her way to Perth, the better.

***

A massage and a visit to the hairdresser took up most of the afternoon, then it was time to have her dressing changed again. Stacy was pleased with the ear, and Carol went up to get ready for dinner feeling more positive. She was getting better, and tomorrow would fix things completely. The upbeat feeling lasted until she was squirting some perfume on her neck and wrists and staring at her reflection in the en suite mirror. If inconspicuous was the look she was aiming for, she'd missed it by a mile, with that wad of dressing in her left ear. And it would take more than freshly washed hair and her blue and silver blouse to make her look glam, too. Carol smiled wryly – cheer up, woman, at least you're well enough to go down for dinner and the Christmas biscuit demonstration.

She pulled a face at the mirror and went back into her new bedroom. It was smaller than the old one, but having a room to herself more than made up for that, and there was even a tiny balcony overlooking the lake. Stacy had helped her settle in, and it was a relief to think she wouldn't disturb Maureen if she was restless in the night, and Maureen wouldn't disturb her, either. There was a lot to be said for having your own space.

A tap on the door heralded the arrival of her friend. 'You look very nice. I'm glad to see some colour in your cheeks again – the pills must be doing their work.' Maureen held the door open as Carol collected her handbag and cardigan.

'That's antibiotics for you. I'm glad I'm feeling less zombie-like, even if I do look like a clown with this dressing.' Ralph's face flitted into Carol's head. He hadn't looked at her as if she was a clown, had he?

Downstairs, a hum of talk was coming from the restaurant, which was almost full, and Carol took her seat at their table beside the dais where the tree stood. The lighting was subdued, giving the candle decorations on the tables a chance to shine out and be reflected in the silver and red. It was all very festive. Carol lifted the menu and browsed the long column of main courses.

'Saffron risotto – that looks perfect,' she said. 'And a side salad. No starter.'

The waiter appeared and asked about drinks, and Carol ordered mineral water, trying not to feel envious of Maureen and her large glass of Féchy.

'I'm glad to see you're so much better!' Ralph was standing by their table, looking very elegant in a dark grey suit. His warm brown eyes shone down at her.

Carol touched the side of her head. 'I'm sure I'll be fine, once this stupid hole in my ear's been repaired.'

'And you never know – you might make the plane at the weekend after all!' said Maureen, and Carol saw a shadow pass over Ralph's face.

'We'll cross everything you can join your family as soon as possible,' he said.

He liked her... he did. Carol watched as Ralph moved on through the restaurant, stopping to talk to several people on the way. She turned back to the table, slightly disturbed to see Maureen's eyes gleaming at her. Oops. It was time to talk about something completely different.

'Do you think I should have red nail varnish for the Gala Dinner, or silver to match my outfit?'

Maureen fell straight into the trap, and they chatted about manicures while Maureen ate her grapefruit starter. Carol relaxed. No way did she want to talk about Ralph until she knew what was what with him – and with her.

The risotto was delicious, and Carol listened while Maureen told her about the various things she'd done that day. The fitness room was apparently excellent, and so was the café in Rorschach where Maureen and a couple she'd chummed up with in the spa had gone for lunch. Carol nodded in all the right places, and now she was definitely envious. She was glad to be able to sit back for the Christmas biscuit demo, due to begin at eight o'clock.

At five to, Rico and Alex appeared carrying a table, followed by Stacy with a trolley holding a selection of ingredients and baking things. They set everything up on the dais, then Rico pulled down a screen at one side and turned to the room.

'Chef's on the way,' he announced, and a spatter of applause came.

The chef, a tall man with a shock of dark hair, bounced in from the kitchen and clicked on the microphone he was holding.

'Good evening, everyone – my name's Rob, and first of all I'm going to tell you something about our beloved *Weihnachtsguetzli* – Christmas biscuits – tradition here in Switzerland.'

His English was fluent, and Carol settled down as he explained about the dozens of different Guetzli, which were only made in December. They were cut into festive shapes, decorated, then eaten or put into bags and gifted to friends and family. A series of images accompanied the talk, and Carol's mouth watered at the cinnamon stars, coated with shiny white icing sugar, and the round hazelnut macaroons with a whole nut pressed into the middle. Rob showed pictures of eight different biscuits, some decorated within an inch of their lives with hundreds and thousands, silver balls, and even ribbons. He told them how he'd always made Guetzli with his grandmother while his mother was at work, and Carol smiled as a thought struck her. She could make some with her little granddaughter, in a week or two. Swiss biscuits in Australia… Her ear gave a twinge as soon as the thought entered her mind, and she crossed her fingers under the table.

'And now I'll show you how to make lemon nut biscuits,' said Rob. 'It's a fifteen-minute demo, and please feel free to move around so that you can see properly.'

Several people came down the room to watch from the side, and Carol was glad to be sitting so near the front.

The recipe appeared on the screen while Rob took his place behind the table and slid the contents of three small bowls into a large one. 'Easy peasy – melted butter, sugar, and egg yolk, and then you beat them together.' He lifted a hand mixer and suited the action to the word. 'Add your flour and ground nuts, and mix.'

He mixed with a spoon this time, then held up the result for them to see. 'Now we have a nice soft dough, and at this point we put it in the fridge for an hour or two, but don't worry – and Stacy tells me you say this a lot in Great Britain – here's one I made earlier!'

The audience laughed as he lifted the new dough from under an upturned bowl and proceeded to roll it out. 'About four millimetres is best. And now we're ready to cut shapes. We have different cookie cutters – heart shapes, Christmas tree, star, of course, half-moon – whatever takes your fancy.' He held the different cutters up, then swiftly cut a selection of shapes and placed the biscuits on a baking tray. 'Now we leave them to rest before they go into the oven for ten minutes, and again – here are some I made earlier.'

The audience cheered, and for the first time, Carol was glad she'd come to the hotel. This was fun, and she was getting ideas for things to do with little Emma.

She watched as Rob made the lemon icing and brushed it over the final batch of biscuits.

'And there we have them. And to make sure none go to waste, we're going to serve coffee and a selection of Christmas Guetzli, and tomorrow morning you'll find a little bag of these biscuits, plus a booklet with a few of the most popular recipes, waiting for you at breakfast time.'

Carol joined in the applause. Rico and Alex began clearing the table away, and the waiters came out with jugs of coffee and started a round of the tables. Carol gazed around the room and met Ralph's eye. Had he been watching her? She gave him a brief smile and looked away. Oh, dear – now her heart was beating faster again, and this was *not* what she needed. Or wanted. Was it? And Maureen was gawping at her too, oh help.

'How's your ear? You're looking much better!' Stacy slid into one of the empty chairs at the table and squeezed Carol's hand.

'I've almost forgotten about it,' said Carol. 'Do you think–'

'I think you need this operation,' said Stacy, looking at her sternly. 'Definitely. Don't worry, it isn't a big deal – preferable to root canal treatment, anyway. But you need it done now, Carol. You don't want Australian bugs flying into that ear.'

Carol pulled a face, but in an odd way, it was comforting that Stacy seemed so sure Australian bugs would have the chance to fly into her ear.

11

Wednesday, 5th December

Rico spent the night rolling around and fighting the duvet as weird and scary dreams flitted through his head, dreams where Ralph, Edie and Carol were chasing after each other, leaving him desperately trying to catch up with them, yelling, *stop, stop, Mum, Dad* – but they didn't hear him, and he fell further and further behind. He came to with a jerk and was immediately wide awake, not comfortably dozy like he usually was. Rico wiped the sweat from his brow and lay there taking deep breaths. Heck… what a start to the day.

He rolled over, stretching a hand out to Stacy then letting it flop back again. It wasn't even six yet; he couldn't wake her this early to talk about something he should have told her yesterday. They'd both been done in after the biscuit demo, though, then Stacy'd wanted to practise her New Year Healthy Eating Plan talk on him. After that, Rico didn't have the energy to start a complicated conversation about what he'd seen, and what he'd seen had caused this nightmare, hadn't it?

A lump the size of a football rose in Rico's throat as he thought back to the previous day. He'd been standing at a window overlooking the terrace and spotted Dad and Carol walking up from the lake path, shoulders almost touching and deep in conversation. It had all looked very cosy. A lot cosier than he liked. Heck again. Was Stacy right? But Dad couldn't have forgotten about Mum already... Rico grabbed a handful of duvet and wiped his eyes. Thinking about Mum was still so bittersweet; surely his father felt the same way. Maybe he and Carol had gone for separate walks and met on the way back? Dad was being polite to a sick guest, that was all. Rico blinked hard. That wasn't what his gut was saying, was it? His gut agreed with Stacy and was telling him loud and clear he hadn't read the signs wrongly, and oh, how it hurt to think his father might be ready to welcome the idea of another woman in his life. And as Carol would be jetting off to Australia soon, then back to England a few weeks later, where that would leave Dad was anyone's guess. Rico rolled out of bed and charged into the en suite. Time to start the day and think about something else.

The coffee machine was droning by the time he emerged, and he stumbled into the kitchen feeling as if he'd run a marathon backwards.

Stacy slid a mug of coffee in front of him. 'Drink. You look like you need it. There was a lot of tossing and turning on your side of the bed last night – what were you dreaming?'

Rico opened his mouth to tell her, then a cheerful whistle came through the door, followed by Ralph, who headed straight for the bread bin.

'Can't remember,' said Rico. 'I'm fine, honestly.'

Stacy raised her eyebrows with an 'I don't believe you but I can see this isn't the time' expression, and Rico helped himself to a croissant and dipped it in his coffee. She was looking tired today too, and he had disturbed her sleep. Welcome to the Lakeside Hotel, run by your friendly neighbourhood zombies... It was going to be a long day.

Stacy put down her mug and looked from Rico to Ralph. 'Who's going to take Carol to St Gallen this morning? She has to be there at ten o'clock. I'd do it, but I'm needed in the spa.'

Rico leapt in immediately. 'I'll do it. I want to visit the factory to have a word with the tubs people, and that's in the same part of town. I can collect your Samiclaus beard, too, Dad.'

Ralph almost choked on his coffee, and Stacy slapped his back. Rico ducked his head, not meeting his father's eye. Wanting a word with the tubs people wasn't quite a lie, because they'd been thinking about getting that planned tub in the garden installed next spring, but... He'd said that because it was the only way he could think of on the spur of the moment to make sure Ralph and Carol didn't have time together. And how despicable was that?

His guilty conscience tripled when Stacy leaned over and kissed him.

'You're a star. Maureen's going with Carol, so you don't need to do anything except drop them off at the day surgery unit. I'll tell them to be downstairs at nine-thirty.'

At half past nine, Rico was in the office behind reception, checking through the emails that had come overnight. The lift doors opened with their usual ping, and he stood up. Hopefully that was Carol; it was time to go.

A sibilant whisper pervaded the front hall. 'He's not here yet. Such a pity it's Rico driving us, and not Ralph! I bet he'd have liked to – Ralph, I mean.'

Maureen's speech ended with a loud chuckle, and Rico clenched his fists. What an awful woman.

'Maureen, for heaven's sake. I'm having an operation. I just want it over with.'

Carol sounded as fed up as Rico felt. He waited until the two women had moved towards the front door, then strode up behind them. 'Ready? Let's go.'

Carol sat beside him as the car sped up the motorway, winter sunshine streaming down, the snow-topped hills of the Appenzellerland to their left and Maureen in the back seat yakking away nonstop about the scenery. Rico gritted his teeth. He was being unfair; that conversation in the hallway hadn't been Carol's fault, and if the situation had been different, he'd probably have been amused by Maureen's chatter. As it was, he was glad to pull up outside the *Hals, Nasen, Ohren Klinik,* a large 1930s grey stone building in the east of St Gallen.

Carol peered unhappily at the sign above the door. 'I guess Hals is throat?'

'That's right. Inside, you'll see signs for the *Ambulante Tagesstation* – that's the day surgery ward. They'll speak English, don't worry. Text Alex when you're ready to come home, and someone will collect you. Good luck!'

The two women disappeared inside, and Rico slumped in the driving seat, old memories flashing through his head. He'd had his tonsils out here. Mum had brought him, and stayed right beside him all the time from walking in the door to ice-cream and discharge afterwards. He hadn't been nervous; he'd known everything would be all right as long as she was there. And now she wasn't here any longer, and so much wasn't right. Rico shook himself. No matter how much you wanted to, you couldn't change the past, and right now he had errands to do in town. He'd talk to Stacy about it as soon as he got back to Lakeside.

She was checking through an order of disinfectant in the medical room off the large spa when he arrived home.

Rico stood in the doorway. 'Got a minute?'

She stared, then pushed the box to one side. 'Yes. Shall we go upstairs for coffee? You look like some privacy would be good.'

'It would, but I don't want Dad to hear us.'

'He's gone to Rorschach. Come on.'

She led the way upstairs, and Rico sat in the kitchen while she made his cappuccino and plonked the biscuit tin on the table. Sudden tears rolled down his cheeks, and Stacy grasped both his hands across the table.

'Spit it out, Rico.'

It sounded petty as he told her about the overheard conversation and his frustration, and the part about his tonsillectomy made him sound like a hormonal teenager, but oh, it was so hard to think that his mother might be losing her place as the most important person in Ralph's life. And that awful Maureen...

Stacy gave his hands a little shake. 'Rico–'

'I know. I'm being stupid and childish.' Now he sounded peeved as well. Rico closed his eyes in despair.

'No, but I think we have to accept that Ralph's life is his, especially when it comes to his friends and his relationships. He loved Edie and I'm sure he always will, but – it's a different kind of love now she's gone, isn't it?'

The fact that she was right only made Rico feel worse. And it didn't mean he had to like what was happening, did it? He glowered into his mug, then stood up abruptly. 'Talking isn't going to change how I feel. I'm going for a walk. I'll see you later.'

Her sigh as he exited the kitchen touched a raw nerve. Rico slammed the flat door as hard as he could behind him.

***

The clinic staff were kind, and Rico was right; they all spoke excellent English. Carol submitted to being examined and prodded, then dressed in the usual kind of hospital gown, and boy, this wasn't half making her feel vulnerable. It was years since she'd last been in hospital, and although the medical scenario here was familiar in some ways, in others it was totally alien. For instance, while the staff all spoke more or less good English to her, when they were talking to each other they spoke Swiss German and she didn't understand a word. To make matters worse, Maureen seemed to be thoroughly enjoying the whole experience, gaping around avidly with bright, interested eyes and a little half-smile on her face. She'd be dining out on this for years to come, no doubt. Butterflies the size of squirrels were crashing around inside Carol by the time the staff left her on her trolley in a little room to wait for the anaesthetist.

Maureen pulled her chair up close. 'They're very efficient, aren't they? Though I must say, they seem to be more casual about staff wearing jewellery and things like that. Not like when I was in hospital for my hallux operation. That was–'

No, no-no. No way did she want to listen to a long story about Maureen's left foot today. Carol interrupted her friend in mid-flow. 'This is day surgery, though. That makes a difference, I expect.'

'Yes. Ooh, I do hope it's Ralph who picks us up afterwards. I'm sure he really likes you, Carol – isn't it lovely? I wonder if...'

No no no no no. She was *not* going to lie here and have Maureen speculate over her head like this. Carol gripped the front of her gown with both hands.

'Maureen, I'm going to be ages here – why don't you pop into town for an hour or two? There's no sense you sitting here twiddling your thumbs while I'm out for the count, is there?'

A nurse appeared before Maureen opened her mouth to reply, and Carol seized the chance. 'Is there a bus into town from here? My friend could do something else for a couple of hours, couldn't she?'

Five minutes later she was alone again, and Carol lay drinking in the peace. Maureen meant well, but she was a dreadful gossip, and all those insinuations were just – cheap, somehow. Like something in an Agatha Christie novel where two older ladies were deluding themselves that the hotel porter fancied them and it ended up with a body in the dining room, or something. A brief smile chased across Carol's face, but oh, she didn't want to end up like that. She wasn't old, not really. Not at all, in fact.

What did she want? The usual ache was back. Her family, oh, she wanted to see Barry and Diane and the children so much; she wanted to be with them and never leave them and if that meant moving to Australia, well, that's what she would do. Decision made.

Ralph's face swam in front of her eyes, and Carol pushed it away. If things had been different, they might have had something together one day. But it was what it was – too soon for him, too far for her, and there was no use hankering after the impossible. Forget it, Carol.

12

WEDNESDAY, 5TH DECEMBER, AFTERNOON

Rico and Alex were doing something complicated on the office computer when Stacy went downstairs after lunch. Was he still uptight? She put her head round the door, eyebrows raised, and Rico gave her a tight smile and shook his head. Stacy left them to it and went on to the medical room. Frustrating as it was, if Rico wanted to ignore what was happening with Ralph, right this minute there was nothing she could do about it. Okay. Her Healthy Eating Plan talk for tonight was prepared, and she had plenty of time before she'd have to leave to collect Carol. This would be a good time to call Denise, Alex's mum. Stacy pulled out her phone and tapped.

'Hello, Stacy, love, good to hear from you.'

Guilt seared into Stacy's middle. She should have done this a week ago at least. 'Sorry, Denise – it's been manic here. As well as all the Christmas stuff we have a sick guest. Alex said you're doing very well with your therapy, though?'

Denise sounded more upbeat than Stacy had ever heard her. 'I feel I've turned a corner. I went right down to the street today, by myself, and I know if Alex or someone was with me, I could go further. I really hope I can hold onto the progress this time. But tell me more about the hotel – is it flu your guest has? And let's get a visit sorted, lovey. It's been too long.'

Stacy explained about the ear infection, leaving out the Ralph complication. Denise used to work in a big international hotel in Sarajevo, so she knew how stressful hotel work could be. The outbreak of war in the nineties meant she and her husband had to flee, and the resulting agoraphobia had cost Denise her marriage and Alex his dad, who worked in India now. Stacy had supported Denise at the start of her therapy, and it was a two-way thing now too – Denise was a motherly soul. And a visit was long overdue.

She glanced at the medical room clock. 'I'm going to collect Carol and her friend in a bit. How about I visit you tomorrow morning? We could go for a walk if it's nice. I'd like to see your progress.'

They arranged to have elevenses together, giggling like two schoolgirls about the fact that it was 'elevenses' in English but 'nineses' in Swiss German, which gave you an idea about working times here. Stacy ended the call and sighed. No wonder she was half-dead on her feet; she was up with the larks every morning and hadn't seen her bed the right side of midnight since last week. And now she had to drive to St Gallen. Stacy grabbed her things and hurried through the spa.

Ralph was standing in the hallway, a perplexed expression on his weather-beaten face. He grabbed her on the way past.

'What's up with Rico? He nearly bit my head off when I went into the office just now. What on earth are they doing?'

'He has a lot on his mind,' Stacy replied, and fortunately Ralph took this as having something to do with tomorrow's Gala Dinner and decided to have another look at his Samiclaus speech. Stacy left him waiting for the lift – what a mess this all was.

Half an hour later, she was running up the steps of the Ear, Nose and Throat clinic. The day surgery ward was on the ground floor, and Stacy went in with fingers firmly crossed that Carol's op had gone well. What would they do if it hadn't? She asked for Carol at the nursing station, and a nurse directed her to a room at the end of the corridor. Carol was waiting in an armchair, with Maureen on a smaller chair beside her, and the moment Stacy stepped through the door she could see the procedure had gone well – Carol's entire posture was more relaxed.

'You're looking good, all things considered,' said Stacy. 'The nurse said you're ready to go. Shall we?'

She gave Carol her arm on the way out while Maureen carried the bag of dressings and meds they collected from the nursing station. Outside, Carol heaved a huge sigh.

'I wish I'd had a burst eardrum after my flight home the year before last. If I'd had it fixed then, I'd have been off to Perth on Saturday.'

'Won't be too much longer,' said Stacy, clicking the key to unlock the car. 'You're looking good, Mrs.'

'I feel so much better than I thought I would.' Carol lowered herself into the front passenger seat. 'Though I still can't hear normally in my left ear.'

'I'm not surprised, with all that wadding on it,' said Maureen from the back.

'When do you have to see the doctor again, Carol?' Stacy was determined not to let Maureen start her usual chatter. This woman's tactless remarks were causing Rico a shedload of grief, and try as she might to suppress it, resentment rose in Stacy every time Maureen opened her mouth.

'I have to see your doctor again in a week,' said Carol. 'Then he'll decide when I get to fly.'

'So until then we do everything strictly by the book,' said Stacy firmly. 'We want to get you to Australia ASAP.'

Carol sniffed. 'I'd better contact the airline and tell them I'm not flying on Friday.'

Fortunately for Stacy's nerves, silence reigned in the car for the rest of the short journey home, and she left Carol resting in her room while Maureen went to the hairdresser. Job done. And now for the man in her life.

Rico was nowhere in sight and wasn't answering his phone, either. Stacy searched around and eventually found him on an exercise bike in the fitness room, his face shining with sweat. Stacy grimaced. Exercise would get rid of Rico's frustration, maybe, but it wouldn't actually change the problem, would it?

'Hi, there.' She went over and checked the gauge on the bike. 'Fifteen kilometres, not bad.' She glanced behind them. No one was within hearing distance. 'Are you okay, Rico? And are *we* okay?'

He slowed down and sat straight, taking a slug from his water bottle. 'We're okay. I'm sorry. I'm still struggling with – you know. Dad.'

Stacy nodded. 'It's going to be hard, I get that. It's an odd idea for me too, and I didn't know Edie, though I feel as if I did. But it's Ralph's life and we have to be happy if he's happy.'

'In a way, I hope it all fizzles out when she goes to Australia. Actually, I hope even more that we're wrong and he doesn't – he isn't–' Rico pressed his lips together.

Stacy rubbed his arm. 'We'll wait and see, and be supportive to Ralph whatever happens.'

Rico dismounted, and slung his towel round his neck. 'Yeah. I don't have to enjoy doing it, though.'

Stacy watched as he sprayed disinfectant on a paper towel and wiped the bike down, then headed for the showers. Poor Rico. And poor her, too. In exactly an hour and a half, she had to give her Healthy Eating Plan talk, followed by a Q&A session for as long as the guests had Qs for her to A. Stacy sighed. Fourteen people had put their names down for the talk, so probably there'd be even more by the time it started. It was going to be another intensive evening.

To Stacy's relief, her audience of sixteen – mostly women, didn't guys care about healthy eating? – listened with interested expressions and didn't ask too many questions. She piled up the chairs at the side of the medical room to be put away tomorrow, and headed for the lift. And the moment she got back to the flat she was going to make a lovely hot chocolate and blob for twenty minutes before bedtime. She'd earned it. Rico came out of the office and joined her.

'I've wrapped some more of the presents people are ordering. The spa shop was an inspired idea, you know. You should thank your mum from us. It's turning into quite a money-spinner.'

Stacy tucked her arm into his as the lift whirred upwards. 'She'll be pleased about that. I'm going to make some–'

The doors opened on the fourth floor and they stepped out, almost colliding with Ralph, who was heading towards the attic floor rooms on the other side of the landing, a little tray in his hands with a cup of tea and a slice of almond cake.

'What the–' Rico jerked up straight and hissed at his father. 'What are you doing?'

Stacy's heart plummeted. If ever a man had looked guilty, it was Ralph. So much for a hot choc and a blob before bedtime.

Ralph gave Rico a sideways glance. 'I'm taking Carol a cuppa. I know she's still up because I heard her moving around a few minutes ago.'

Mentally, Stacy rolled her eyes. He'd listened at her door, he meant. And if she didn't get this particular situation sorted before they were all less than three seconds older, Rico was going to explode. She seized Ralph's tray and jerked her head towards their own flat.

'Skedaddle, gents. It's a good idea, Ralph, but I'll take it in. Carol might still be up, but she might be in her nightie too.'

She marched up to the door leading to the attic floor rooms and went in, closing it firmly behind her. Please God those two had enough sense to go and finish their argument in their own flat.

Carol *was* in her nightie, but she was pleased to have the tea, and Stacy made a note to put a hospitality tray into the room for her. She'd meant to do that before, but somehow, she'd had other things on her mind. Like the two men who were saying heaven knows what to each other right now. She crossed the landing and went into their own kitchen, bracing herself for an argument.

The room was empty. Ralph's door was closed, and Stacy went on into the living room. The French doors were open, and Rico was standing outside, leaning on the balcony rail.

'Rico Weber! You'll catch your death out here in this weather. Come back in and I'll make us some hot choc. You okay, love?' She put an arm around him and hugged. He was shaking.

'I can't stop him, can I? Even if it's not Carol, he'll find someone, and Mum will be gone from Lakeside.'

Stacy pulled him inside. 'Edie will be here in spirit as long as the chalet's still standing and you're here too. Come on, Rico. Let your dad live his life, because you're right, you can't stop him and you shouldn't want to, either.'

They went into the kitchen and she put a jug of milk into the microwave. Rico was slumped over the table, unshed tears bright in his eyes. Stacy made the hot choc and pushed a mug over to him. 'Tell me you didn't tear strips out of each other while I was with Carol.'

'We didn't say a word.' Rico sipped. 'I do know you're right, you know. I'm just having problems getting my head round the fact that I could have a new mother soon.'

Stacy gave his shoulder a shake. 'Now you're being daft. Leave Ralph alone. Does this have anything to do with your own grief, Rico?'

He stared. 'No. Not really. I'm grieving the life I had, but that won't bring it back and that's…'

'Normal,' Stacy finished for him. 'And we're building a new life and your mum would be proud of us both. Now drink that chocolate and let's get some sleep before we have queues of guests at reception again.'

He smiled, but oh, it was a sad smile, wasn't it? She'd have to help him get on top of this. Stacy sipped her hot choc. The Lakeside Advent programme had started with a bang, but fireworks weren't what they needed at Christmas time.

13

Thursday, 6th December, morning

Stacy flung the duvet back. Six-thirty on Thursday morning, well past time to get up – why hadn't Rico woken her? Probably he thought he was doing the right thing, after last night's upset, but tonight's Gala Dinner was the biggest occasion on their Advent events calendar so far, and it had to run like clockwork. Posh clockwork, even. Not that the food was particularly posh tonight; they were having watercress and celeriac soup or grapefruit cocktail, followed by Raclette, a traditional Swiss meal consisting of cheese melted under a grill and served with potatoes and pickles. There was a mushroom risotto option for anyone who hated cheese, then ice cream cake for dessert. It was the Samiclaus appearance that would make the evening memorable, and the way things were in their family right now, they were going to have to put on several brave faces for the guests.

Stacy showered quickly, making plans. She would take charge of the family mood as soon as she had both Webers at the breakfast table.

Ralph appeared first, and Stacy handed him a steaming mug.

'You're spoiling me,' he said, reaching for the cereal.

'We have to keep our Samiclaus going.' She smiled brightly as Rico banged into the flat and thudded into a chair without speaking, then passed him a mug too. 'Okay, gents, important announcement alert. Listen up.' Two faces gazed at her enquiringly, and Stacy grasped her courage with both hands.

'This is our first hotel Advent, and it's a lot of work. Plus, we've had ups and downs of various kinds this week. But – we're going to put all that behind us, and make this the most successful Gala Dinner ever. *Capisce?*'

She added the last word in Italian – it sounded more humorous than 'is that clear?' Somehow, they were going to have to get into a jolly Christmas mood for the guests, but hotel keepers were good at acting, weren't they?

'*Si, si,*' said Ralph, and Rico nodded in agreement too.

Stacy sat back. Good. Surely it was clear to the men in her life that business was business and the other stuff should be dealt with in a way that didn't hurt the hotel?

Ralph chomped his way through his cornflakes, then stood up. 'Stacy, could we try on my Samiclaus beard before lunch? I don't want to have a panic half an hour before my appearance.'

Rico waved his toast at Ralph. 'Could *we* try on...? Please do not put any beards on my fiancée,' he said, his face deadpan, and Ralph guffawed.

'I'd like to see him try,' said Stacy. Brilliant, they were working with her.

She went down to the spa after breakfast and found the first two guests up to their necks in a tub already. Carol appeared soon afterwards to have her dressing changed, looking much happier. Because her operation was over and the prospect of flying to Australia didn't seem so distant? Or because she had met Ralph and sensed her life could be different? Hard to tell, and impossible to ask.

Stacy put on her nurse's face. 'Looking good here.' She discarded the old dressing and began to clean the ear.

'It feels fine. Do you think I could do my own dressings now? I don't want to be a nuisance.'

'You're not. Why don't you come back tonight and I'll guide you through it, and if all goes well, you're on your own afterwards. How's that?'

'Perfect.' Carol left to go for her manicure, and Stacy started to tidy the dressings tray.

A knock came at the door. 'Excuse me?'

Stacy turned round – oh, it was Elaine Cooper, the mother of the two children in the hotel this week. She gave the woman a smile. 'Hello – how can I help?'

Elaine pulled her bathrobe more firmly around her. 'I'm just about to jump in a tub, but we were wondering – do you have a babysitting service? Joe and I want to come to the Gala Dinner tonight, and that's not really anything for kids, is it?'

'Oh, but–' Stacy swallowed her surprise. A visit from the Samiclaus was exactly right for kids, but of course the guests knew nothing about what was planned for the evening.

She dropped her voice so that no one else would hear. 'Please do bring them tonight. There's a surprise, and without telling you too much, I can say it's something that kids all over Switzerland look forward to at this time of year. Believe me, the Gala Dinner tonight is *exactly* the right place for Sharon and Simon.'

Elaine's shoulders drooped. 'Oh – okay. I was kind of hoping for a nice peaceful evening with my husband, for a change. We've spent the entire week doing things for the kids.' She gave Stacy a very tight smile and flip-flopped her way towards the hottest tub.

Stacy stared after her. Gawd. The woman had two lovely children, they were on a family holiday, and she was trying to... Stacy went back to the medical room to gather her thoughts, and common sense kicked in. She should stop right there. Just because she was longing to have a family didn't turn every tired mum who wanted an evening away from her kids into a monster. And heaven knows, she knew what it was like to be tired, too. And now it was more than time she was heading off to see Denise.

Rorschach was a five-minute drive up the lake, and Stacy took a moment on the way to go into the village patisserie for a couple of Denise's favourite pastries. She parked under Denise's apartment building on a hill a few minutes early. Time for a quick breather. Stacy stood by the car, gazing right and left over Lake Constance below. The opposite bank was hidden in clouds today, and the water stretched into infinity. Peace...

The church clock further up the hill struck nine, and Stacy hurried inside and up to Denise's first-floor apartment.

'You're spoiling me.' The older woman hugged her, and Stacy hugged back, unexpected tears in her eyes. It felt like a long time since she'd had a hug. Ralph was more a pat on the shoulder person, and Rico – well, they barely saw each other these days, never mind hugging. And when they did find themselves in the same space, she always seemed to be preaching at him in some way. Well, not preaching, exactly, but it was heading in that direction and she hated it. She sat down on Denise's squishy sofa, and Snowy the cat immediately jumped up for a cuddle. Oh, this was lovely.

Denise came through from the kitchen with coffee. For a while they chatted about Alex and Rico and Christmas in general, then Denise put down her empty plate.

'You're as pale as I've ever seen you, Stacy. What's going on? Alex said on Tuesday that the hotel was busy, but everything was going well. Has your sick guest been keeping you up at night?'

Stacy flinched. Nice to know you were a terrible advertisement for your wellness hotel… She'd better use more blusher or she'd be frightening the guests. 'No – well, only once. But there's so much more to do than I'd anticipated, and this is just week one. Rico and I barely get a moment to breathe, and I'm totally crabby and tired.' And worried about Ralph and Carol and Rico, but that was better kept to herself.

Denise frowned. 'You need extra Christmas staff, like you have in the summer. They could do the day-to-day hotel stuff for you, and free you up for the special Christmas work.'

'Another year, that's what we'll do, but it's too late for this season now. A good night's sleep will sort me, though, and after this week we only have another two before we close on the twenty-second. I'll be able to relax then.' If another two weeks didn't kill her first, that was.

Denise nodded thoughtfully, then drained her mug. 'Let's go for that walk, shall we? Our first ever walk on the streets of sunny Rorschach!'

Stacy laughed. 'You're on! Today Rorschach, tomorrow – who knows where you'll land!'

***

The tubs were buzzing when Stacy arrived back at Lakeside. Everyone seemed to want a soak before the Gala Dinner. Alex was at the desk, dealing with a short queue of guests, and Stacy frowned. Why wasn't Flavia, the hotel's all-rounder, out here helping him?

He jerked his head towards the office. 'Believe it or not, she has fifty-three orders from the spa shop to gift wrap.'

Glory... Or – good in one way, but a touch intensive. Stacy looked in on Flavia, who was pink and frowning over a silver ribbon. 'Oh, Flavia. I'll get someone to help you ASAP.'

To Stacy's horror the girl promptly burst into tears. 'I have to help in the restaurant and look at the queue at reception and I still have all these–' She gestured towards a long list of who had ordered what from the shop. 'And Margrit said she'd started a new list, too!'

Alex put his head in the door. 'All good out here, now. I'll help you for a bit, Flavia.' He sat down beside her at the desk and gave her shoulder a little pat.

Flavia gave him a shaky smile. 'Thank you, Alex.'

Her eyes lingered on his face, and the expression in her eyes... Stacy reeled. Please, somebody tell her she didn't have another one-way romance on her hands here. There was no use at all in Flavia getting all starry-eyed over Alex when his eyes were firmly fixed on Zoe – who'd be leaving soon for a five-month tour with the orchestra. This was dire... But right now, it was definitely a case of 'least said, soonest mended'.

Stacy grasped the door frame. 'Thanks, both of you. Do your best for now, and I'll find someone to help out later.' But who? Ralph was no gift-wrapper, and – heck – Ralph! She was supposed to be helping him with his beard right now.

Stacy fled, and took the lift up to the flat, and oh, her brief respite with Denise had been exactly that – brief. How was it possible that a hotel Christmas would generate so much work? Upstairs, Ralph was in the bathroom, peering anxiously at the little tube of glue supplied by the shop. Stacy sat down on the edge of the bath. Good, she wasn't late – or not very.

Ralph glanced up. 'I've never used this stuff before. Supposing it won't come off?'

Stacy pressed a tiny amount onto her fingers. 'I think it's like that gum they sometimes have in magazines. You know, when they stick a sachet of face cream or whatever to a page. Let's try it.'

Fifteen minutes' work convinced Ralph the beard wasn't going to be a problem, and he grinned at Stacy. 'Sorted. Um – how's Carol this morning? Have you seen her?'

'Recovering well. She's looking forward to the dinner tonight.'

He fidgeted with the tube of glue. 'When will she be able to fly?'

Oops. Stacy packed the beard back into its box to give herself time to think. Patient confidentiality might be about to raise its head. She spoke carefully. 'She sees the doc again next Wednesday, and he'll decide about flying then.'

Ralph's face brightened noticeably at this. Stacy hesitated. Should she say something? But why not? She and Ralph were as good as family now. She grabbed her courage before it bolted. 'You like her, don't you?'

He stared at her, then spoke in an unexpectedly bitter tone. 'I'm allowed to, I guess? But either way, she'll be gone soon, so that's sorted. For Rico. Not being blind, I've seen what he thinks about it, you know.'

He swung round and left the room, and his bedroom door closed behind him. Stacy headed back downstairs. By the looks of things, she'd be spending the next few hours wrapping presents. But oh, poor Ralph. Poor Rico, too. It would need a really good family discussion to put things right – if they could be put right.

***

Carol emerged from the massage room that afternoon feeling literally lighter. All the tension in her shoulders was gone, and the pummelling had loosened up her entire body. This was how she'd imagined she'd feel after a holiday in a spa hotel. Okay, her hearing was still dull on the left side, but the niggling pain was gone. The only worry was she might miss Christmas with her family, and–

Ralph leapt out of the room behind reception and strode across to her. 'Hello there! Feeling better today?'

Carol stopped dead. Had he been watching out for her? Or was she conceited to even think that? 'Almost normal, thank you. Everyone's being so kind.'

'I was wondering – would you like to go for a coffee, or another little walk by the lake? It's pleasant out today if you wrap up well.'

His brown eyes gazed at her hopefully, and Carol's heart thumped. Oh, why weren't things different? If they'd met in London another year down the line when Ralph was properly over his wife's death, this could have turned out well. Things weren't different, though, and she should be sensible and say 'no, thanks' to Ralph, potentially saving both of them more heartache and agonising. Her heart decided for her. Sensible was boring... though it would have to be a walk. The last thing she wanted was to sit in the restaurant with him and run the risk of Maureen spotting them there when she came out of the spa. Knowing Mo, she'd pull up a chair and join them.

'Some fresh air would be lovely,' she said. 'I'll get my jacket.'

They left the hotel via the terrace and wandered along the lake path, heading in the other direction this time. Not many people were out; in spite of the sunshine it was cold, with a bitter wind blowing across the water. Carol tucked her dressing more firmly under her hat and thrust her hands into her pockets, her thoughts in turmoil. She was out walking with a man she could easily fall in love with, but she wasn't sure he was ready to fall in love with her, no matter what he thought. And soon now she'd be leaving Switzerland, so she'd never see him again and maybe it was better like that. You didn't get much more bittersweet than this. Help... This walk was a bad idea.

'It's a *Bise Wind* today, it comes from the north-east,' said Ralph. 'See how the colour of the lake is different, out in the middle? And the waves are another typical sign. It's normally pretty calm.'

Carol gazed over the water, dark blue with an almost-turquoise stripe up the middle today. 'That wind could be blowing straight from Siberia. Do you think you'll have snow soon?'

'They're forecasting it for next week. So you might see some more before you leave us for warmer places.'

Carol didn't know whether to be pleased at the prospect or not. 'I think if I came back to Switzerland, I'd come in the summer. There must be so much to do then.'

Ralph was silent for a moment, then he began to talk about summers in Grimsbach and in Lugano. They exchanged views on how much heat was desirable when you were on holiday, and Carol couldn't help laughing at Ralph's tales of some of the tourists who arrived at the hotel in summer, expecting the weather in northern Switzerland to be cold.

'I'd like to see a Swiss summer,' she said, pulling the zip on her jacket as high as it would go.

'I hope you will,' said Ralph. 'And you'll have plenty of winter heat in Australia, too.'

'I might be living in that heat soon,' said Carol, then nearly bit her tongue off. Heavens, why on earth had she blurted that out? Ralph's eyes were shocked, and she hurried to explain. 'Barry wanted me to join them permanently, and of course I'd love to see the children grow up. But nothing's settled.'

He was silent for a moment, then smiled a strangely sad smile. 'Watching the children grow up would be wonderful. But for now, we should go back. I'll need some time to make myself glamorous for the Gala Dinner tonight.'

Neither of them said much on the way back, and Carol fought against a tide of doubt swirling in her head. His face when she said she might make her home in Australia had been telling. Maybe that thought that he only liked her because of her resemblance to his wife was wrong. Burning tears rose in her eyes, and she blinked them back, glad to blame the wind. Yes, she could easily fall in love with this man. He was kind, he liked her, yes, he did – but he didn't know if she liked him, did he? And yet… maybe it was better like that. Wasn't she too old for all this, anyway? What did she want for the rest of her life? *To live with her family in Australia,* her head answered immediately, but oh, she didn't know what her heart wanted.

Ralph left her in the front hallway literally ten seconds before Maureen came out of the spa, and Carol grinned inwardly. Sometimes things did go right...

Maureen took her arm and pulled her towards the restaurant. 'Have you been outside? Isn't it cold? Let's go for coffee. Have you seen Ralph today?'

'Maureen, for Pete's sake, don't be such a question mark!' said Carol. 'A quick coffee, then. I have to see Stacy about my dressing.'

To her relief, Maureen said nothing more about Ralph, and Carol escaped twenty minutes later to have her dressing technique checked.

'That's fine,' said Stacy, after talking her through the change. 'Fingers crossed you'll be on a plane soon. Remind me how long your son's been in Australia?'

Carol told her, and they had quite a conversation about parents and children who lived far away. Apparently Stacy's mum had problems with that too, and Carol could only sympathise.

'Will I be able to stay on here next week?' she asked, crossing all her fingers. It would be awful if she had to find a B&B, and live with people she didn't know.

Stacy nodded. 'Your room's empty until January, so no problems there. The attic floor rooms are smaller than the regular ones and we decided not to use them for the Christmas package. I'm sure you'll be on a plane in no time, though. That ear's looking good.'

Carol went upstairs to get ready for the Gala Dinner feeling much more positive. Very soon, she'd soon be toasting in Australia, making Swiss Guetzli with little Emma. *Far away from Ralph*, said her heart. *That's what you want*, said her head. *Hm...* said her heart. *Would you even be wondering about making your home in Australia if you had someone here to love?* Her head was silent.

14

Thursday, 6th December, evening

Rico pulled at his bow tie. He so rarely wore a dinner suit he didn't have one, and this hired one wasn't sitting comfortably. The shiny black lapels on the jacket made him look like a Christmas decoration, and weren't dinner jackets meant to be longer? He'd be a whole lot more comfortable in his own single-breasted black suit. The one he'd bought for Mum's funeral... Oh, heck. He twisted in front of the wardrobe mirror, then went through to the living room in search of a second opinion.

'No, it's fine,' said Ralph. 'And think how much cooler you'll be in that than I'll be in my Samiclaus gear, so stop complaining.'

'You look fab, Rico,' said Stacy, who was looking gorgeous in a long dark blue dress with sparkly bits down the front.

'So do you. I wish we were going somewhere just the two of us.'

A wistful expression flashed across Stacy's face as he spoke, and Rico sighed inwardly. They were both feeling the pressure, but there was no time to do anything about it. He tugged at his jacket again. It would have to do. He turned back to his father and Stacy.

'Okay, team. Stacy and I go down and mingle as the guests arrive, then I'll do my speechifying, then it's starters, then Raclette, then another speech to introduce Dad as the Klaus. I suppose Alex has everything he needs to be Schmützli?'

'Yup. We filled the goodie bags for the guests this afternoon and packed them in his sack,' said Stacy. 'Shall we get the show on the road?'

Downstairs, Rico walked round the restaurant chatting to the arriving guests while the waiters distributed Prosecco. The room looked great – the lights on the Christmas tree were twinkling away in dimness on the dais, and each table had a Christmas decoration as centrepiece. The two Cooper children were wide-eyed as they took their places, and regret stabbed into Rico. Stacy so wanted kids... He pushed the thought away and glanced over to the tables along the far wall, where four large Raclette grills were set out, ready for the waiters to bring portions of cheese to the tables. The Raclette was to be served *à discrétion*, which sounded better than 'all you can eat'.

When everyone was seated, Rico went to the dais and switched on the microphone. The buzz of chatter died down.

'Ladies and gentlemen, welcome to the first ever Advent Gala Dinner here at Lakeside. December the 6th is a very special day in Switzerland, but I'll explain more about that when our guest of honour arrives after the main course.'

A murmur ran through the room, and Rico smiled round at the guests. Some of them would have an idea of what was to come, but others would be clueless – whichever way, hopefully they'd all have fun.

'I won't keep you longer now, so I'll wish you all *en Guete* – have a lovely meal!'

He walked among the tables as he headed for the door, hearing Sharon Cooper's loud whisper as he passed.

'Is Santa coming, Mummy?'

Rico stopped, and bent to whisper loudly in the little girl's ear. 'We don't have Santa in Switzerland. It's the Christ Child who brings the presents here, but nobody ever sees him and he never visits shops or parties, either. But don't worry – I promise you'll enjoy our visitor!'

He followed Stacy from the room as the waiters brought out the starters. In the office, Alex had arrived and was hanging up his long brown Schmutzli robe.

'I'll come out and tell you when to get dressed,' said Stacy. 'You don't want to be waiting around too long in that lot, especially as the restaurant's going to be warm after all the Raclette-grilling.'

Ralph appeared with his outfit over his arm. 'Go back and mingle, you two,' he said. 'Alex and I can entertain ourselves.'

Rico wandered down one side of the restaurant, chatting to those guests who had finished their starters, while Stacy did the same on the other side. They made a good team, he thought, glancing over to her, then standing still as he saw another wistful look flash over her face. She was looking at the table with the Cooper family, the children chatting away non-stop. And right beside them was another table where four young people were laughing and talking and clinking glasses. Heck. But that was how it worked when you had a hotel. Other people had the fun and you did the work. On the other hand, Stacy did a lot of that work, and he and Ralph hadn't made things easier for her this week, had they? Rico caught her eye across the room and she gave him a tiny smile then looked away. Rico flinched. They would need to take time for themselves soon. This whole Advent thing was causing chaos in their relationship.

He returned to his mingling, realising he was about to hit Carol and Maureen's table.

'Nice to see you looking so much better,' he said to Carol. Like virtually everyone else in the room, she was sitting there with pink cheeks and a happy smile. Did Carol's rosy cheeks have anything to do with Ralph? But surely not...

'Everyone's been so kind,' said Carol.

'I don't see your father here, Rico,' said Maureen, and Rico noticed Carol's sudden frown.

'Oh, he's around somewhere,' he said, trying hard to keep the stiffness out of his voice. 'Enjoy your Raclette!'

He escaped into the kitchen, memories of long-gone December 6th parties crowding into his head. How Mum had loved it. They'd had Samiclaus parties at school, too, but the family ones were the best. Usually, a couple of families had come together in someone's house or garden on the sixth, and a mate of one of the dads would be Samiclaus, and it had all been so special and magical. How could his father just throw away the past like this? Even wanting to start another relationship was–

With an effort, Rico pulled himself together. He was being ridiculous, but it hurt to think that Dad might want to 'move on'. Horrible expression.

Soberly, Rico went through to the hallway. Stacy was in the office now with Alex and Ralph, but she emerged when she saw him.

'I told them twenty minutes,' she said. 'Shall we grab some soup to keep us going?'

Half an hour later, the waiters were clearing the last of the Raclette plates away, and Rico went back to the dais. At the side of the room, Stacy dimmed the main lights, leaving the dais illuminated by the tree. An expectant hush fell over the room.

Rico gazed around the assembled guests, his face carefully solemn. 'Ladies and gents – as some of you may know, in Switzerland we have a very important visitor on December 6th. He only comes on this one day, and the rest of his time is spent in the Black Forest. We're very lucky that he's come to Lakeside to see you all tonight – but if you've been bad this past year, you'd better sneak out immediately or you'll find yourself bundled into a sack and taken to the Black Forest.' He stopped, shaking his head at the guests. Several people were laughing, while others looked intrigued – good, this was going down well.

'His name, ladies and gents, is the Samiclaus, and he'll be here soon. Does nobody want to leave? What good people you all must be. Aha – too late – I hear a bell!'

The bell – a high-pitched hand bell previously owned by Rico's grandmother – jingled again, and complete silence fell as the restaurant doors opened and the red-cloaked Samiclaus entered, a long staff in one hand and a golden book – a photo album covered in gift-wrapping – under one arm. Rico almost applauded. Ralph really looked the part – sovereign, untouchable and benign all at the same time. The Cooper children were sitting with open mouths, the little boy holding onto his mum's hand. Rico swallowed painfully; oh, he remembered that feeling. Slowly, the Samiclaus moved down the room, Schmutzli following on, looking nervous with a sack over one shoulder and a handful of birch rods in his other hand.

Solemnly, Rico shook hands with both when they reached the dais, then the Samiclaus took his place on the throne and spoke to his audience.

'Schmutzli and I are pleased to be here,' he announced, and Schmutzli nodded vigorously. 'I'm happy to see you all and glad most people have behaved this year. But–' He waved the golden book and dropped his voice as he glared around the room. 'Some things in here aren't quite what we'd like to see, are they, Schmutzli?'

Schmutzli lowered his head sorrowfully, though his lips were twitching under the grey beard. Rico hid a smile.

'We'll come round and have a little chat with each of you,' said the Samiclaus, his voice ringing round the room again. 'And Schmutzli knows what to do if anyone has misbehaved...'

Schmutzli waved his birch rods, and the audience tittered. Solemnly, the Samiclaus rose to his feet and bowed to Rico before moving regally to the first table. At Rico's signal, the waiters began to distribute dessert to the other tables, grinning at the guests' faces.

***

'Oh my – I wonder what he's saying to them!' Maureen gaped down the room, where the red-cloaked Samiclaus was holding his book open and conversing seriously with the couple at the first table. 'And who can it be?'

Carol picked up her spoon. 'I don't know, but let's get on with this before it melts!' And no, she didn't know for sure who it was, but she had a pretty good idea, because she'd spent quite a lot of time recently with someone whose voice was remarkably similar to that of the Samiclaus...

After ten minutes, she and Maureen were at the coffee stage, the Samiclaus was at the next table, and Maureen was hyperventilating beside her. Carol hid a smile, squinting across the table. Heavens, her friend would explode if the suspense lasted much longer.

But it didn't. The red figure and the brown one moved over to their table and yes, it was Ralph. There wasn't much of him to be seen beneath his outfit, and he must have been boiling hot wearing it, but there was no mistaking those eyes twinkling down at her. Carol suppressed a giggle.

'Ladies. It's lovely to have you here in our beautiful country, but – what's this I read?' The Samiclaus opened his golden book and leafed over a few pages. 'Something about not taking enough exercise?' He waggled his eyebrows at them both.

Maureen answered, looking surprised. 'Oh, my goodness, yes – there never seems to be enough time after work!'

Carol gave Ralph a careful grin – she'd complained about not doing enough exercise during one of their walks. Maureen was staring straight at Ralph, and Carol wondered if she'd realised who the Samiclaus was.

The Samiclaus shook his head at Maureen. 'Aha. Could do better, then. And – too much chocolate?!' He whirled round to face Carol square on.

'Guilty as charged,' she said. They'd talked about chocolate, too.

'Should we take them with us, Schmutzli?'

Schmutzli shook his head, and Carol almost exploded as his hood fell forwards over his face, revealing too much of Alex's profile. He pushed it back again, and the Samiclaus coughed.

'Very well. Do you promise to do better?'

'Oh yes!' Maureen giggled, and Carol nodded, grinning into the brown eyes fixed on her face.

'Then all is well. Schmutzli?'

Schmutzli produced two small bags from his sack and handed them to Carol and Maureen. He and the Samiclaus bowed, and moved on to the next table.

Carol picked up her bag, laughing. 'What's in here?' She opened it to find chocolate, a mandarin orange, and some peanuts. 'I assume we're allowed to eat this before we start doing better!'

Half an hour later the Samiclaus finished his round of the tables, having spent an extra-long time with the two children. He waved cheerily to the guests as he shouted goodbye and exited the dining room, leaving a buzz of chatter and laughter behind.

Rico took the microphone again. 'And that was a little peek at our Samiclaus tradition. It's mainly for children, of course. Parents can organise for a local Samiclaus to visit them at home, and there's a system for the parents...' He glanced at the children, and cleared his throat significantly. '...and then the Samiclaus can talk to the children about what they've been doing all year. Traditionally, he should arrive with Schmutzli and a donkey, but you'd be amazed how often the donkey is "sick" on the 6th of December!'

Carol joined in the laughter, and oh, she was tired. It was a good tiredness, though. Rico ended with a few more remarks about the first Advent week, now almost over as several guests were departing the following day, and the lights came back up.

'Feeling okay?' Stacy stopped by the table as Carol and Maureen were getting up to leave.

'Ready for bed. It was a lovely evening. Well done, all of you.' Carol touched the younger woman's arm.

Stacy looked gratified, then Maureen leapt in.

'Who was the Samiclaus?'

Stacy wagged a finger. 'The Samiclaus, of course! There's only one of him!' Her eyes were twinkling as she went on to speak to other guests.

Ralph and Alex were nowhere in sight as Carol and Maureen walked round to join the queue for the lift. Carol hugged herself. She would see Ralph tomorrow, no doubt, and ask him more about the Samiclaus and his doings. It was a good thought to end the day with.

15

FRIDAY, 7TH DECEMBER

Stacy finished explaining about different kinds of heat packs to a couple of guests in the spa the following morning, aware that her mobile in her tunic pocket was vibrating for the second time in five minutes. She pulled it out as soon as the pair were gone, and found a missed call and a text from Ralph. *Leaving about 11. Got time for a goodbye coffee upstairs?*

With you in 2, she texted back, and shot off up to the flat, leaving the spa assistant in charge. In most ways it was a pity Ralph was going back to the Ticino today. It was always lovely having him here, and he hadn't half worked for his keep this week, but his presence had turned into a mixed blessing. Maybe whatever was going on between him and Carol would fizzle out once he was gone, which would make things easier for Rico, though not necessarily for Ralph. Gawd. Stacy pushed the flat door open. Why was life so complicated?

Ralph was alone in the kitchen, one steaming mug already on the table and another in the coffee machine, while two large Danish pastries were sitting on a plate on the table.

'Where's Rico?' Stacy pulled out a chair. She could do with the caffeine and the energy; they'd all been too wired up to sleep after Ralph's Samiclaus appearance last night. Ralph had told them some very funny stories about various 6th of Decembers throughout Rico's life, and it was after one before Stacy had eventually left the two men to it and gone to bed. More kip would have been better than extra caffeine, though. This coffee had yet another sleep-deprivation headache to deal with.

Ralph slid a mug over the table and sat down. 'Herr Ammann from the town council called. Something about the boathouse – I gather Rico has inquired about planning permission to extend it next year. He's gone to the town hall to see about it, anyway, so we've already said goodbye.'

Stacy sipped her coffee. It was the first she'd heard about extending the boathouse as soon as next year, but that could wait for now. 'Right. Bet you're looking forward to seeing Guido and Julia again – give them my love. And send lots of pics of Lugano with all the Christmas decs up.'

Ralph's eyes were sombre. 'I will, but Stacy – I'm coming back at the beginning of the week.'

For a moment Stacy didn't know how to reply to this. There only could be one reason, but...

'Is this anything to do with Carol?'

He sighed. 'Yes and no. There might be something there, Stacy, but I don't know. I don't know what she thinks, to be honest I'm not sure I know what I think, either, and she'll be leaving soon.'

Stacy cupped both hands round her mug. Poor Ralph. It was a difficult situation before you even thought about how Rico might feel. 'Whatever happens, Ralph, Rico and I are behind you. If you're–'

He leaned across the table. 'Stop right there. I know. But I also know Rico's struggling, so I'm leaving it up to you to tell him I'm coming back. Let's wait and see how things go. Eat your *Plunder*.' He took a large bite out of his pastry and pushed the other over to Stacy.

Stacy rubbed her aching head. 'Have you seen Carol this morning yet?' She lifted the pastry and began to work her way through about four hundred calories of deliciousness. She'd have to adopt her own New Year Healthy Eating Plan at this rate.

Ralph shook his head, his lips pressed together, and Stacy continued. 'Maureen was going into the spa when I left, so Carol will be on her own for the next–' She checked the time on her phone. 'Twenty minutes at least. Off you go. Wipe your face first.'

For half a second Ralph was motionless, then he jumped up and dived into the bathroom. Stacy sat back. Oh, please let this Advent time end happily for them all.

It didn't sound like the easiest of asks.

Downstairs again, she found Alex and Flavia in the office, gift-wrapping spa shop items while a small queue of guests was waiting at the desk.

'Alex...' Stacy jerked her head towards reception.

He leapt up, thrusting the sticky tape at her. 'Heck – they've been here less than half a minute, don't worry.' He strode out to the desk. 'Sorry, everyone...'

Stacy gaped at Flavia, who at barely twenty was the youngest staff member, and was horrified to see tears swimming in the girl's eyes. Hell, this kid was as exhausted as she was and it wasn't even lunchtime yet. Countless bottles of salts, tubes of various creams as well as other spa shop bits and pieces were waiting on the table to be wrapped. Who'd have guessed their shop would be so popular?

Stacy grabbed the scissors and set to work. 'This is manic. You're a star, Flavia, and I promise we'll work something out so that next week isn't so busy.'

Flavia sniffed. 'It's not that. I don't mind wrapping stuff, but I did it almost all day yesterday too and every time I close my eyes now, I see ribbons and tinsel waiting to be tied onto parcels. I even dreamt about it last night! And my fingers are sore with all the pulling and tying and sticky tape.'

That was too much. Stacy reached across and took the almost-wrapped parcel from the girl. 'You've gone above and beyond. Go home right now and relax for the rest of the day!'

Flavia's face lit up. 'Are you sure? There's still another sixteen to do and they're all being picked up tonight.'

'We'll cope. Go.'

Flavia didn't need telling again, and Stacy peered dismally at the list of items still to be wrapped. She'd be running back and forward between here and the spa for the rest of the day.

'Stacy?' Alex was standing in the doorway, frowning. 'How about I ask Mum if she'd wrap some for you? She might be able to come here, otherwise I could take them to her at lunchtime, and someone could pick them up later.'

He'd spoken Swiss German, and Stacy stared. 'That would be brilliant. D'you think she'd mind? Call her first, in case she has a dressmaking or baking session on this afternoon.' Denise worked from home, but that didn't mean she could drop everything to help them.

Alex reclaimed his chair and made the call while Stacy organised items for the five parcels room 203 had ordered. She frowned as he spoke. Her Swiss German was pretty good now, but had she really understood Alex properly here? That Denise would even consider coming here, so far away from her home? He ended the call and looked at her with an indescribable expression on his face.

'She has time, and – she said she'd come here if I picked her up. She thinks she'll be okay as long as I'm nearby – or you, of course.'

Tears shot into Stacy's eyes. 'Oh, Alex – that's wonderful. She's doing so well, isn't she?' Even thinking she could do that was amazing progress for the woman who, just a few months ago, hadn't been outside for over a year. At least something was going well...

***

Carol arranged her hair over the new dressing on her ear, and stared at her reflection. Not bad for someone who'd had a general anaesthetic two days ago. She was still pale, but the scrunched-up look around her eyes was improving by the hour, almost. A slosh of make-up, and she'd be ready for the day.

A tap on the door interrupted her as she was packing her handbag for the lunch trip to St Gallen she and Maureen were making that day. Heavens – that had been a short last soak in the tubs for her friend.

'Come in!' she called, opening the wardrobe for her jacket.

'It's me.'

Ralph's voice in the doorway made Carol jump so hard she banged the wardrobe shut harder than she'd intended. *Ralph.* What did he–

She moved a step nearer the door where she could see him, her heart pounding under her ribs. Nerves? Or more than that? He was looking anxious too, his eyebrows lowered and one hand gripping the door as if it was about to fall from the hinges.

'Hi there.' Carol managed to sound upbeat, pulling herself together as hard as ever she could. 'And congratulations on a very successful performance last night. It must have been exhausting!'

His face creased into a smile. 'I'm glad you enjoyed it. Um, I'm here to say I'm going home to Lugano for a day or two, but I'll be back at the beginning of the week, and – perhaps we could go for a meal, or a coffee?'

Carol sank down on the bed. He wanted to see her again, and now she had a few days to think in, and she needed to think. But with Maureen gone she'd have plenty of time to do that at the weekend.

'That sounds like a good idea,' she said. Glory, her voice was trembling like an old woman's now.

'I'll come and find you, then.'

Carol nodded dumbly, then reached for her phone and passed it over. 'Here's my number. You could text me when you're back.'

He manipulated her phone and his, then handed hers back. 'It'll be Tuesday morning sometime, depending on when I start out. Take care of that ear!' He gave her a brief smile, and was gone.

Carol sank down on the bed clutching her mobile and waiting for her heartbeat to return to normal. There *was* something between them, but oh, how awkward that had felt. What good would going out for dinner with Ralph do, really? She'd be setting herself up for a fall, that was all. There was no half way here; a relationship, even a friendship would only work if they were both ready and if she didn't go permanently to Australia. And if she had to choose between life with Barry and Diane and the children, and life with a new, uncertain relationship... no, no. Some things were too risky. She was too old, or too set in her ways, her life. Carol clasped her hands together hard. She was being ridiculous – people her age started relationships every day of the week. *Not if they're going to Australia*, said her head, but she pushed the thought away for later. At least she had some thinking time now.

Twenty minutes later, she and Maureen were stepping out of the front door when Ralph's car drove away from the side of the building and vanished through the gates. Carol gazed after it, the cold sensation of being bereft sweeping through her.

'Penny for them,' said Maureen, taking her arm as they trudged along to the bus stop.

Carol pulled her gloves further up her wrists. 'If it gets much colder, I wouldn't be surprised if the snow they're expecting next week came early,' she said, forcing the bright tome into her voice. 'I might have to buy some snow boots!'

'Ugh. Rather you than me. Come on. Let's get into a nice warm bus.'

Carol sat in the bus as it rumbled round a few little towns, travelling ever upwards to St Gallen. Her ears popped at one point, but it was a normal pop. At last they hit the edge of town, and Carol gazed out as the bus drove through the usual kind of urban scenery, grey buildings with shops and offices on the ground floor and flats on top. They could have been in London, on this street. Forty minutes after leaving Grimsbach, they arrived at St Gallen *Marktplatz*, where Alex had told them to get off.

Carol made sure her hat was covering her ear. It was noticeably colder here than in Grimsbach, but then it was three hundred metres higher, too.

'Look – that'll be the street up to the cathedral, and the Abbey Library's round there too.'

Maureen led the way with the enthusiasm of someone who was determined to make the most of her last day, and Carol hoped fervently she'd be allowed some lunch between sights. And that thought she'd had about London was way out, in this part of town. The centre had nothing English about it; look at those old houses and wow – was that the cathedral at the end of the road? She gazed at the church, which had tall, arched side windows and lofty twin towers soaring up towards a blue sky. That was definitely worth a visit. Carol took Maureen's arm as they crossed a wide forecourt and pulled open the heavy wooden door of the cathedral.

Inside, she strolled round with wide eyes, gazing at the ornate and colourful frescoes on the vaulted white ceiling, and the very baroque décor of the entire building. Marble statues and curly cornices everywhere you turned; she'd never seen anything like this back in England.

'The town's named after an Irish monk called Gallus,' whispered Maureen, peering at the brochure she'd picked up in the hotel. 'This is the fanciest church I've ever seen. Do you like it?'

Carol decided she did; the feeling of airiness and hushed peace here was comforting. She should come back sometime, and sit and have a quiet think.

A visit to the neighbouring Abbey Library with its ancient books and almost equally ancient wooden floor – they made you wear felt overshoes – was another 'wow' experience, and Carol emerged feeling that her soul was lighter. And oh, my goodness – tiny little flakes of snow were floating down on the town, turning the cobbles outside the cathedral white. How magical…

Carol took Maureen's arm and pulled her into the Christmas market in the streets surrounding the cathedral.

'Food,' she said firmly. 'Look, there's a stand with *Bratwurst* – Alex recommended those. Let's have one for lunch, and get some mulled wine to wash it down.'

The sausages on the Bratwurst stand were sizzling aromatically, and Carol accepted hers wrapped ready to eat in a piece of grease-proof paper. They were given bread rolls, too, but fortunately the mulled wine stand had high tables to stand at. Quite a lot of people were having the same lunch; the sausages seemed to be popular.

And all around, people were talking, mostly in Swiss German. Carol soaked up the wintry atmosphere. If everything had been different and she and Ralph had a future, she might have understood this language one day. But no. Her future lay in Australia.

***

'You haven't had lunch yet, have you? Shall we grab half an hour and make some spag?' Stacy stood in the office doorway. She'd spent the rest of the morning sorting through the spa shop orders and creating little piles of items for Denise to wrap that afternoon. Alex was going to collect her at half past one.

Rico closed the laptop. 'Sounds good. Heard anything from Dad yet? I hope it isn't too snowy for him going up the San Bernardino.'

'I checked the weather satellite online. I think he'll be fine. Come on, we could both do with a break, and you can tell me how your meeting went this morning.' And she could tell him Ralph was returning next week, which was going to be easier said than done.

Rico pushed his chair back and followed her to the lift. 'Herr Ammann doesn't see any reason why a larger boathouse shouldn't be approved, and what we put in it is our business. I thought we could get Andi to draw up plans to extend the building with the sauna and fitness rooms there. We can apply for planning permission as soon as we have them.' He opened the flat door and stood back to let her go in.

'Good idea. Lakeside's not half growing, isn't it?' Stacy led the way into the kitchen. It was a good idea and they'd talked about it last spring, but it would still have been better if he'd run it by her before the meeting. Teamwork, and all that. Still, with them both so rushed, she could see why he hadn't. And this was a time to choose your arguments, so she'd let this one go. She told him about Flavia and Denise while they were eating spaghetti with pesto sauce, then took a deep breath. Go for it, Stace.

'Did Ralph mention he was thinking about coming back next week? I suppose he'd borrow Guido's car.'

Rico gaped at her. 'Not a word. Why would he – aw, heck, no.' He clutched his head with both hands.

Stacy reached out and grabbed his wrists, pulling them away from his face so that she could see him properly. 'Let him work things out for himself, Rico. Whatever happens, you don't want to antagonise him and I think he's already upset you're not happy.'

Rico grimaced. 'Too right I'm not happy. But I'll be nice, don't worry.'

'He doesn't want you to be nice. He wants you to understand.'

'Okay, I'll try. I can't say more than that, can I?'

Stacy got up to put her plates in the dishwasher, patting his shoulder as she passed. And this was awful. A couple of weeks ago she'd have given him a big hug. Her phone trilled out on the table while she was running water to rinse the pans, and Rico peered at it.

'It's your mother. I'll leave you to it.'

He stomped off, leaving Stacy with the ridiculous feeling that she should feel guilty about having a mother to call her. She wiped her hands and lifted her phone.

'Hi, Grandma! How's things?'

Janie launched into a description of the latest doings of baby Tom, now five months old and best grandchild in the world, according to his doting grandmother. Stacy grinned, glad her mother couldn't see it. Thank heavens Gareth and his wife Jo had presented Mum and Dad with the perfect distraction from Stacy and Rico's as yet unplanned wedding – though no doubt Mum would get right down to the planning bit when she and Dad were here at New Year. Stacy put the phone down twenty minutes later wondering again how she would feel in Rico's situation, with no mum, but really, there was no way to imagine it.

Downstairs again, the hotel was jumping, and she spent the next two hours running between the spa and the office, where Denise was parcelling up gifts while Alex was kept busy on reception. Friday and Saturday were the two main 'leave and arrive' days, and people didn't like being kept waiting at these times.

'Thank you so much for jumping in like this, Denise,' she said warmly, bringing the older woman a coffee at half past three. 'I'm so glad you can do this for us.'

Denise smiled briefly. 'Having Alex close by helps, I'm not sure I would manage without him. About those parcels, though. You're making twice the work for yourselves, and wrapping paper hides all your lovely gifts, too. Why don't you get some of those fancy cellophane bags to put the things in, then all we'd have to do would be to fill them and add a nice festive bow, or some tinsel?'

A wave of relief crashed over Stacy's head. Why on earth hadn't they thought of that? She'd been dreading having so many orders every week, and Denise was right – this would more than halve the work. She beamed at the older woman.

'That's a brilliant idea. I'll get some at the weekend.' And even more brilliant was Denise's '...all *we'd* have to do...' It would make a real difference to Alex if his mum was able to get out and about. Stacy sighed. What with her and Rico, and Ralph and Carol, and Alex and Zoe, it seemed that relationship problems were looming all over the place. The youngsters would sort themselves out eventually and so would she and Rico, but Ralph and Carol? That might not be a happy ending.

By five o'clock all the expected guests bar one couple had arrived, and Alex and Denise went home, leaving Stacy drumming her fingers on the desk. She had a million other things to do, but she'd sent Flavia home so it looked like she was on desk duty until Maria arrived at six.

The lift doors opened, and Maureen and Carol came round to reception, both jacketed up and Maureen pulling her suitcase.

'That's me off,' said Maureen. 'Thank you so much, Stacy, for being such a help.'

Stacy checked her out. 'No problem. Have a safe flight home. Is someone taking you to the station?'

'Me,' said Carol. 'The walk will do me good, and it's a lovely night.'

The two left, and Stacy tidied the desk. Glory be, she was done in. This had been the longest week ever, and it wasn't over yet. And even when it was, the next two weeks would be repeat performances – normal duties during the day, then Advent events nearly every evening. Business might be booming, but it was flattening them all at the same time.

The front door swung open, and Stacy glanced up to greet the new arrivals, a very glamorous young couple, each with one arm wrapped around the other's waist and pulling a suitcase with their free hand. This must be honeymooners.

'Mr and Mrs Andrews? I'm Stacy. Welcome to Lakeside.'

The couple nodded, beaming at her, then gazed for a long moment into each other's eyes.

'How amazing that sounds,' murmured the woman. 'Mr and Mrs Andrews.'

Her husband kissed her forehead, and an overwhelming desire to giggle swept over Stacy. This pair were so loved-up... *And lucky them*, said a little voice in her head. *You and Rico barely see each other nowadays, and when you do you have to spend the time sorting other people's problems.*

She booked the couple into their room and sent them on their way upstairs, then tapped out a quick message to Ralph to check he'd arrived in Lugano without landing in a snow drift. She knew all too well what conditions on the San Bernardino route could be like in winter. The answering text pinged in. *Arrived safely, about to relax with a pizza and a glass of red. Have a lovely evening. Xxx*

A shriek from the spa made Stacy jump, and she sprinted through to find Sabine had spilled an entire drum of disinfectant on the floor between the two largest tubs. The normally discreet pine aroma was heavy in the air, Sabine was in tears and several guests were hanging out of each tub offering advice in at least three languages. Stacy went for a mop.

A lovely evening? Chance would be a fine thing...

16

SATURDAY, 8TH DECEMBER, MORNING

Rico waved off the last of the day's departing guests and tapped into the computer for a quick look through the expected arrivals. Good, they were only expecting six this afternoon, after the influx they'd had yesterday. He walked down the hall to check the front drive and wow, someone would need to sweep those steps soon. The snow wasn't heavy, but it was lying. That would be a good job for him to work up an appetite for lunch with.

Stacy arrived from the cellar, a drum of disinfectant in her arms, and Rico went to open the spa door for her.

'That's heavy. You should put it on a trolley.'

She glared at him. 'And exactly how am I supposed to heave a trolley up from the cellar? We decided against a stairlift, remember? We should keep the spares on this floor, that's what we should do.' She shoved the drum into his arms and took his place behind the desk.

Oops. 'Where do you want it?'

'Medical room, far right corner.'

Rico walked through the spa, greeting guests in the tubs as he passed. The pine smell had faded to a more normal intensity after yesterday's spillage, thank goodness, because today's weather was the perfect inducement to have a spa day, and most of the guests were up to their necks in water. When he returned to reception, Stacy was still frowning.

'You shouldn't walk through the spa in shoes, Rico. How are we to get the guests to stick to the flip-flops only rule if we don't?'

Rico opened his mouth to ask what was bugging her when a young couple arrived at reception, arms wrapped around each other.

'Hi. We're going for a coffee and then later we'd like to try your tubs – what should we do?'

Stacy's explanation was almost word-for-word the same as the one in the brochure the couple obviously hadn't taken the time to read yet. They stood listening, each stroking the other's back, and twice the young man dropped a kiss on his partner's head. Rico could barely hold back a grimace – this must be the honeymooners, and a more clichéd couple he had never seen.

'...so if you find me or the other spa attendant for your BP check before you go in for your first soak, we'll get you started.' Stacy finished with a bright smile, and the pair moved away into the restaurant.

'Love's young dream, aren't they?' said Rico.

To his horror Stacy turned on him, hissing into his ear. 'And lucky them, that's all I can say. At least they have some romance in their lives and the chance to have fun together. When did we last do anything even remotely non-hotel-related? Every moment of every day seems to be filled with being there for other people and I'm tired, Rico, and there's no end in sight. And you'd better get the snow off those steps before someone breaks their neck.' She stomped off to the lift, leaving Rico rooted to the spot.

He was about to follow her when a woman emerged from the small spa and approached the desk, smiling hopefully. And when he'd dealt with her the snow had come on again. Rico called to a passing waiter to watch the desk, and went to get a broom and some salt. Someone should grit the car park, too... His father was right, they needed more staff.

That was what was wrong with Stacy, too. She was exhausted because she was doing double-duty, but how on earth they were to find extra staff less than three weeks before Christmas, Rico had no idea. Perhaps it *was* a good thing his father was coming back next week.

***

Carol stepped off the train at Rorschach and stood waiting for the level crossing barrier to lift and allow her to cross the track to the harbour area. Eek, that wind was cold – but the dressing on her ear and her pink woolly hat would keep her right. She gazed over the lake, mid-blue with a more turquoise stripe in the middle and yes, waves were slapping against the harbour wall. It was a Bise wind again, and how weird she knew enough about the weather conditions here to be able to tell. That was down to Ralph, and what she was going to do about him was still a major mystery in her life. But there was nothing she could do, was there? Feelings were feelings, and circumstances were something quite different. She had the choice of avoiding him entirely until she left for Australia, or enjoying his company while she was still here, knowing that would risk hurting them both even more at the end. Because an end there would be.

The gong-like sound that rang out while the crossing was closed stopped abruptly, and the gate swung upwards. Carol crossed the track and turned left along the pathway by the lake, thrusting her gloved hands into her jacket pockets as a flurry of snow hit her face. Help... maybe her idea of walking the couple of kilometres back to Lakeside wasn't the best one. Her phone rang while she was passing a large, square building right by the water, and she ducked into the entrance to get some shelter from the elements. It seemed to be some kind of museum, so at least she wasn't trespassing, and ooh – Barry was on Facetime.

'Hi, Mum! Emma's just off to bed in a moment, so we thought we'd call and get the latest on your ear before she goes.' He beamed at her, then the picture lurched and Emma came into focus.

'Hello, Grandma! Are you better now?'

Warmth flooded through Carol as Emma's high-pitched Australian accent came down the phone as clearly as if she was standing beside Carol.

'Much better, darlings, and I'm so looking forward to seeing you all again!' Surely the doctor would say on Wednesday that she could rebook her flight. Maybe by this time next week she'd be basking on the beach, not freezing in Switzerland. Carol chatted for a few minutes, then rang off and dropped her phone back into her bag. For a moment she stood still, gazing out over the blustery beauty of Lake Constance. No. She was lovely and warm now after talking to her loved ones, and she wasn't going to fight against a cold north wind in a snowstorm for the next however long it would take her to get back to the hotel. She would have a nice window-shopping spree then fight with the ticket machine instead, and get the train back.

Something over an hour later she was walking up the drive at Lakeside. The car park was pretty full, and someone had been out sweeping the snow from the driveway. Everyone would be wanting a lovely hot soak in the spa this afternoon, and they probably had the best idea, too. Carol pushed the front door open, fishing for her phone as a message pinged in. Oh – this was from Ralph. She would take it up to her room to open.

Her heart was thumping away by the time she got her jacket off and was sitting on the bed with her phone. And tap. It was a photo of a sunny market square with a Christmas tree in the middle and little stalls set out around the sides. Underneath was: *Saturday market at Lugano – get your Christmas decorations here! How's Lakeside? Rx*

Yikes. A kiss. Carol thought for a moment, then tapped. *Chilly out (snowing) but lovely inside as usual.* And now – should she sign off with a kiss too? Oh, how complicated, and really, after her lovely conversation with Barry and Emma, complications were the last thing she needed. She added: *C* to her message, and put a snowman emoji beside it. Thank heavens for emojis. Her phone was silent for a moment, then it pinged as Ralph's reply came. It was a smiling emoji with sunspecs, so she didn't need to answer it. Was she pleased about that, or not? Carol put the phone down and gaped at it. What was happening to her life? And more to the point, what was she going to do for the rest of the afternoon? Maybe a coffee downstairs would be a good idea; it would fill half an hour or so, anyway.

Downstairs, she caught a glimpse of the young assistant receptionist – Flavia, that was her name – wrapping presents in the office. Carol abandoned her coffee idea and went for a peer at the spa shop stand on the other side of the hallway. She wanted to order more things to take home, and she'd have space for a couple of tiny bottles in her Australia case too. She made her selection and went to the desk for an order form.

Flavia came out and handed over the form and a pen, and Carol couldn't help noticing the girl's fingers. Had she been in an argument with a very scratchy cat?

'Do you have a cat?' She pointed to the row of plasters on Flavia's hands.

Flavia blinked hard, and Carol winced. Had the cat succumbed to whatever had made it scratch poor Flavia? She stretched out a hand to the girl.

'Oh dear, I'm so–'

'It was the presents! They all needed paper and ribbon and it was so many and it–' Flavia gestured with her fingertips, then summoned a very unconvincing smile and nodded. 'But it's all sorted now. Stacy has a new wrapping method, much better.'

Carol lifted the pen. 'Tell you what, Flavia. I'll make my choice now, and then I'll help you wrap it all up. How's that? Your fingers need time to heal.'

Flavia gave her a watery smile. 'Very good. Thank you. You're a special guest!'

Carol laughed. Twenty minutes later they were sitting in the office putting tiny bottles and sachets into cellophane bags to go to Australia, and Carol was attaching little premade bows and stars. The things going to London needed no gift wrap. Alex came in when they were nearly finished and raised his eyebrows at her.

'Do we have a new member of staff?'

Carol waved a parcel at him. 'Not quite. I'm just saving poor Flavia's fingers from further destruction by tinsel!'

He gaped at Flavia's hands, looking even more startled. 'Wow. I'm glad to see Stacy has adopted Mum's suggestion about bags. Poor old Flavers. Have you seen my sunspecs?' He added a sentence in Swiss German, and Flavia got up and opened a cupboard.

Alex accepted his sunglasses and put them on top of his head. 'Forgot them yesterday,' he said. 'Okay, ladies, I'll love you and leave you!' He winked, and strode from the office.

Carol turned to say something to Flavia, then stopped. The girl's cheeks were pink, and her head was bowed over the sachet she was filling with bath salts. Carol reached for the scissors, frowning. Did Flavia have feelings for Alex? But hadn't Stacy said something about Alex's girlfriend being a musician? Oh dear, poor Flavia if she was right. The Lakeside Hotel did seem to be a complicated place when it came to people's relationships...

17

Saturday, 8th December, afternoon

Stacy finished her rearrangement of the spare spa things in the cellar storeroom, and wiped her face with a grubby hand. Oops. Now she'd look like a chimney sweep, and oh, no, poor Rico. She shouldn't have unloaded all that about not enough staff and too much work on him; he was working as hard as she was. Another couple of weeks would see the end of their Advent project, and they'd be able to relax. She wiped her face on a tissue and headed back to reception to apologise.

Rico was outside, however, and Stacy dived into the staff loo to check her reflection properly. And what do you know, as soon as she re-emerged, the honeymooners were heading into the spa, all kitted up in their bathrobes and still with their arms firmly around each other. They'd have to let go in the tubs…

The humorous thought kept her going as she took their medical history and blood pressure – they had to let go for that, too – and informed them apologetically that no, they couldn't drink prosecco in the tubs.

Rico was waiting when she left the pair in a tub and went back to reception.

'Sorry…' They both spoke at once, then grinned sheepishly.

He leaned over the desk. 'I've just seen Flavia – Carol helped her wrap the things she was ordering. I guess if you needed another pair of present-wrapping hands, you could ask her.'

Stacy nodded. 'She's a gem. But with Denise mucking in too now, I imagine we'll manage the new bagging system.' She joined him behind the desk, noticing that no one had lit the candle on the Advent crown today. She rectified the situation and stood watching the flickering flame as its 'winter' scent wafted across reception. How peaceful. Deceptively peaceful? Maybe not. Tomorrow the second candle would be burning too, and things *would* get easier, now the first week was over. They'd altered the timing of some events to spread things out a little – the Christmas biscuit demo was on Monday, and her Healthy Eating talk on Tuesday.

Rico vanished into the restaurant to talk through the plans for this week's Gala Dinner with Rob the chef, and Stacy pulled up the guest list on the computer. Full house again, good. For the bank balance. She pulled a face as she looked at the plan for the week. A Winter Wonderland trip tomorrow again, though this time they didn't have to go all the way to Davos. They could drive through the Appenzellarland, which was much closer and lovely too, if rather less imposing. The hotel events were okay, but they didn't have anything special for the Gala Dinner. The Samiclaus was a one-off, and Rico'd been wondering about getting some carol singers in for this week's do. Stacy tapped her fingers on the mouse mat. Carols were lovely, but ordinary. They needed something Swiss. Inspiration struck, and she leapt up and dived into the snug bar, where Peter the restaurant manager was checking through the cocktail cupboard.

'Peter! We need you on Thursday night!'

He gaped at her, a bottle of Tequila in one hand. 'I'm already here on Thursday night.'

'I know. Can you bring your Alphorn and be a secret feature at the Gala Dinner, like Ralph was as Samiclaus?'

Peter rubbed his chin. 'I could. Do you want me to dress up and look Swiss, too?'

Stacy clasped her hands beneath her chin. 'That would be perfect. I'll tell Rico now, and we can sort out the details later. You're a star!'

He saluted, and Stacy went back to see if Flavia was coping on the desk. That had been easily sorted. If only all the other niggles were as easily put right.

'Smells lovely, doesn't it?' An older couple, dressed for outside, smiled at her as they passed reception hand in hand and vanished outside.

Loneliness almost overwhelmed Stacy. Everyone was loved up and holding hands except her and Rico. They were being nice to each other, because they couldn't fall out at Advent. Christmas at Lakeside was a triumph for the hotel, but...

***

Rico flung himself down on the sofa and looked around the empty living room. Stacy was waiting for Maria to arrive, then she'd be up too and at long last they'd have an hour or two off before they collapsed into bed. He grimaced at a photo of his mother on the bookcase. Mum had always said the days over Christmas when the hotel used to be closed were what set her up for the rest of the year, and he was beginning to see what she'd meant. The Advent programme was a huge success financially, but talk about a steep learning curve. They'd need to plan it differently next year, that was sure.

The flat door banged shut as Stacy arrived. 'Rico, if I don't have a glass of house red in my hand in three seconds flat, I'm leaving you.'

'House red coming up.' He opened a bottle and poured, and they clinked. 'We'll make it, Stace. One week down, two to go, then we're off for Christmas.'

'Bring it on. I'm just thankful your dad's coming back on Tuesday.' She squinted at him.

Rico swirled his wine, watching as the ruby liquid caught the light from the standing lamp in the corner. 'I suppose I am too, but...' He took a big swallow of Merlot.

She came over and rubbed his arm, and Rico almost flinched. What had happened to giving the love of your life a big hug?

'Rico. You have to–'

Bitterness flooded through him. 'I know. I have to accept that my father's looking to replace my mother. I do know, Stace. I don't have to like it, though, do I?'

She pulled him over to the sofa. 'Come and sit down. Tell me more about Christmases when you were a kid.'

Rico relaxed beside her as memories came flooding in. Christmas had always been at Lakeside – opening presents after dinner on Christmas Eve, after the Christ Child had flown in when no one was looking. All carefully orchestrated, of course. Mum had packed him and Dad and Guido and Michael off to do something in the garden or the village while she and Julia flung up the Christmas tree in the living room and organised all the presents beneath it. When the rest of them were home again, the 'Christ Child' had been... They'd had dinner with the piles of presents glistening tantalisingly all the while, and then after dinner, they'd sung carols by candlelight, and then the big moment, the present-opening. How magical it all seemed, even when he was older and knew who the Christ Child really was.

He looked around the living room. They had no decorations at all up yet; they'd need to change that before Stacy's parents arrived for New Year, or knowing Janie, she'd take over the decorating of the whole flat. And oh, if only Mum was still here. One day, hopefully, he and Stacy would have kids, and the magic would begin all over again, with some shadowy woman there with Grandpa Ralph instead of Mum. He wiped his face with one hand. Some things, you just couldn't fix.

18

SUNDAY, 9TH DECEMBER

A crowd of excited and well-wrapped up guests was waiting in the front hall when Stacy went down after breakfast.

'Everyone ready for the Winter Wonderland tour?' She smiled round the sixteen waiting people, mostly older adults, though the honeymooners were there too. They were locked together as usual, and Stacy stifled a grimace. They'd need to stop gazing soulfully into each other's eyes if they wanted to appreciate the scenery... Oh, how cynical that was. She gave herself a shake. She was still tired, even after seven hours' sleep, and she was envious, too, of this pair who had more than enough time for each other while she and Rico were either at opposite ends of the building, or tearing chunks out of each other on the rare occasions they were home together.

Alex arrived and waved the minibus key at the guests. 'Ready for some proper snow and fabulous mountain scenery, folks?'

Stacy joined the crowd as they made for the door. You'd never guess Alex hadn't grown up somewhere in the south of England. His English had been excellent when he started work at Lakeside last summer, and now it was virtually at native speaker level.

'Where are we going?'

The honeymooning husband was beside her, and Stacy smiled to herself. Was the 'eyes only for each other' stage over already?

'First stop, the Säntis, the highest peak in the Alpstein range,' she replied. 'We'll get the cable car to the summit, and you can have a walk around if you like, or a coffee in the restaurant, but beware, it's not cheap. Then we'll go on to a little village called Urnäsch for lunch.'

The guests piled into the minibus and they set off. Tiny snowflakes were floating down, but they weren't lying and the weatherman said it would be Tuesday before real snow hit the low-lying banks of the lake. Stacy gazed out as they drove along, taking the motorway up past St Gallen and then a smaller road through what would normally be rolling green countryside and was now white. Halfway there, the sky cleared and the sun came out, and there was a general scramble for sunspecs on the minibus.

'That's the Säntis straight ahead,' she called down the bus, and people leaned over to get good views and photos. Stacy was reminded of the first time she'd come here, with Emily and Alan, and oh, now she was here with Alex and all those others – and she'd never been with Rico. And for heaven's sake, she'd better snap out of this grumpy mood pronto or the guests would notice.

They parked at the cable car base station, and Alex went up with the twelve guests who wanted to see the views from the top. Stacy remained in the base station restaurant with two older couples who weren't up for mountaineering, even by cable car. They strolled around the snow-covered restaurant terrace taking photos, then went in for a coffee and some postcards.

Stacy made sure her charges were happy with their cards and drinks, then went out for a tramp along the road, taking a couple of pics of the red cable car as it slid up the mountain. They could use one of these pics and one from Davos last week to show next year's guests what they could see on the Winter Wonderland tours. The cable car was rocking into its dock when she arrived back at the base station, and Stacy watched expectantly as a crowd disembarked, but none of the Lakeside guests were there. She glanced at her watch. They should be leaving soon; they had lunch booked in Urnäsch.

It was two cable cars later before the rest of the party arrived, though, and then of course they all dived into the loos. Stacy felt her patience deserting her.

'Sorry,' said Alex. 'It took ages to get them all together at the top. Still plenty of time, don't worry.' He whistled cheerfully and went to put the minibus heating on.

Stacy stared after him. It was somehow more reassuring when Ralph was her co-host on the WW tour. On the Davos trip, it had felt as if he was in charge, which lifted some of the responsibility from her shoulders. Here, she was the boss and she wasn't in control of her party. Were people her age supposed to feel so tired all the time? Okay, she'd been working eighteen-hour days for the past week, but still.

Lunch passed uneventfully, apart from Sadie, one of the older ladies, having left her medication at the hotel. She was rather sniffy with her husband, who assured Stacy that this particular pill could be taken a little late, but they had to be back by six on the dot for Sadie's Warfarin. Stacy put on her most reassuring manner – but if they weren't back at least two hours before six she'd be a total wreck. Margrit could go on next week's WW tour. Definitely.

In the end, they only just made it by six. After a visit to the little village of Appenzell and a walk there, plus Kaffee und Kuchen, they got stuck in the slowest traffic jam in Switzerland all the way back down to St Gallen. It was a narrow road and it was snow-covered, and Alex sat with his face as glum as Stacy had ever seen it while the honeymooners cooed at each other and Sadie fretted about her meds and the rest sat in gloomy silence as darkness fell and the scenery vanished. Stacy had never been so glad to turn in the Lakeside gates at ten to six. Thank goodness tomorrow was a quieter day.

***

Carol left the restaurant as soon as she'd finished her evening meal. She'd have coffee in her room and a blob on her bed with her iPad, and thank goodness she had it, because the attic bedrooms at Lakeside didn't have TVs. She jabbed the button for the lift, waving to Stacy as the younger woman shot out of the stairwell and on towards the restaurant, looking like the definition of someone who could use a good holiday in her own hotel. Stacy had too much work, anyone could see that. Carol sighed. It was a pity she couldn't take a paid job here while she was stuck in limbo, because her holiday-spending budget was fading fast. She hadn't reckoned on a second week of hotel life, and the really stupid part was, the worry about what it was all costing meant she wasn't even enjoying it. The room was smaller, yes, but it was a single and she had no idea what they'd charge for it. Then there was being alone in a crowd all day – Maureen had her quirks as a travelling companion, but she'd been company.

Upstairs, she made a cup of peppermint tea – something she never drank in London, but she'd developed quite a taste for the selection of fruit and herbal teas they provided here, and arranged her pillows so that she could blob in comfort. A tap through today's text exchange with Barry and family was cheering, and so was the row of emojis Emma had chosen to end it with. Carol touched the little face on the photo they'd sent. Maybe she'd be able to do that in real life next weekend... Oh, please, she must be able to fly soon.

Ralph had sent a couple of Lugano photos too; it looked a lovely place, though apparently it had rained all day today. She'd replied with a heart emoji which hopefully he'd realise was for Lugano and not for him. It didn't need further comment – he'd be here on Tuesday, all going well. *Supposing it doesn't?* said her heart. *Supposing he doesn't come and you get the all-clear and fly to Australia and leave without seeing him?* Carol gave herself a shake. Heck, the mood she was in, you'd think she'd broken both legs and was facing major surgery with no prospect of improvement this side of next Christmas. Get a grip, woman. You're stuck here for the moment, yes, but it's a lovely place with great people and heaven only knows when or even if you'll ever be back in Switzerland, after you leave. Which could be as early as next week, so pull your bloody socks up and cheer up, too. She swung off the bed and went for her toilet bag. There was a family bathroom up here with a lovely big rolltop bath; she would pamper herself with some of her Lakeside smellies. Go.

***

The next morning, Carol woke up to sunshine streaming through the curtains – heavens, what time was it? Nine o'clock... goodness, it was years since she'd slept for so long. She'd need to get her skates on to have breakfast before they cleared everything away.

Unusually, it was Flavia who brought her coffee. 'Eva is sick,' she said glumly, when Carol commented. 'I should help Alex with presents and the desk, too.' She stared towards the hallway, her face resigned.

Carol watched as she wound her way round the tables with the coffee jug. Poor Flavia, she would undoubtedly be happier helping Alex. But then, if he had a girlfriend already, it might actually be best if Flavia didn't spend too much time with him. An idea came when she was leaving the restaurant, and she stopped at the desk. Alex came out of the office and gave her a grin, but he wasn't looking his usual cheerful self either, was he? Carol came straight to the point.

'I hear you're short-staffed. Would it help if I gave you a hand with the present-wrapping? I have the whole day on my hands and nothing to do except change the dressing on my ear.'

Alex's face cleared, then he frowned. 'That would be amazing, but I'll have to run it by Stacy or Rico first. My mother helps out too, but she's starting a cold, so we're a couple of people down. Thanks, Carol. I'll call you as soon as I get hold of someone to ask.'

Twenty minutes later, it was Stacy who called. 'We'd be very grateful if you gave Alex a hand to assemble the presents for an hour or two, Carol. I had no idea our mix 'n' match scheme would be so popular – we have a ridiculous number of orders to prepare. As soon as people set foot in the spa, they want all the products. It's a good money-spinner for us, but we'll have to rethink it for next year.'

'My pleasure. I'll go down now, and we can see how far we get today.' And good – she'd be repaying some of the kindness Stacy had shown her, too.

Down in the office, Alex showed her the pile of order forms. 'You put the bottles, etcetera, into the cellophane bags and add a couple of decorations, then put a post-it with the room number on too, and leave each room's order on the table here. The products are either in these boxes–' He waved at a row along the floor and beneath the table, 'or in the storeroom beside the hairdresser's if we've run out here.' He grimaced. 'And if you can think of a quicker system, shout very loudly.'

Carol could see why it took so long to get the gifts ready. A bigger space to work in would speed things up, but that couldn't be available or they'd be doing it already. She set to work, and was just finishing her third bag of assorted jars and bottles for room 205 when her phone buzzed. A text from Ralph: *Looking forward to being back at Lakeside tomorrow. Hope they're treating you well!*

Spontaneously, Carol took a photo of the table in front of her. *I'm having a lovely time – helping in the 'shop' this morning!* The message was barely en route to Ralph when Stacy came in, and Carol's face flamed. Help, it was ridiculous to feel guilty about taking a moment to send a message... or was it because it was Ralph she was texting? Still ridiculous, though. She shoved her phone back into her pocket, noticing that Rico was at the desk talking to Alex.

Stacy piled the finished bags into a large box. 'You're doing great! This is such a help, Carol, though I do feel we're imposing on you. I'll get these delivered and free up some space here.'

'Alex helps when reception's quiet. I'm happy to do this, Stacy, don't worry. It's too much for one person. I was wondering... I think the problem is, you're giving people too much choice. Every one of the bags I've put together has been different. If you gave people a smaller selection of mixed bags to choose from, you could prepare them in advance next year.'

Stacy thought for a moment. 'Yes. That might work. We'll definitely need something different in the long run. Thanks, Carol.'

***

Rico's phone buzzed as a message came in, and he stepped away from the desk to answer it. It was Dad: *Definitely coming tomorrow, be with you before midday.* Rico's stomach churned. Would Dad be coming back if Carol hadn't been here? Hardly. Oh heck, this really was happening. After three years of not looking at another woman, his father was going to replace his mother. Rico clenched his fists. Part of him knew it was idiotic to think like that, but the thought of someone else in Ralph's life was just – nauseating.

He became aware that Mara, the second spa attendant, was waving at him from the spa room. 'We need Stacy in here – a guest isn't feeling well.'

Not another one... Rico gave her a thumbs up and put his head in the office door. 'Stace, you're wanted in the spa.' He nodded at the box of presents. 'Thanks, Carol. I imagine Dad will give us a hand when he's back.' For the life of him he couldn't keep the chilly tone from his voice, and oh no, she'd noticed, and so had Stacy. Rico spun round abruptly and left.

Stacy whizzed past him. 'We'll talk later.' She vanished into the spa.

Rico stood for a moment in the spa entrance, watching as Stacy and Mara helped a woman from a hot tub. Stacy vanished into the medical room with her, leaving Mara to keep an eye on the other spa-goers. Nice to know the procedure for dealing with an emergency in the tub room was working.

It was lunchtime before Stacy caught up with him. Rico was upstairs, having shoved a frozen quiche into the oven in the hope they'd have time to eat it, when the flat door banged shut and Stacy appeared in the doorway.

Rico opened the fridge for the salad dressing. 'How's your patient?'

'Fine. She has unstable diabetes, but we sorted her out. But Rico, the way you were with Carol down there was out of order. You do know that, don't you?'

Rico shrugged. 'You can't expect me to like what Dad's doing.'

She put both hands on her hips. 'Rico, a) I would hope you're pleased if Ralph is happy, and b) it's not Carol's fault. I suggest you have a good hard think about what's important.'

Rico sagged. She was right – but he couldn't help how he felt, could he?

19

TUESDAY, 11TH DECEMBER

Something was different. Carol sat up in bed, staring around. It was after seven and the darkness outside was beginning to lift, as it did around this time every morning, so what was going on? Then she realised – it was the silence. Usually, she could hear traffic on the road in front of the hotel: a few cars, the twice-hourly post bus, the odd lorry. Today, there was nothing. She jumped out of bed and pulled the curtains back from the window, which was on the side of the building, meaning she could see both road and lake.

Snow. Carol gasped. Thick white flakes were floating down and oh, my goodness, there must be almost a foot of it out there. Everything was shining eerily in the half-light and the glow provided by the streetlights, and the shrubs and bushes bordering the driveway were heavy with whiteness. It was impossible to tell if the snow on the ground was covering grass, pavement or street. Oh, my – that was serious snow, every bit as much as she'd seen up in the mountains on the trip to Davos. As Carol watched, a snow plough grated noisily along the road, leaving a grey and white pathway behind. Two cars followed on, then a group of schoolchildren, who were having a wonderful time – goodness, were the schools open in weather like this?

She headed into the ensuite for her shower and started Tuesday morning, a disturbing thought crossing her mind. Would Ralph still drive 250 kilometres from Lugano in this weather? Carol had looked up his route on Google maps, and the road went pretty high on either side of the San Bernardino tunnel. That sounded dangerous… Worry niggled inside her as she dressed and went down for breakfast, but there was nothing she could do except wait. Or should she ask Stacy? But the younger woman was on the phone at the desk, and Carol passed by with a brief smile. Maybe he would text her to say he wasn't coming. That would please Rico, wouldn't it? His expression yesterday had been revealing.

No new messages had come into her phone, though, and Carol toyed with her croissant without tasting it. Stacy was still at the reception desk when she went past after breakfast.

'Morning, Carol! I was thinking – why don't you try the tubs this morning?'

Carol touched her ear, still with a light dressing on it. 'I'd like that, but – would it be okay?'

'As long as you're careful. See Margrit for a check-up before you go in the water.'

'I'll do that. What a lot of snow – I was surprised to see the children going to school.'

'Yes, no snow days here! It's pretty, isn't it? Until it melts, and then we have a monumental mess for a day or two. But hopefully we'll have a white Christmas now.'

She turned to deal with a waiting guest, and Carol went on upstairs. Stacy didn't seem worried, anyway. Of course, she might know Ralph wasn't coming...

At half past eleven Carol climbed out of the tub, feeling much more positive after a good soak that had done her shoulders the world of good. The chat with the other two women in the water had been fun, too. This was actually why she'd come here in the first place – to set herself up for her Australian summer. She pulled her bathrobe around her, then froze as Stacy's voice rang through reception.

'Ralph! You lunatic – you must have driven like the clappers to get here so quickly in this weather!'

He laughed. 'We were snow-free in the south, and I drove behind a plough all the way to Chur on this side. The motorway's been cleared, and Guido's car can cope with any weather.'

'Come upstairs and have some lunch. Rico's gone to...'

The voices faded, and Carol went to get dressed, the niggly-worry feeling in her gut gone. Ralph was safely here, and whatever happened now, she knew one thing. He was important enough for her insides to have turned somersaults at the idea that he was in a difficult situation. That didn't mean he would be part of her life, just that – well, he was here and soon they would talk. Carol went for lunch feeling ravenous, and thoroughly enjoyed her spinach and ricotta ravioli.

She was in her room adjusting her make-up – the advantage of being forewarned – when her phone pinged.

Coffee in the bar in 10?

See you there! she texted back, swallowing the nervous fluttering in her middle.

The snug bar was tucked behind the restaurant, and seemed to be a new addition, judging by the freshness of the décor. Ralph was sitting in the far corner when she arrived, and Carol hesitated. The awkwardness was still there. She didn't know what he was thinking, now that he'd had the chance to mull things over for a few days. Maybe he regretted telling her he'd come back? But then, he could easily have used the weather as a reason not to come. Fortunately, a waiter approached him while she was on the way across the floor, so they didn't have to gawp at each other for her entire journey across the room – which admittedly was on the small side, but still. Carol slid into the chair opposite Ralph, trying hard to breathe normally.

'A flat white for me,' she said to the waiter, then smiled at Ralph, clasping her hands on the table top to stop them shaking. 'Welcome back! You must have had a snowy trip north.'

'The second half was – but we're used to it here,' he said. 'How's the ear?'

'Good. I hope. I can hear normally again, so that's a relief. We'll see what the doctor says tomorrow. Stacy's been very kind.'

He smiled at this, but his eyes were thoughtful and Carol wondered suddenly what Stacy thought about him returning like this. Rico's face betrayed his negative feelings, but maybe Stacy was just better at hiding hers? It wasn't a comfortable thought. Carol stirred her coffee when it arrived, more for something to do than anything else, and when she lifted her head he was grinning his old grin again.

'I was going to invite you for a walk, but you may not want to go out in this weather?'

Carol seized the idea. Anything was better than sitting here gaping at each other while waiters were wandering about the place. 'I'd love to go for a tramp. I'll need to change my shoes, but that's no problem.'

'Excellent – we'll drive to Rorschach and walk along the promenade there.' He lifted his coffee cup.

In spite of her nerves, Carol enjoyed the afternoon. It was as if they'd agreed beforehand to take time to get to know each other better before moving on to anything controversial. They talked about anything and everything, and Carol's apprehension lightened with every step. They had the same sense of humour, they were both tennis fans, and – so many little things were just 'right'. And yet... she still didn't know what he thought about it all, and as for where this would end – who could tell?

'Can I take you to dinner tomorrow night?' he said, as they drove back to Lakeside. 'I'd ask you tonight, but I haven't seen Rico yet. He's away today and won't be back until four-ish, so Stacy's planning a family meal.'

'Tomorrow's perfect,' said Carol. 'I'm booked into Stacy's healthy eating talk after dinner tonight anyway.'

He held the front door open for her, then followed her in. 'Look – have you noticed these?'

Carol turned round. He was standing beside the coffee table, where the white vase containing the forsythia cuttings they'd gathered on St Barbara's day stood, and – yes, Carol could see tiny leaves were forming all the way up most of the branches.

Ralph removed one that appeared to be dead and beamed at her. 'See? We'll have good luck, now!'

Carol touched one of the stems and met his eye. It was an omen, it had to be, and the way he was looking at her, he thought the same. Carol's heart lurched. But then – it changed nothing.

Back in her room, she sat down to do some serious thinking. Supposing she and Ralph did start a relationship – what would that mean? Nervous dismay thudded into her middle. One of them would have to relocate, that was what. And she was the one with fewer ties to her home town. Did she really want to leave London, give up her life there, not to mention her job, for the chance of being one of a pair again? And that was before you even considered Barry and the family in Perth. What would they think? It was odds-on they'd ask her again to join them in Australia – what on earth would she do then?

For the life of her Carol didn't know.

***

Rico toyed with his minestrone and crusty bread, the appetite he'd worked up this afternoon while out buying new supplies for the spa shop deserting him the moment he lifted his spoon. Dad was looking very chipper. According to Stacy, he'd taken Carol out for a walk, but no way was Rico going to mention that, or – or he didn't know what he'd end up saying. And as neither of the other two were mentioning it either, it was fair to say there was an elephant in the room all through dinner. Fortunately, Stacy wanted to talk about her plan for a snowman competition that evening, and she and Ralph batted ideas back and forth across the table until Ralph went downstairs to organise the floodlights.

Stacy gave him a stern look as soon as Dad was out of earshot, and Rico noticed her pale face for the first time that day. She was still tired, shit.

He gave her his best managerial smile. 'Do you think the guests will appreciate the change of plan?'

'I'm sure they will. They'll get all the healthy eating material in their email inbox tomorrow, and this could be a one-off. Come on – they'll be gathering downstairs by now. And Rico, I know you're not happy about Ralph and Carol, but – play nice, huh?'

He nodded dumbly, then followed her down to the medical room, where her talk was planned. Eleven people were waiting, mostly women – but Stacy was prepared for that.

'Evening, everyone – we have a proposition for you in the form of an alternative programme for this evening. Those who wish can stay here for the New Year Healthy Eating Plan talk, given tonight by Margrit, our other trained nurse. Or you might like to join another group on the back lawn where we're holding a snowman competition. Fun, exercise, fresh air – need I say more? Floodlights are up and we have prizes. Snowmen people have ten minutes now to collect your jackets, gloves, spouses, etcetera – see you on the back terrace!'

Her eyes danced at the guests, most of whom shot off to get ready to go outside, and Rico grinned too. She was such a natural at hotel-keeping and all that went with it. Just like Mum had been, in fact, and yes, he would do his bit here.

Nineteen guests were gathered on the terrace when he and Stacy arrived ten minutes later.

Rico stood up on a stool so that he could count the guests. 'We'll have three groups of five and one of–'

'Count me in too,' said Ralph, appearing behind Rico. He strode over to join Carol and three other guests.

Rico swallowed, but there was no time to brood about what his father may or may not be thinking. He switched on the floodlights, sent the groups of guests to different corners of the lawn, and yelled, 'You have forty minutes – go!'

He watched for a few moments as the construction of large-sized snowballs began. Ralph's group disappeared into the darkness, and Rico's lips twitched. There would be a lot of snow on the path down to the landing stage, and plenty of moonlight to gather it by – talk about a home advantage. He and Stacy went round the groups together, advising on the best places to find twigs, and handing out carrots for noses. Quite a few non-participating guests appeared on their balconies above, shouting encouragement, and Rico was glad they had no neighbours close enough to be disturbed. When the forty minutes were up, he blew his whistle.

'Time! Everybody back on the terrace, please, and we'll send the judges round to pick the winner!'

He waved towards the terrace, where Stacy and Rob the chef were setting up a table with mulled wine and hot punch for the guests, plus a selection of Christmas biscuits.

'Who's judging?' asked Rob, and Rico grinned.

'I'd reckoned with you and Dad, but he's messed that idea up. We'll have you and–'

'Margrit,' said Stacy, as the nurse appeared with the people who'd attended her talk.

Rico stood sipping his punch as the judging pair made a solemn round of the snowmen. Ralph was deep in conversation with Carol at the edge of the terrace, and Rico's stomach lurched. Carol was a nice lady and Stacy was right, it was Dad's life. His mother's face swam before Rico's eyes, and he blinked. He literally couldn't stand this.

Rob and Margrit picked the best snowman, made by the honeymooners and an older threesome, and the crowd cheered as Stacy presented them each with a voucher for the spa shop. So the evening had been a full success, proving that you could be flexible in your event planning. Rico went inside, trying – and failing – to ignore the fact that Ralph and Carol had disappeared off in the direction of the lake. Hot frustration rose, and Rico clenched both fists and pressed them against his chest. He could do nothing at all about Dad and Carol, and nice lady or not, he wasn't about to stand back and watch while his father made such a monumental mistake. Yet there was no way to stop Ralph doing whatever the hell he liked. Or – Rico pressed his lips together and blinked back tears. Maybe he could do something. With his father here for the foreseeable, he didn't have to stay and watch. He could pack a bag and leave any time he wanted.

20

Wednesday, 12th December

Stacy worked her way through a bowl of muesli to the sound of Ralph singing under the shower in the family bathroom. At least someone was cheerful, after last night. It might be an idea if she had a word with him and asked him to have a frank talk with Rico about whatever was going on with Carol. One part of Rico's problem must be the uncertainty about it all, and she could see it would be unsettling, with the three of them all on top of each other, like they were here. Stacy lifted her mug and cuddled it. The other part of Rico's problem was, he was still trying to integrate his mother's death into his own life, and that wasn't so quickly dealt with.

She stood to push her mug into the coffee machine for a refill. In a different way, things would better at the hotel with Ralph here for a few days. He'd run the place for nearly three decades, so he could easily take care of the managerial duties and free them up to see to the festive programme. It didn't change the fact that she and Rico would be on duty for eighteen hours out of twenty-four, but it would make them eighteen easier hours. And hopefully the love of her life would be thinking the same way. The pair of them were behaving more like people who'd been married for a million years, not like the engaged-and-desperate-to-be-married couple they were. Where was the romance in her life? And this was the worst time ever to be mulling this over, because the Advent programme simply didn't give them time alone together. They'd plan next Christmas differently, that was sure, but in the meantime, they'd just have to get on with it. January would soon be here, and having Mum around at New Year, talking about wedding plans, would help too. Stacy's lips twitched as she remembered how desperate she'd felt earlier that year when all her mother wanted to talk about was wedding plans... come to think of it, the hotel had taken up all her head back then too, with the flooding they'd had. Lakeside had a lot to answer for.

'Nice to see you smile – penny for them.' Ralph squeezed past to drop bread into the toaster.

'I was remembering last summer,' said Stacy.

'Busy time.' He stirred sugar into his coffee. 'Like now. What's happening this morning? Where's Rico?'

'He went downstairs early – I was barely awake when he left. I'm in the spa first thing, then I'm taking Carol to the doctor. Rico's looking after things here, and you're going with Rob to buy a large-sized load of food,' said Stacy firmly. She didn't want him anywhere near Lakeside while Carol was hopefully making decisions about flights.

To her relief, Ralph accepted this without comment, and Stacy went down to open the spa. Flavia was on at reception, and she waved an envelope as soon as Stacy stepped out of the lift.

'Rico said to give you this. He had to go out somewhere.'

'Okay.' Stacy took the envelope and went through to the spa, switching on the tubs on her way to the medical room. Where on earth had Rico gone that he couldn't take two minutes to come and tell her – or even call her, if it was super-urgent? And why on earth hadn't he texted? She tore the envelope open and sat down to read the note in Rico's sprawling handwriting.

I'm sorry, Stace, but I can't stay here and watch Dad and Carol getting cosy together. I need some time to think it all through, so I'm going to Dad's in Lugano. He doesn't know, so can you please tell him for me? I'll be in touch soon, but I can't stay at Lakeside with all this hanging over me. Rico xx

No! Stacy ran from the room and charged outside, stopping abruptly on the top step. From here, she could see the staff spaces in the car park, and thank heavens, the car was still there. He must have gone by train. This was awful; how could he do this to her? They were rushed off their feet, and he swanned off to have a think. A *think*? It was outrageous – whatever he was doing, it wasn't thinking, that was sure. She ran back to the lift, calling to Flavia to keep an eye on the spa for ten minutes.

Upstairs, Ralph was loading the dishwasher. Stacy thrust Rico's note at him, watching as he went pale, then red, and finally whipped out his mobile.

'He won't answer,' said Stacy. 'We should leave him for a few hours.'

Ralph listened to his phone for a few seconds then thumped the work surface, swearing in Italian. 'I'll tell Guido to watch out for him.'

'Good idea. I have to go back to the spa. Can you take charge here later while I'm at the clinic with Carol?'

He opened his mouth, and she put a hand on his arm. 'Yes, I'm going with her. I'm the nurse, remember?'

'Fine.' He snapped his phone case shut and stomped into his bedroom, where he was soon talking Italian at a hundred miles an hour to presumably Guido. Stacy took a long, cold drink of water. At this rate, she would kill Rico before they had a chance to get married, but right now, she had a job to do and unlike her beloved, she was going to do it.

Carol was waiting at quarter to ten when Stacy arrived in reception with the car key.

'I hope this is going to be good news. I don't want to have to call Barry to tell him I won't make Christmas.'

'You feel well, your ear's dry and you've no temperature,' said Stacy, trying to sound encouraging. 'All good signs.'

Doctor Erisman was running late, and they had to wait nearly half an hour, which Stacy could tell was doing nothing for Carol's peace of mind. She watched the other woman fidget around on her seat as she leafed through a magazine. Was this all to do with being desperate to get to Barry and family in balmy Australia, or was some of it because of Ralph in snowy Switzerland? At last they were called in, and Stacy took a seat at the side of the room while the doctor peered into Carol's ear.

'It's healing very well,' he said, straightening up and smiling at Carol. 'I'll tell you now – you had the largest perforation I've ever seen.'

'When can I fly?' said Carol, her knuckles white, and Stacy held her breath.

'In an emergency I'd say, go, but waiting a few more days wouldn't hurt,' said the doctor.

Carol heaved a huge sigh and slumped in her seat. 'Thank you. I'll get onto the airline today. I don't imagine they'll have a seat for me immediately, anyway.'

Stacy hugged Carol on the way back to the car. No matter what was going on with Rico, and with Ralph and Carol, it was good news for the family in Australia. 'Christmas in Oz, then.'

Carol's eyes were suspiciously bright. 'Christmas in Oz.' She wiped her eyes with a glove.

Stacy pulled out into the main road. Were those tears of happiness at the prospect of seeing her family soon – or something else?

At Lakeside, Ralph was in the office, head-first in the computer while Alex manned the desk. Stacy closed the office door and sat down beside her future father-in-law. Fond as she was of Alex, this was family-only stuff.

'Any word from Rico?'

He shook his head. 'He's probably only just arrived in Lugano. I thought we could let Guido pick up the pieces for now, and try Rico after lunch?'

Stacy chewed her top lip. Suppose Rico wouldn't talk to her? Or Ralph? And any second now Ralph was going to ask–

'What did the doctor say?' He clicked out of the file he was in and stared straight at her.

'Carol's free to rebook her flight.' She could say that much without breaking confidentiality, surely.

Ralph slumped in his chair. 'Stacy, I'm – horrified that Rico feels like this. I've no idea what to say to him.'

Stacy put a hand on his arm. 'It's Rico's problem. To be brutally honest, I don't think you can help him. But I could – maybe. So I'll pack a few things and join him in Lugano, if you can look after the hotel for a day or two?'

***

Frustration filling her head, Carol banged her iPad down on her table, then checked guiltily she hadn't damaged it. Okay, it was Christmas; everyone and their dogs were en route to visit family in Australia, but how boring that she couldn't get flights until the eighteenth – that was nearly a whole week to wait. *And nearly a week more with Ralph*, whispered her heart, and Carol grimaced. If only, only they'd met at the Thursday night pub quiz in her local back home. It would all be so easy then. As it was, she couldn't possibly afford to stay on at the hotel until the eighteenth so she'd better see Stacy about finding somewhere else ASAP – and she'd better call Barry, too. What time was it in Perth? Seven at night, perfect.

As usual, Barry sounded as if he was in the next room, not several thousand miles away.

'Hi, Mum! What's the verdict?'

Carol relaxed. She would soon be there, and she'd see about extending her holiday to the end of January. She'd get a sick line, wouldn't she?

'Flight booked for the eighteenth, and I'm down for a cancellation place if one becomes available, though they said that was unlikely.'

'Brilliant. Your lounger on the beach is waiting, and I'll tell Emma you're definitely on your way now. Can't wait to see you here, and Mum – we have news, don't forget!'

Carol pricked up her ears. Was this the surprise he'd mentioned before? There was an underlying excitement in his voice. Whatever the news was, it was big.

'What?'

He laughed. 'Curiosity killed the cat! It's part of your Christmas pressie.'

It was the surprise. Nothing Carol said could persuade him to say more, and she rang off a few minutes later with her head full of question marks. What on earth was it? He'd already said it wasn't another grandchild. A thought swooped into her head, and Carol held her breath. Diane was one of twins. Barry had said it wasn't another grand*child* – could it be grand*children*? Oh, my...

She was on her way downstairs to have her nails done when a more likely thought struck. Barry could have a concrete job offer for her down under. It might even be combined with a place to stay, warden or administrator in a complex for the elderly or the like. He'd mentioned that as a possibility before; it could have turned into something more immediate. How very complicated that would be. *No, it wouldn't*, said her head. *You'd just pack up your stuff and go to your family...*

'Brilliant news!' said Kim the manicurist, when Carol told her about the booked flights. 'Over Singapore? Will you have time to see the city?'

'No. Maybe on the way back,' said Carol, watching as Kim filed her nails. 'I wish I was going sooner. I'll have no spending money left for Australia, at this rate.' She smiled ruefully. Which was why she was sitting here having her nails done... ha. Tonight's dinner with Ralph was going to be a turning point. They'd talk about her trip to Perth, and either decide there might be a possibility for them in the future, or... or they'd let it go. And oh, if only she knew what she wanted. A picture of his face, brown eyes shining at her, slid into her head and a lump rose in her throat.

Carol emerged from the manicure booth half an hour later, admiring her turquoise nails with silver sparkles. She'd never had anything like this before, but now she'd started she would carry on; they were fabulous.

Ralph was at reception with Alex, but he came round the desk when she appeared. 'I was waiting for you – and what glamorous nails!'

Carol stretched them out for another look. 'I'll have to be careful with them. Though I do have the varnish for a touch-up.' She patted her bag.

He tipped her shoulder with two fingers, his eyes soft. 'Excellent. I wanted to ask – can we bring our dinner tonight forward a little? There's a carol concert in the marketplace beside the cathedral in St Gallen, one of those singalong things, and I thought you might like to go, after we eat? It should be fun. I'm sorry I can't entertain you this afternoon, too, but I have to help Stacy.' A little worry line appeared between his eyes.

'No problem. A concert sounds lovely.' Pleased, Carol went up to her room, the memory of Ralph's eyes looking at her bittersweet in her head. Somehow, she was going to have to come to a decision about what – and who – she wanted in her life, and it might not be easy.

21

WEDNESDAY, 12TH DECEMBER, AFTERNOON

Stacy hurried across Zurich main station to platform eight, where the Lugano train was waiting. Last time she'd made this journey by train was when she and Rico were joining Ralph and Mum and Dad in the Ticino last summer. How very different today's journey was... She found a window seat and shrugged out of her jacket before settling down to spend the next three hours staring out at winter in Switzerland and worrying about Rico. She'd need to work out what on earth she was going to say to him when she arrived, mind you, and that might take up most of the three hours because right now, she didn't have a clue.

A group of about fifteen children hurried past on the platform outside, and Stacy watched as the two women with them – teachers? – ushered them into the next carriage. It wasn't very long ago that she'd been longing for the day when she and Rico would have a family. Somehow, that felt very far away this afternoon. The train jerked and moved off, and Stacy closed her eyes as a wave of sleepiness almost overwhelmed her. Maybe a nap would be the best preparation for her talk with Rico...

The Ticino was noticeably milder than the north. Stacy emerged at Lugano's lofty train station and headed for the funicular down into the town. Ralph's flat was within walking distance of the city centre, so she'd be there in quarter of an hour – fortunately, because it would be dark soon. The funicular was still on the way up, and she stood for a moment, looking round the wooded hills that surrounded Lugano. Monte Brè and Monte San Salvatore, the two peaks that flanked the bay and rolled down to the lake. Both had a sugar-coating of snow, but none was lying underfoot.

'Fancy some company?'

Stacy jumped at the voice immediately behind her, then wheeled round to hug Julia, Guido's wife. She replied in the same German Julia had used. 'How did you know which train I was on?' As if she couldn't guess...

Julia took her free arm. 'Ralph called us. I didn't bring the car, but I'll treat you to the funicular. Oh, Stacy. What a mess this is.'

The blue and white funicular arrived at the hill station and spewed out a handful of passengers en route for their trains. Stacy followed Julia into the front section, where they sat on a hard bench for the few minutes' ride down to the centre.

'Have you seen Rico?' Stacy hardly dared ask how he was.

Julia shook her head. 'Guido has. He said he's angry and upset and needs time. I hope you can help him, Stacy. He hasn't had it easy for the past few years.'

Stacy was silent. This was true. There was the sudden death of Rico's mum, then the worry when Ralph let the hotel go to the extent that it almost went out of business and was only saved when Rico stepped in – but to save the hotel he'd had to give up his dream of doing a master's degree in IT and then opening his own business.

Between them, though, they'd turned things round and made a success of Lakeside, and as Rico was due to start his postponed degree in February, theoretically it had all been sorted – until Carol arrived. What he'd done now was hot-headed, but maybe it was understandable.

Now, she pulled a face at Julia. 'He has to let me help him. What do you think about Ralph and Carol?'

Julia grimaced back. 'I think if Ralph is happy, it's a good thing. Don't you?'

'Of course. But Rico isn't over Evie's death yet. In a way, he's still living in the past, and that's what we have to fix.' Which sounded easy when you said it quickly, though it was going to be anything but.

They arrived at the block of flats where Guido and Julia lived on the top floor, with Ralph a couple of floors down.

Julia pressed the button in the lift, and they glided upwards. 'I'll leave you to it, Stace, but you know where we are.'

'Thanks, Julia.' They jerked to a halt on the sixth floor and the doors opened. Stacy stepped onto the landing, gripping her overnight bag. She rang the bell at Ralph's flat and waited. This was where she'd need all her tact and love and – everything – to help Rico. Footsteps sounded behind the door, and Stacy blinked back sudden tears. Please let her be able to help Rico.

***

Carol logged out of her online banking and went into the en suite to check her face before she set off in search of Stacy. It was a touch embarrassing to ask, but if she knew how much her hotel bill was likely to be, she could organise her travel money better. She was a planner; it didn't feel right to float around not knowing how much of a bill she was running up. And she wasn't so well off it didn't matter, either.

She took the lift down, then put her head into the spa rooms. The other nurse was on duty, though, and there was no sign of Stacy in the restaurant, either. Carol hesitated. She'd prefer to talk to Stacy rather than young Alex, who was organising something in a drawer under the desk.

He closed it, and saw her. 'Looking for Stacy? She's not here this afternoon. Can I help?'

Oh, well. It wasn't super-urgent. 'It's okay, thanks. I'll catch her later.'

'Ah – I'm not sure when she'll be back. She took an overnight bag with her.'

His face was troubled, and Carol's radar beeped. Something was wrong. Rico didn't seem to be around either. Was Ralph?

She found him in the snug bar, staring out towards the lake. 'I was looking for Stacy,' she said, joining him at the window. He squinted at her, and yes, something was definitely wrong.

'Rico and Stacy have gone to Lugano. I'm hoping they'll be back tomorrow.'

His voice had an odd edge to it, and Carol's breath caught. Was she being hugely conceited to wonder if this was anything to do with her? Her and Ralph? There was only one way to find out.

'Does this have anything to do with me being here?'

Ralph's face tightened. 'Yes. And no. It's me. Rico would have a problem with anyone – any woman – he thought I might replace his mother with.'

Carol blinked. 'You'll never be able to replace his mother, that's not how it works. Doesn't he want you to be...' Yikes. Who was she to suggest she might make him happy?

Ralph put a hand on her arm. 'I know. It's all right. He's not thinking straight, that's all, he needs time. Now, why don't you fetch your coat and we'll get for our dinner in St Gallen. Don't worry about Rico.'

Carol trailed back to the lift, her thoughts in turmoil. And maybe it was a good thing her ticket to Oz was booked.

The restaurant was in the centre of town, and Carol was glad to get inside out of the cold. They'd come up in the post bus, as Ralph liked a glass of wine with his meal and Carol definitely didn't feel able to tackle a left-hand drive on snowy streets – and she liked wine, too. She settled down and gazed around appreciatively. It was all golden pine panelling and rustic charm here.

'Traditional Swiss grub in a traditional Swiss restaurant,' said Ralph cheerfully. 'Not a tourist in sight. Have you tried *Züri Geschnetzeltes* yet? You can't say you've been a fortnight in Switzerland and not had that. With rösti potatoes?'

Carol agreed apprehensively. As far as she knew, she'd never had veal, but Ralph pointed out a woman a couple of tables away who was having it, and he was ordering the same so it must be okay – mustn't it? The waiter arrived with wine first, and Ralph raised his glass.

'To Christmas!' His eyes twinkled at her.

It was a pretty safe toast, all things considered. Tactful, too. Carol clinked glasses, then took a big swallow for courage and sat back as their main course arrived. It looked like creamy stew and tasted amazing.

'See?' said Ralph, waving his fork at her. 'We have the same taste. We go well together.'

This was the kind of remark Carol would rather have avoided. Feeling rather mean, she told him about Barry's planned barbeque Christmas dinner.

Ralph nodded. 'I know, you want to get to your family,' he said. 'It would be best to leave all talk of the future until you've done that.'

Carol nodded dumbly, not knowing what to think now. Even talking about not talking about the future meant they were... talking about the future. Oh hell, this was complicated and all she wanted to do was hug her grandchildren more often. But he was right. For the rest of the meal they talked of families. He spoke so sweetly about his wife, and she told him about her husband, then over coffee they worked their way through politics and holidays, and Carol's heart ached. They did 'go well together', the two of them. But what if Barry had other plans for her? The thought of having normal, everyday contact with her family again would be hard to resist.

The carol concert in the old town centre was freezing but incredibly atmospheric. Ralph had arranged to meet Alex, who was coming up in the minibus with a collection of guests, at half past seven. The floodlit cathedral towered in the background, and a few tiny snowflakes were floating down from a dark sky. Song sheets were given out at the start, and Carol leafed through hers. *Stille Nacht, Heilige Nacht* was there, and *Oh Tannenbaum* – that was *Oh Christmas Tree*, wasn't it?

'You have the right name for this time of year, don't you?' Ralph took her arm, and Carol laughed. It was an old joke, but it felt good that he was making it, after the upset – was it an upset? – about Rico. She sang along to the carols she knew, glad that a couple were in English. The concert ended with a rousing chorus of *Rudolph the Red-Nosed Reindeer*.

'Space for two more in the minibus?' Ralph said to Alex, as the crowd dispersed through the medieval streets of the old town centre.

'Oh, I think we'll manage to squeeze you in,' he said.

The minibus was parked at the edge of the old town, and Carol settled into her seat beside Ralph. Alex drove off and St Gallen vanished behind them, leaving Carol with a sudden lump in her throat. Would she ever be back there? Ralph and Rico didn't know how lucky they were, having all their family in the same country, never mind on the same continent. Ignoring the buzz of chatter in the bus, she stared out into darkness beside her as they drove through flurries of snowflakes back down to the lake. It was an odd feeling, not knowing where she would live for the rest of her life.

22

THURSDAY, 13TH DECEMBER, MORNING

Rico lay awake, watching as the radio alarm by his bed ticked round. Midnight, half past, one o'clock. and still sleep was a long way off. He stretched a hand out to the other side of the bed, but Stacy wasn't there. Nausea rolled over him. They'd talked for hours, but there was no way she was ever going to make him be happy about Ralph finding another woman to share his life with. He rolled on his side, pulling the duvet under his chin and cuddling the downy warmth to his heart. His heart was the problem. His gut knew he was being ridiculous. Millions of people were widowed and went on to love again, so why couldn't he accept that Dad could, too? In the end, Stacy had left him to it and gone up to Guido and Julia's to sleep; that was how pissed off she was with him. So right now, she'd be asleep in the bed that the two of them had shared last summer. The bed they'd made love in and laughed, in the days when their only problems had been a lake in flood and Stacy's mum wanting to take over the wedding. The wedding that might never happen, now. Oh, heck. What had he done? He rolled onto his back again and stared into the darkness above him.

He'd pushed her away, that was what. They'd started out okay, talking about what it meant to lose your partner or a parent, but then she'd suggested, for about the millionth time since they'd met, that he should go for bereavement counselling. What would that bring? It wasn't counselling he needed, it was his mother. Or, if that sounded too childish, he needed his life back. The evening had ended with him refusing to talk any more and Stacy in tears. He was going to have to fix that.

Sleep came eventually, and the alarm was showing 07.40 when Rico opened his eyes again. He hauled himself to his feet and stumbled into the bathroom. Twenty minutes later he was on the top floor ringing Guido and Julia's doorbell.

No answer. Rico frowned. Guido would be at work at the family boatyard, but in the circumstances, wouldn't Julia have stayed at home with Stacy? He pulled out his phone and tried Stacy first. Her phone was switched off. Heck... He tapped to connect to Julia.

'Hi, Rico. No, I'm at the yard with Guido. Stacy left early this morning.'

His mouth went dry. 'Where was she going?'

'She didn't say exactly, but not to Lakeside. She wants time to be by herself and think.'

Rico dropped his phone. Oh hell. Oh no. She'd left him.

***

Reception was deserted when Carol came out of the restaurant after breakfast, but the door to the office was half open. Alex was wrapping presents. Carol went round the desk and tapped.

'Only me. I'll give you a hand with those, shall I?'

She settled down with the latest list, and Alex went back to the desk to help a couple of locals who were talking about the sauna in a very heated way, but as "sauna" was the only word Carol understood, there was no knowing what the problem was. Eventually, Ralph appeared and the discussion adjourned somewhere else. Carol raised her eyebrows at Alex when he came back.

'They sounded cross.'

'They were. They wanted season tickets and we don't do those.'

Carol could see that season tickets for a relatively small sauna might mean guests were crowded out at peak times.

'You could work out your capacity, then sell a limited number of tickets that cover ten visits and then the eleventh is free, or something like that. Make them personal to stop folk sharing them round the family.'

He lifted the present list. 'I'll run that by Rico. Or Stacy.'

Carol reached for the Sellotape. It would be very nosy to ask if there was any news about Stacy or Rico, so she wouldn't, but hopefully someone would tell her soon.

Twenty minutes later, she was almost at the last bag of creams and salts when Ralph put his head round the door.

'You can take your break now, Alex, and I'll mind the desk.'

Alex didn't need to be told twice. When he was gone, Ralph leaned in the doorway, his face sombre.

'I'm finding it hard not to call Rico or Stacy, but I think it's best to leave them to it.'

Carol put a room number sticker on the newly wrapped bag. She should tell him what she was thinking, though it wasn't going to help because it was way too late now. 'I don't feel good about this,' she blurted out. 'If I'd never come here–'

He stepped into the office and closed the door. 'If you'd never come here, I wouldn't have realised I could ever find happiness again. I was like a shell of a person, Carol. Ask Stacy. Whatever happens now, I know I'm alive.'

She gaped at him. Were those tears in his eyes? She opened her mouth to say heaven only knew what, then closed it again when his phone rang. He fumbled it from his pocket.

'Rico! Are you–? ... No, she's not ... I don't know. I haven't spoken to her ... All right. I'll see you soon.' He ended the call and looked at Carol. 'He's on his way back. I'll meet his train at Romanshorn.'

He strode from the office, and Carol tidied the present-wrapping material away, her head whirling. Rico would be coming back here. And she was the one person he definitely didn't need to come into contact with. Ralph had vanished, so she waited at the desk until Alex came back, planning her next move. It was the thirteenth, so another five nights until her flight on the eighteenth. It was time to go elsewhere. Maybe Kim the manicurist would be able to suggest somewhere.

'You can prepare my bill, please,' she said to Alex. 'I'll be leaving later today.' She hurried off before he'd opened his mouth. She was causing these good people too much grief; she should pack.

Her suitcase was on her bed and half full when a knock came on her door and Ralph walked in without waiting for an invitation.

Carol glared. 'You'd have looked pretty silly if I'd been standing here in my undies, wouldn't you?'

He wiped a hand across his face. 'Sorry. But I'm not letting you leave like this.' He pulled out the chair by the small table and sat down.

Carol went on folding blouses. 'You can't stop me. And I truly think you and Rico will be able to work through his problems much better if I'm not here, don't you?'

'No, I don't. I do think he'd be able to continue ignoring his problems if you're not here, and that's not going to help anyone, is it?'

Carol hesitated, and he seized his chance. 'Tell you what. Let me show you something now, and afterwards, if you still want to leave Lakeside, you can. Meet you downstairs in ten minutes. Wear your jacket.' He strode from the room without looking at her.

Carol abandoned her suitcase and pulled on her duvet jacket and woolly hat, wrinkling her nose at her reflection in the wardrobe mirror. At least no one could accuse her of trying to look seductive in this outfit, could they?

Alex at the desk gaped as she emerged from the lift, but Ralph was already waiting and bundled her out of the front door and down the driveway to the car park.

'It's only a two-minute drive,' he said, as she settled into the passenger seat.

It wasn't even two minutes. Carol gazed out as they drove along the main road for fifty yards, then turned into a series of side streets to come to a stop at the cemetery, a small plot enclosed by a high wall and containing a tiny chapel at one end. Her heart rate went up a notch, but he was out of the car and round opening her door before she had a chance to speak. He'd only bring her here to show her one thing, wouldn't he? Was it really what she wanted to see?

'Edie's grave. Come and see.' He didn't touch her as he led the way down a side path and along a row of very small plots to a white marble headstone, where he crouched to remove a few stray dead leaves from among the winter pansies planted there.

Carol read the inscription, which was very short. Just her name, Edith Martina, her dates, and 'beloved wife and mother' in English. At the top of the stone was an engraving of the hotel, a simple chalet shape. Two tears trickled down Carol's cheeks, and she wiped them away before he noticed.

'We were together for twenty-seven years,' said Ralph, standing up. 'We were happy. Now she is here, in an urn grave.' He spun round to face her. 'Look around you. This is a pleasant spot, but it's in the past, isn't it? None of this has a place in today's life, except maybe in a little corner of our hearts, we who loved Edie. She'll always have that corner. But I want to live, too.' He stared at the grave, blinking fast with both hands thrust into his pockets.

Carol cleared her throat. 'Thank you for bringing me here.' *And thank you for not saying more than you did*, she added mentally. 'I have David in the same corner of my heart, so I do know. But let's give ourselves time now, Ralph. We'll see what Christmas brings, and then...'

'Then we'll know.' Now he did touch her, taking her hand and leading her away from the grave. 'Will you stay at Lakeside until you go to Australia? Please?'

At the end of the row she turned for a last look back. 'If Rico agrees, I will. Deal?'

He nodded, then held her hand against his cheek. 'And now I have to meet his train.'

23

Thursday, 13th December, afternoon

The intercity jerked to a halt at Romanshorn, and Rico swung his bag down from the rack. Having spent the entire journey itching with impatience to get home and wishing with all his heart he'd run away by car, another twenty minutes or so would do it. He'd be walking up to the hotel and God only knew what kind of reception he'd get from Dad. And Stacy... please, please let her have come home since he'd called Dad. It was a bit of a useless wish, given that the call had been less than an hour ago. Rico joined the queue to leave the train, misery engulfing him. Or self-pity. He was a mess.

The doors opened and he stepped down, turning towards platform one where the lake train was waiting. A hand slapped his shoulder.

'Good to see you, Rico. I've got the car here.'

Dad's face was serious, but calm. Rico nodded, and followed silently to one of the 'fifteen minutes only' spaces Ralph had parked in. Ralph said nothing either, which didn't make Rico feel any better. But then, he was too old to be told, 'don't worry, son, Dad'll fix this for you'.

He tossed his bag into the back seat. 'I'm sorry if I've made things difficult at Lakeside.' It was as good a start as any.

Ralph shrugged. 'The hotel will be fine, Rico. That's not the problem, is it?'

Rico slumped in the passenger seat as they joined the queue of cars at the lights, waiting to get away from the busy harbour and station area. Dad looked weary, just bone tired and older, somehow, and that wasn't because of any extra work he'd had at Lakeside. Nausea surged, and Rico sat breathing carefully. What had he done? Stupid question. He'd abandoned everything he cared about and now his fiancée had abandoned him, and the only way to put things right was to accept the unacceptable, a new woman in Dad's life. In place of Mum.

He squinted at Ralph. 'Have you heard from Stacy? She left Lugano early this morning.'

'Not a word.'

Rico glanced at the dashboard clock. If Stacy was coming home, she'd have been there by now. This could really be it; he could lose her, and Dad was uncharacteristically silent. He wouldn't lose his father, but the relationship could easily be damaged. Badly. A picture of the three of them watching the Christmas lights go on at Lakeside slid into his head. Just... heck, just two weeks ago they'd been happy, planning the celebrations for the hotel and looking forward to their own Christmas. If he lost Stacy now, he'd never have what Mum and Dad had had all their years together.

He buried his face in his hands, took a deep breath, and sat up straight. 'I've been a class A prat, haven't I?'

'Yup.' Ralph patted his knee. 'Call Stacy when you're home, son. You have to start sorting this.'

Going through reception was like some kind of walk of shame. Alex at the desk gave him half a nod then looked away, and he'd seen Carol dive into the office as soon as they appeared in the doorway. The only good thing was, the lift was waiting and no one got in along with them. Rico went straight into his bedroom and flopped down on the bed he and Stacy might never share again. Call her, man.

Her phone rang, two, three, four times, and Rico's stomach twisted more with every ring. Then on the fifth ring, she took the call.

'Rico?'

'Stace. I'm sorry. I'm so sorry, please, we have to fix this. I'm back at Lakeside, please…'

'I'm at Kim's. We can talk here.'

The connection broke, and Rico leapt up and into the en suite. He hadn't even showered today yet.

The walk to Kim's home in the village was the most nerve wracking he'd ever taken. The manicure booth at the hotel was empty, so it was odds-on Kim was at home too. Rico clenched his fists in his jacket pockets. He and Stacy needed to talk alone, but maybe that wasn't his call to make, now. The door opened as soon as he rang the bell, and Stacy stepped out.

'We can walk and talk.'

She was pale, but the tilt to her chin showed she was determined about something. They fell into step, heading for the lake path, exactly as if this was a normal, out for a breath of fresh air kind of walk. Rico reached automatically for her hand, then clasped his own and swung round to face her.

'I want to get through this.'

'So do I. And so does your dad. Rico, you have got to let him decide about his own life. He'll do it anyway, and you want to be a part of whatever comes after his decision.'

'He and Mum–'

She stopped dead. 'He and Edie will always be part of your life. Edie will always be part of Ralph's life. It's not an 'either – or' thing, don't you get that? He can love Edie in the past and someone else now and in the future *as well*, Rico. Like having a child and loving it doesn't mean you love it any less when the second baby comes along.'

They came to the stony beach and Rico sat down on one of the slabs at the water's edge. 'I think I'm starting to see that. Will – can you help me? Can we go back to Lakeside and work together like we meant to?'

She perched beside him. 'Yes. At least, we'll go back and work on the Advent programme and make it the success we wanted it to be. As for the rest, you know what I think. But tiredness is a big part of this right now, Rico. We bit off more than we could chew, didn't we?'

Relief flowed through Rico like a refreshing wave on a Bahaman beach. This wasn't a solution, but it was a good start.

'Done. We'll get to Christmas, then take stock. I'll think about bereavement counselling. And I'll leave Dad alone.'

'Promise?'

'Promise. Come on. We have a hotel to run.'

He held out his hand, and she took it. Cold reality replaced the relief as they started back to Kim's for Stacy's things. They would make a go of it, the two of them, but would he ever be able to accept another woman in his father's life?

***

Stacy slid behind the desk at reception and peered at the Gala Dinner bookings on the computer. 'Sorry, you two. Business as usual from now on in. Have I missed anything important?'

Alex shook his head. 'Flavia's just about caught up with the present orders this afternoon, you'll be glad to hear. She's worked like a Trojan, though Carol helped too.'

Stacy smiled at Flavia. 'You're a star! Do you want to take your break now? I'll be here to help Alex for the next half hour.'

Flavia sloped off. She didn't seem frantically pleased at the prospect of a break, and Stacy remembered her thought that the girl was keen on Alex. Hm, might be best to limit Flavia's reception tasks.

'Is everything really okay, Stacy?' Alex was frowning.

It was nice of him to care, but the last thing they needed was worried staff. Stacy made her voice as brisk as possible. 'Don't worry. You know yourself life kind of spins away from under you sometimes, but yes, it's going to be all right.' She hoped... Stacy closed the Gala Dinner file and turned back to Alex. 'How's your mum?'

'Much better. She–'

Margrit stuck her head out of the spa. 'Stacy – got a minute? Now?'

Stacy hurried across the hallway. So much for helping on the desk. Margrit stopped her in the spa entrance.

'Mr and Mrs Andrews are having a real old barney in the changing rooms.'

The honeymooners, and heavens, yes, she could hear them, muted by the two doors between the changing room and the spa, but still, supposing someone else wanted to get changed? That pair would put anyone off. She hurried up the side of the spa and into the changing area. The couple were in the middle changing booth, the door firmly shut – not that a closed door was muffling the argument.

'…if all we do is sit around in hot water all the time!'

It was the honeymooning husband and he didn't sound happy.

'It's a spa, Craig, that's what you do here and anyway, it's our honeymoon! We're supposed to be pampering ourselves. We can sightsee any time.'

'Not in Switzerland, we can't. You're being selfish, Lolo. We should both have a say about what we do each day!'

Lolo? Ah, it was Laura, wasn't it? Well, now she knew what the problem was. Stacy tapped briskly then pushed the door open. The pair were fully dressed, and by the look of Mrs A's make up, they hadn't been in the tubs yet.

'Hello – is anything wrong? Can I help?'

Craig Andrews glowered. 'Nothing's wrong. Sorry if we're disturbing the peace. I'm going for a walk and my wife is going into the spa.' He thrust his towels into Laura's arms and marched past Stacy, whereupon his wife burst into tears.

'Oh, dear. Come and have a lovely soak. I'm sure he'll be fine after he's had an hour to himself and some fresh air.' Stacy handed over a tissue, and really, who was she to be handing out relationship advice?

Fortunately, Laura dried her eyes and emerged a few minutes later for a soak in the hottest tub. Stacy exchanged looks with Margrit, then left them to it. Time to get ready for the Gala Dinner.

Tonight's Gala menu was Fondue Chinoise, thin slices of beef and pork skewered on forks, cooked in a pan of simmering consommé at the table, and eaten with different sauces from little bowls arranged around the pan. There was a veggie option too, and several people had gone for this. Accommodating everyone's choice had taken a bit of table juggling. The guests seemed happy as Stacy walked down the restaurant, chatting briefly to each table as she went. Rico was doing the same, and Stacy noticed gratefully that Carol was on her side of the room, chatting to an Irish couple. Ralph had gone to visit his cousins up the Rhine Valley and wouldn't be back until late, so Rico wouldn't have to confront him with Carol beside him today, anyway. He was talking to the honeymooners now. The pair looked happier than they had this afternoon, though for once they weren't holding hands on or under the table.

Tonight's highlight was Peter the restaurant manager and his alphorn. He carried it out and set it up while the waiters were going round with dessert, and a little hum of conversation ran through the room. Stacy sat down at an empty table, remembering the first time she'd heard Peter play, down at the stony beach on a cold autumn night when she'd only been on the job for two days and the hotel was still unrenovated and Rico merely her boss. Tonight, Peter was wearing the traditional black trousers with a white shirt and red waistcoat, and a flat black hat with the emblem of his music club on the side between the Swiss one and the one for the canton.

Rico stepped up to the microphone. No one looking at him now would ever guess all the angst and heartache he'd gone through – and was still going through, for that matter. He was every inch the successful hotel manager, and a little stab of pride pricked into Stacy. She joined in the spatter of applause, smiling encouragingly when he caught her eye.

'Ladies and gentlemen, I hope you're enjoying the hotel's second Gala dinner. Tonight's guest isn't really a guest, it's someone you'll all have seen about the place – Peter, our restaurant manager. He's the guy who's coordinated all the lovely grub you've been eating this week.'

More applause, and Stacy relaxed. It wasn't just a case of they could do this, they *were* doing it, her and Rico.

'What you won't have seen is his alphorn, but here it is – you don't get much more Swiss than an alphorn, and we hope you enjoy the traditional melodies too. Peter.'

A nod from Rico, and the lights went down in the room, leaving only the dais lit. Rico came to sit with Stacy as the music started, and she gripped his hand. The first two pieces were relatively up-beat, then came a haunting melody that shivered around the room, echoing strangely through the old chalet. He'd played this one down at the stony beach, too. The guests were silent, then the final note faded and was replaced by a crash of applause.

'Thanks, folks. If anyone wants to have a go, be my guest!' Peter wiped the mouthpiece and raised his eyebrows invitingly at the room.

It didn't take long for an enthusiastic group of wannabe alphorn players to gather on the dais, and the resulting red faces and rude noises that parped through the restaurant in the next half hour had Stacy – and everyone else – in stitches. This was what these guests would take away with them, and what better encouragement to come back one day for a second visit? The evening ended with another turn from Peter and applause from a group of people who'd gelled together tonight even more than the first week's guests.

Stacy and Rico stood at the door, saying goodnight as the guests dispersed.

'Good job, Mrs.' Rico hugged her, and Stacy's breath caught.

'Let's leave them to it. Peter's in charge tonight.' She took his hand on the way up to the flat. Surely they were going to be all right now.

24

Friday, 14th Decemer

Stacy put her head into the reception office, where Rico was scowling at the laptop. In some ways, it really did feel like back to business today, but there was still an uneasy undercurrent rippling through the Weber family, and it wasn't a good feeling. Ralph was being very quiet, and as far as she'd seen there had been no heart-to-heart chat between him and Rico. Okay, guys weren't big on the emotional stuff, but they'd have to thrash this out eventually. Poor Carol was caught in the middle; the woman had positively slunk past into the spa this morning. They'd have to do better than this.

She went into the office and peered over Rico's shoulder. 'Coffee time? What's up?'

He jabbed a finger at the screen. 'We have someone in a wheelchair booked in for next week and I've just noticed they're in a room with a small en suite. How on earth did that happen?'

'I guess Alex booked them in without thinking about the wheelchair, but it's easily fixed, Rico. All you need to do is swap them with someone. 203 on the same floor has a large en suite.'

He stood up, still looking like thunder. 'It shouldn't have happened. Supposing I hadn't noticed? That would've made a terrible impression.'

Stacy followed him into the restaurant and signalled for coffee. He was right. There was so much to learn, and they were still finding their feet as a spa hotel. A bad review wouldn't help.

'I'll go through the computer and designate rooms as wheelchair-friendly,' she said. 'We've caught it in time, so stop worrying.'

Ralph strode into the restaurant, gave a little start of surprise when he saw them, then paused at their table. 'I'm just collecting a picnic lunch. Carol and I are going to Appenzell today, then tonight we're going for dinner on the fondue ship, so I won't be around much to help.'

Stacy put her cup down. He was avoiding them, wasn't he? But she was going to get this sorted soon or her name wasn't Stacy Townsend. She grinned at Ralph. 'Sounds lovely. I'd love to go on the fondue ship!'

'We'll do it in January,' said Rico. 'Enjoy your day, Dad.'

Ralph saluted and marched on into the kitchens, and Stacy exchanged looks with Rico. He was at least now trying to be supportive to his father, but the fact that it was so obvious meant it wasn't working and in a way, she could see the problem. If Carol made her home in Australia, Ralph was going to be hurt, end of. And after all the upset this week, it might be an idea to have a word with the other woman anyway. Stacy glanced at her phone. Half past ten; Carol would be out of the tub room now.

After coffee, she took the lift upstairs and tapped on Carol's door. The older woman was looking through a small selection of pullovers laid out on the bed.

'Stacy, well timed. Which do you think would be best for a trip to the Appenzellerland?'

Stacy went to stand beside her. 'You have a good winter jacket, so I'd wear the thin blue pullover and take the cardie in case you need it too. Layers are the best way here in winter. Your trip's why I came, actually. I wondered if you'd like to borrow some snow boots, so you could go for a tramp if you wanted to?'

'That would be kind, thank you.'

Carol folded the unneeded knitwear into the wardrobe, and Stacy perched on the bed. Now for it. 'Ralph's looking forward to your trip to Appenzell,' she began. To her surprise, Carol interrupted.

'And you and Rico are worried about him. I know, Stacy, because I'm worried too.' She sank down beside Stacy, her face unaccustomedly grave. 'I don't know what to say to you. None of this should be happening. I was on my way to visit my family, and when you're my age in my situation, your family is the most important thing.'

Stacy was silent. Carol was right, of course, but where did that leave Ralph? Wasn't love enough to make people into a family?

As if she had read the thought, Carol went on. 'Anyone can be family, of course, but you know – or maybe you don't know, but I hope you will, someday – the strongest love of all is the love you have for your children. I won't know what fate has in store for me until I see my son and his family. I hate having them so far away, so... I'm sorry, Stacy.'

Stacy felt like crying. She reached out, and for a brief moment they hugged. Carol's family came first, that was clear. Would she feel like that? Would she put her child before Rico? There was no way to know, and what it came down to for Carol was a potential new relationship versus a child and grandchildren on the other side of the word. It didn't leave Ralph in a good place, but it was up to Carol to decide.

She left the older woman to get ready, and popped into the flat to check her face after all that emotion. Help... she looked about a hundred and fifty. The weariness caused by the last week or so had settled around her eyes like a giant panda. Hopefully someone would give her a large parcel of energy for Christmas, that was all.

Reception was quiet when she arrived back downstairs, good. At least the hotel was running smoothly again. The thought had barely entered her head when the honeymooning Laura Andrews ran out of the restaurant.

'He's not there! He's not in the hotel!' She burst into floods of noisy tears.

'Oh, dear. Come in here and tell me what's wrong.' Stacy bundled the woman into the office, evicting Flavia, who was wrapping presents. She sat Laura down and passed the tissues.

'Is it your husband?'

Laura dabbed her eyes. 'Yes. We had an argument about what to do today. We're leaving tomorrow and I wanted to have a last time in the sauna and the spa, but he wanted to go out and now he's left me here alone!'

'Have you tried calling him?'

'He's not answering.'

Stacy rubbed her face. It wasn't her job to sort this, but the woman needed advice, nothing was more clear.

'You know what I'd do? Text him and say it's fine if you both do your own thing today, and you'll see him here for dinner tonight. Then I'd have my last sauna and soak in a tub. You obviously want different things for your last day, and there's no reason you can't both do what you want to.'

'But we wouldn't be together!'

Stacy patted her arm. 'Sometimes an hour or two apart is a good thing. Believe me.'

Laura didn't look convinced, but she dried her eyes and went off upstairs for her spa kit. Stacy fetched herself another coffee. She'd earned it, hadn't she?

***

The snowy hills of the Appenzellerland rolled against a deep blue sky as they drove through the village and on upwards, the lake view vanishing behind them to be replaced by hills and mountains that would look fabulous on a postcard. Carol gazed out as Ralph's car droned uphill, trying to swallow her apprehension about the gradient long enough to admire the way the glittering silvery whiteness of the snow was broken up by dark green splodges where woodland interrupted fields. Sun on snow was dazzling; thank goodness she'd brought her special super-efficient sunglasses, the ones she'd thought would be so useful in Australia.

Ralph spoke mainly about the places they were driving through, and Carol was glad. That conversation with Stacy had made her think. She couldn't decide anything until she'd seen Barry, of course, but the lives of so many people would be changed by whatever decision she made in the next couple of weeks. It wasn't just her and Ralph.

They stopped for a walk at Gais, and Carol gasped as she opened the car door and breathed in frosty cold air.

'This is the highest point we'll reach today,' Ralph told her. 'Unless you want to go up in a cable car again, but I think that's best left for another time.'

Would there be another time? Carol perched sideways on the back seat and wriggled her toes into Stacy's snow boots. Ralph was doing the same at the other side. She stood up and took a couple of careful steps. 'How high are we?'

'Over nine hundred metres, that's three thousand feet above sea. Cool, huh?'

Carol managed to laugh. 'Literally!'

The village was beautiful – typical white houses in the village centre, four or five storeys high with curved gable roofs joined onto each other. It was the poshest terrace anyone could imagine. Deep snow lay everywhere, giving the place a fairy-tale Christmas-card appearance. They stamped around the village square and had a look at the church, which was lovely, though less ornate than the cathedral in St Gallen. Half an hour was enough, then Ralph's car tour continued downhill into the next valley where Appenzell was. Carol gasped as the Säntis, along with the entire Alpstein range, filled the windscreen. Real, proper snowy mountains and so close. This truly was Switzerland. They stopped for photos, then went on to the village, where they parked by the church.

Ralph led the way along a little track to a cold sunny bench by a river. 'Time for a Lakeside lunch.'

Carol accepted a ham and pickle roll and a cup of tomato soup from a flask. She was having a December picnic outdoors in Switzerland, how surreal was this? And this man – being here, with him, was all she wanted from today, and yes, her heart was beating faster, but oh, was it enough? They *were* on the same wavelength. He knew she needed time and was respecting that. Didn't that show they could have a future?

'Thank you for today,' she said, when they were on the way home again, driving along the main street in Teufen with the mountains in bright sunshine to her left. 'It's given me a wonderful sense of the place. It's beautiful.'

Ralph gave her an odd little smile and pulled up for her to take yet another photo. 'Something to tell your grandchildren.'

A strange thought struck Carol as they continued their journey home. Would Emma and Jonny ever see mountains and snow? The Alps? They would visit Europe one day, surely, but would they come to Switzerland in winter? And an even stranger one – if she relocated to Australia, would she ever return to see scenery like this again?

***

The fondue boat left from Rorschach at seven that evening. Carol stared at the ship, where coloured Christmas lights shone festively into the dark night as the passengers embarked. There was even a little Christmas tree on the front deck.

She'd done some thinking since she and Ralph had returned from their drive. The only thing to do was enjoy the rest of the time here in Switzerland, go to Australia and make up her mind where her life was to be. Then she'd be able to give Ralph a definite answer to the question that hung unformulated between them every moment they were together.

They settled down at their table on one side of the dining room in the mid-section of the ship, and the waiter brought drinks as the boat pulled away from Rorschach and set course towards Lindau on the German bank. It was a lovely, different kind of evening – in between courses they could go on deck to stare out at lights shining all around the lake as the *MS Thurgau* cut though dark water.

'If you'd come in summer we could have gone out in our boat, *Lakeside Lady*,' said Ralph.

Carol had heard about the cabin cruiser from Stacy. 'Do you serve fondue?'

Ralph chuckled. 'What do you think?'

For the main course they were having cheese fondue, and Carol smiled to herself. Different fondues two nights running... she really was in Switzerland. The starter was salad, and Ralph ordered a crisp white wine to go with it.

'Cheese fondue's quite heavy, and so is Fondue Bourguignon – that's when you get chunks of meat and cook them in oil in the pan,' Ralph told her, when the waiter deposited a large pan of bubbling cheese on the burner on their table.

Carol speared a chunk of bread on her fondue fork and dipped it into the cheese. 'Mm, this is lovely. Thank you so much for bringing me here.'

'I thought you'd like it,' he said, his eyes twinkling at her.

They dipped and ate until Carol could eat no more. She leaned back and sipped her wine, fanning her face with the menu card. All these burners made it hot in here.

Ralph stood up and lifted his jacket from the back of his chair. 'Shall we go on deck and–'

Whatever he'd been about to say was interrupted by Carol's phone ringing in her bag.

'Sorry.' She fished it out, then caught her breath. It was the airline. Fingers sliding on the phone case, she took the call and listened intently, hardly able to believe her ears.

'I'll take it,' she said, then ended the call and blinked at Ralph. 'They have a flight for me on Sunday at one, via Dubai. They're sending the details now and I've to check in online immediately. Oh God, I've never done that on my phone before.' She didn't miss Ralph's little start of dismay, but his voice was steady as he pulled his chair round the table so that they could look at Carol's phone together. 'We'll work it out.'

It was easy enough, but Carol's heart was racing as her boarding card came through and she saved it in her phone. This time on Sunday, she'd be well on her way. This time on Monday, she'd be in Perth.

'I'll need to pack,' she said, staring at Ralph. 'And email Barry.'

He nodded. 'I'll take you to the airport. You can leave your Switzerland case at Lakeside, and we can make arrangements about it when we know what you're doing about your return flight.'

Carol took a shaky breath. 'Thank you. Can we go on deck for a while? I need some fresh air – my second last night in Switzerland!'

'You're in German waters now,' said Ralph, holding her jacket for her to slip into.

Carol led the way outside and leaned on the rail, staring across the dark waters of Lake Constance. Clusters of lights showed where the towns and villages were – a large cluster for Rorschach, a much smaller one for Grimsbach and the other villages. Some of those lights would belong to the hotel. She shivered. This time on Sunday…

25

Saturday, 15th December

Rico switched off the TV and stretched. Two minutes past midnight, and Friday night had turned into Saturday morning. He should have been slumbering in bed beside Stacy a long time ago. Hotel owners needed to grab their kip while they could, not watch long films, especially when tomorrow – today, now – was the main changeover day. Still, this was the start of the final week of their advent programme; the end was in sight.

The flat door closed with a click, then Ralph looked in. 'Still up?'

He perched on the edge of an armchair, frowning, and Rico swallowed. What was coming now?

'How was the fondue boat?' He leaned forward. They had to talk about Carol sometime, and maybe this was an easy way in.

'Good. Same as ever. Carol got a call to say she has a place on a flight on Sunday.'

Rico blinked. Oh no. Ralph's whole posture was stiff; he looked like a man only barely holding it together.

'I'm sorry.'

'Are you?' Ralph stood up, then sat down again. 'No, that was mean. I'm sorry too. But Rico, know one thing. What Carol does is in no way influenced by you, and not by me either. It's all about her family in Australia.' He stood again and went to the door, where he looked round. 'You can put her minibar bill on me, please. We pretty much emptied it when we came back.'

'Okay, and Dad, I – I...'

Ralph smiled sadly. 'I love you too, Rico.'

Rico buried his face in his hands as Ralph went into his bedroom. What could he do now? Damn all. He took his mug through to the kitchen, frowning as the lift on the landing droned into action. Surely it wasn't supposed to be quite as loud? They'd have to get it checked; they didn't want a repetition of someone getting stuck in it. Or maybe it only sounded loud because the hotel was so deathly silent. He opened the flat door and stood listening. The lift stopped at the ground floor and Rico waited, but it didn't come up again with a late guest or two. Was someone going out? It wasn't quite the weather for a moonlight stroll. Someone leaving without paying their bill? Heck...

He grabbed his jacket from the coatstand and sped down the wooden stairs, realising halfway that he'd left his phone on the coffee table. Downstairs, reception was deserted and the restaurant area was in darkness. Rico stepped out of the front door and gaped at the car park. Nothing going on there, but a small figure was standing by the gates, only just visible in the light from a streetlamp opposite. As he watched, it turned and trailed back towards the hotel. What on earth...? It was the female half of the honeymooning couple. Laura Andrews, yes.

He zipped up his jacket and walked towards her. 'Mrs Andrews, um, Laura, is anything wrong?'

She clasped her hands under her chin. 'My husband hasn't come back yet! And he isn't answering his phone.'

Rico held the door open for her, listening to the story of the argument and Stacy's advice and the long wait all evening. He did his best to sound reassuring. 'It's only just gone twelve. There are still trains running, don't worry. Do you know where he went?'

If the bloke was having a look round somewhere remote, he might have missed the last connection back, but there wasn't much point in saying that. Mrs Andrews was upset enough already.

She shook her head. 'I'll try his phone again.' She tapped, with no result, and Rico was wondering what on earth he was supposed to do now when her phone pinged as a message came in.

'It's him!' She tapped again. 'Oh.'

Rico leaned over to see. *Missed bus from Waldkirch. Back 9 tomorrow.* Well, it was reassuring in one way, but the guy might have added a kiss. 'Good news, then. Sort of.'

She was looking daggers at him now. Rico ushered her into the lift, and she left it on the third floor with a muttered 'goodnight'. Whoopee, another happy customer,

Ralph was waiting for him upstairs. 'What's going on?'

'Guest AWOL, sorted now.' He explained briefly, and Ralph nodded.

'See you in the morning, son.'

He reached out and hugged Rico, and Rico hugged back. A proper hug. And the whole chilly Andrews episode was worth it for that hug.

***

Rico was still sleeping like a baby when Stacy woke up, so it was Ralph who told her the story of the honeymooning husband as far as they knew it. Heavens, you didn't half see life when you ran a hotel. She'd better try and make sure Laura didn't throw the furniture at Craig when he eventually appeared.

It was Alex's day off, so Stacy sent Flavia into the office to wrap a few presents in an attempt to pre-empt this week's orders. If they made a few sets and put them into the shop cabinet with a price attached, hopefully that would help. Meanwhile, she'd look after reception and sort out the January staff rota, which was way overdue, and keep an eye out for Craig's return. It was ten to nine now, so he could appear any minute.

She leaned over her iPad on the reception desk. With Rico starting his master's in mid-February, they'd need to have a general reshuffle of duties. Flavia was being promoted to part-time receptionist, and a new general assistant was starting in March, so hopefully it would all work out. January and February were usually quiet months in the hotel. Bring it on…

Carol emerged from the lift and marched straight into the restaurant for breakfast, giving Stacy a wave as she went. Stacy stifled a sigh. Ralph had told her about tomorrow's flight too, so this was the couple's last full day together. Not that they were a couple, and they definitely weren't together. She tapped a finger on the desk. Should they do something, a family – oh heck – a family dinner, or…? But maybe better not.

She was still mulling over the pros and cons of this when the front door opened and Craig Andrews came in. His wife must have been hiding behind the lift, she appeared so promptly, and Stacy didn't have time to draw breath before they were standing in the middle of the hallway hissing at each other. It wasn't what you'd call an amicable reunion, but at least it was quiet. She cleared her throat, and the two glared at her before stamping off to the lift. Well, they had an hour before they had to check out, and hopefully she wouldn't have to play referee before then.

One of the families who'd checked in yesterday was approaching the desk now, all jacketed up, and Stacy beamed at them. This was the Walker family – mum and dad with three-year-old Lily, who was so incredibly gorgeous it made you want to eat her up. Well, almost. But those shiny black curls and brown eyes were to die for.

'Hello! I hope Lily's cot was okay?' They'd had to buy a folding cot when the family booked, as the old ones from the hotel's previous incarnation had been disposed of in the renovation. Lily was only just three, and her mother hadn't wanted one of the two child beds the hotel had.

Lily's mother beamed back. 'It was perfect, wasn't it, Lil?'

The child nodded solemnly, and Stacy's heart melted. One day... The father asked about soft play areas nearby, and Stacy told them about the only one she knew of, in a shopping centre just outside St Gallen. It didn't seem a very 'holiday in Switzerland' kind of thing to be doing, but the Walkers went off quite happily and Stacy returned to her iPad. Maybe now she'd have time for–

'Stacy! Alex called. His mum's coming to help me make some gift packs. Is that okay?'

Flavia was beside her now, her face glowing. Because she'd had a chat with Alex?

Stacy gathered her thoughts. 'That's brilliant. How's she getting here?'

'Alex is bringing her on his way to Zürich. I can drive her home again if I can borrow a car.'

Hm... 'Let's sort that out later. Thanks, Flavia.'

So much for trying to keep Alex and Flavia apart. If Alex stuck to Zoe, there would be tears for poor Flavia. Stacy looked up to see the honeymooners come out of the lift, arms around each other and gooey-eyed all over again.

'We'd like to settle our extras bill, please.' Craig fished his credit card from his wallet, rather awkwardly as he kept one arm firmly around his wife all the time.

'Certainly. I hope you enjoyed your stay?' Stacy had to make an effort not to smile too hard.

The pair looked deeply into each other's eyes, then spoke in perfect synchrony. 'Oh, yes!'

Stacy watched as they left the building and tramped up the drive en route for the station. Then she laughed.

Rico come out of the lift, looking sheepish. 'Sorry I'm late. You should have woken me. Did I miss anything? What's so funny?'

Stacy wiped her eyes. 'Saturday morning on reception, that's all. Come on. Let's grab a coffee.'

***

Carol took the selection of chocolate bits and pieces she'd chosen to the cash desk in the *Chocolatier* she and Ralph were in. Hopefully this lot would survive the flight. The children would love those choc animals, and the champagne truffles for Barry and Diane tasted fabulous; they'd given her one to sample. Ralph had suggested coming here when she told him what she needed and it was a good idea, because she'd found exactly what she wanted.

They were in a busy shopping centre just outside St Gallen. It had the chocolate shop, plus a kind of posh Swiss souvenir place where she'd bought some great wooden animals for the kids and a few kitchen textiles for the grown-ups. Next, they were going to a jewellery workshop Ralph thought she might like, and then it would be home to Lakeside to start packing. She joined Ralph, waiting by the door, despair flooding through her at his kind smile. Less than twenty-four hours now…

'Ready? The jewellery workshop's on the top floor. Afterwards, we'll go into the city and have a last walk round there. We'll be back at Lakeside by four, don't worry.'

Carol managed a smile too. 'Sounds lovely.'

He took her arm as they negotiated the crowd. Saturday seemed to be the main 'do the shops' day in Switzerland too, and Carol was wondering aloud about Australian shopping customs when a shrill scream somewhere behind them pierced the air, and they wheeled round. A young woman was running back and forth, shouting while her partner dashed off into a nearby shop.

The woman was completely distraught. 'Lily! Lily, where are you?'

Carol's brow creased. 'They're guests at Lakeside.' She hurried up and grabbed the woman's arm.

'Is it your little girl? Let us help – we're from Lakeside too. I know what Lily looks like.'

Ralph was talking to some security people who'd arrived now. Carol told the mother to wait where she was in case Lily came back by herself, and looked around. What would a little girl find so intriguing that she'd wander off in a busy mall? The chocolate shop came to mind, and she was on her way over when an assistant came out of the shop clutching Lily, whose bottom lip was trembling violently.

'Over here!' Carol waved at them violently, then dashed back to Ralph and the mother. A few seconds later Lily was in her mother's arms and they were both in noisy floods of tears.

Ralph clapped the father's shoulder. 'Can we drive you back to the hotel?'

The young man looked at his wife, who was drying her eyes now. She shook her head. 'We promised her a session at the soft play area. I think we'd better do that. Thank you so much. I expect we'll see you later.'

The family moved off, and Carol looked at Ralph. 'Well! Nothing like a lost child to get your adrenaline going, is there?'

'I know... but all's well now. Come on. Let's finish your shopping.'

Carol took his arm on the way upstairs, but if that little episode hadn't put things into perspective, nothing would. Imagine if something like that happened to Emma. Or Jonny, and she was on the other side of the world, asleep in bed while Barry and Diane went through hell.

No. At the very least, she wanted to live on the same continent as her family. Tomorrow would be goodbye Switzerland, maybe forever.

26

Sunday, 16th December

Carol stood on tiptoe to check the top shelf of the wardrobe. Empty, good. She had everything. She zipped the large case shut, pressing down hard to get it closed. Not much space in there to buy something Australian to bring back to London, was there? But then, maybe she wouldn't need to. Maybe she'd be leaving most of this with Barry while she came back to sell her London home and prepare for the move to Oz. She stood the case upright and wheeled it into the corner. Now to check her in-flight bag, and then she was done. This really was the last day in Switzerland.

She tucked her passport into a handy pocket in her bag, regret flooding through her. Would it have mattered so much if she'd stuck to the original flight on the eighteenth? She'd have had two more days with Ralph. But then, it would only have prolonged the agony. They should have met in London a long time ago, then this might have worked for them. But not now, not here, and not like this.

Her phone buzzed, and she grabbed it. Barry.

'Hey, Mum! Are you on your way yet?'

'Almost. The hotel people are giving me a lift to the airport. We're leaving at ten.'

'That's kind of them. Emma's getting your room ready as we speak. You have floor-to-ceiling drawings and paintings. She's so excited, bless her. And so are we – and so will you be when you hear the news!'

Carol gripped her phone. The surprise news; what on earth was it? 'Give me a clue, you wretched man, go on!'

'Nope. But you'll be dancing in the streets, I promise. See you soon, Mum – love you.'

'Love you more.' Carol ended the call. Whatever the surprise was, it was obviously life-changing. She gazed around the room that had been home for the past couple of weeks, then wheeled her cases out to the lift. She'd leave them at reception and say her thanks to Stacy and the rest of the staff, then have one last, nostalgic look at the lake. Ralph said she might see it from the plane as they flew east; what would that feel like? Lonely, she decided. The sooner she was in Oz, the better.

***

Rico sat in the back of Guido's car listening to the rather strained conversation between Ralph and Carol in the front, and feeling like 'the biggest gooseberry ever', to quote Stacy when he told her he was going to the airport too. Ralph had said no the first time Rico offered, but later had a change of heart and asked his son to come after all, which told Rico plenty about how his dad was feeling about the approaching separation. Or perhaps the approaching goodbye would be a better description. Rico shifted uneasily as Ralph made a too-bright remark about their progress along the motorway and

Carol made an equally bright one back. Maybe, if he hadn't been such a prat, things would be different between those two, in spite of what Ralph had said about Carol's decision being about her family only. He hadn't made things easier for them, but it was too late to change that now. Too late. What sad little words they were.

Rico stared out of the window as the motorway swung past Winterthur. Even the weather was gloomy this morning, but at least it was dry, and no fresh snow had fallen overnight, so the roads were clear. Not long now until they left this road and turned north to the airport, and there was silence in the front of the car now. This was awful, but all he could do was sit tight and be there for Dad when he was needed.

Traffic was heavier now, but still flowing briskly, and a little over an hour after leaving the hotel they were pulling into a space in the Parkhaus at Zurich Airport. Rico accompanied the couple up to deposit Carol's case, disturbed by the drawn expression on Ralph's face. These two needed to have a private talk, and that was exactly what they couldn't do with him standing here like a prize lemon. Would they talk if he left them alone, or would everything remain unsaid, leaving Ralph with only the thought of what might have been while Carol flew ever further into the sky? This wasn't what he'd wanted for Dad; and really, the thought that Carol sharing his father's life would be infinitely preferable to this was pushing further and further forward in Rico's head. He'd been wrong...

'We have time for a coffee before you go through,' said Ralph, and Carol nodded dumbly.

That was it, no way was he going to stay here and ruin their last few minutes together. Rico reached out and gave Carol an awkward hug. 'I'll say goodbye now and have a wander round the shops. I'll meet you at the entrance to security in half an hour, Dad.'

'Thank you,' said Carol, and Rico left them to it. He and Stacy would have to pick up the pieces now, and hopefully Ralph would let them.

He mooched around the shops downstairs, then bought an espresso to go and sat in the central mall watching the crowds. Lucky people, off for Christmas holidays. He and Stace could do that – sometime. After his master's and after the hotel was so well-established that the managers could swan off over Christmas. In seven or eight years, maybe, and maybe by that time they'd have a troupe of kids to take with them. The feeling that life was whizzing by did nothing to make him feel better.

When the half hour was up, he went back upstairs to collect Ralph, and heck, he was early. Or they were late, because there were Dad and Carol standing in front of the machines where you scanned in your boarding pass. Ralph's hand was on Carol's face, his posture tense. Rico pulled up short and stood well back. He didn't want to watch this...

Carol touched Ralph's hand, her eyes fixed on his, then she wheeled round and slapped her boarding pass onto the machine. The barrier opened and she went through, turned round once, raised her free hand, and vanished into security. Ralph stared after her, his shoulders slumped. Rico walked slowly towards him, accelerating into a jog as soon as Ralph turned away and saw him.

'Did she get through all right?' He had to say something, and this would give Ralph the entirely wrong impression that he hadn't been spied on. But they were in the middle of an airport, nothing was private here.

His father had never sounded drearier. 'Yes. Shall we go for lunch?'

'Let's stop somewhere en route. Everywhere's busy here.' Anything to get Dad away from the airport. He put an arm across his father's shoulders as they went, and Ralph didn't object. This was tough.

Rico drove on the way back. They stopped for a motorway hamburger in a very crowded service station restaurant, but Rico was past caring what he ate. Ralph hadn't said much in the car, and halfway through the meal he looked at his watch and heaved a sigh. Rico's heart ached. Take-off time. He said nothing, though, and neither did Ralph. Stacy would be better at this – hopefully, the three of them could have a chat tonight.

It was almost three o'clock when they arrived back at Lakeside, and the moment he walked into the hotel Rico realised they shouldn't have stayed away so long. It was the Winter Wonderland tour today and Alex and Margrit were both away with the guests, leaving Stacy behind reception. A short queue of people was waiting, and judging by her pink cheeks and forced smile, poor Stace was feeling the stress.

'Where's Flavia?' Rico strode round the desk to help her.

Stacy jerked her head. 'In the office wrapping presents with Denise. Some people from the Alpstein Hotel heard about the spa shop and came in to order stuff to collect today. It seemed too good an opportunity to miss, but they didn't half order a lot.'

Ralph took off his jacket. 'What can we do?'

Stacy blinked up at them, and Rico's heart skipped a beat. Hell, she was exhausted.

Her voice was strained. 'If you two can man the desk, I'll get back to the spa. Sabine's holding the fort by herself.' She smiled at the waiting guests. 'Normal service now, people. Thank you for your patience.' She hurried off into the spa.

Rico worked through the queue as quickly as he could, glad no one was annoyed at the wait. He thought back guiltily to that leisurely hamburger he and Ralph had treated themselves to – but then, they couldn't have known that things would be so busy here. On the other hand, they'd been saying for ages that another receptionist wouldn't be a luxury. They should have promoted Flavia long ago, though that wouldn't have solved today's problem. Thank goodness Denise had come.

At five o'clock Maria, the evening receptionist, arrived and Rico left her to it. Ralph had already gone upstairs and Stacy – Rico glanced into the spa – was leaning over one of the tubs explaining something to a guest in the water.

He collected his jacket from the office and went outside to look at the lake. It was a good place to do some thinking.

***

Stacy left the spa at the end of her shift at six and stopped off at the desk, where Maria was on the computer. The Winter Wonderland people hadn't arrived back yet; hopefully they hadn't run into a traffic jam again. 'Any word from Alex?'

'He texted. They'll be back at quarter past.'

Voices were coming from the office, and Stacy went in to find Denise and Flavia making gift-wrap bows for the parcels.

'Heavens, Flavia, you should have gone home an hour ago!'

Denise smiled at the girl. 'That's what I told her, but she insisted on keeping me company until Alex got back.'

Stacy shook her head. It was hard not to think that Flavia might have an ulterior motive here, and she was *not* going to have one member of her staff making eyes at another who didn't want eyes made at him. Time to be tough.

She handed Flavia her jacket. 'Skedaddle! We want you here your usual chirpy self tomorrow, not tired out from making bows!'

Flavia's face fell about a mile and a half, but she said goodbye and left without objecting, and Stacy sat down in the empty chair.

'Denise, you're a star. We can never thank you enough.'

'No need for thanks. Stacy, does Flavia have a thing for Alex? She asked me quite a few loaded questions about him.'

'I think she might. It's not a crime, of course, and he's a lovely guy, but she knows he's with Zoe.'

Denise's mouth turned down. 'I'm not sure how right that is. He told me on Friday he thinks Zoe's going to end it with him. He'll be gutted if she does.'

'Oh no.' Stacy's heart sank. Zoe's career was taking her away for longer and longer now, and maybe she felt it wasn't fair, holding on to Alex, who had made it plain from the start he couldn't live in Zurich and leave his mum to cope with her agoraphobia alone. Denise was in a good phase at the moment, but you never knew what was round the corner.

Denise shrugged. 'I don't imagine she'll say anything before Christmas, but with the tour immediately afterwards... Stacy, do you think he'd have gone with her if I didn't have the agoraphobia?'

'I don't think so. He told me that partners didn't go on tours with the musicians. We can only leave them to sort it out themselves, Denise.' Stacy leaned back in her chair. The problem was, Alex wasn't dealing with it in any way except waiting to see what would happen and hoping for the best. Zoe's life and her career were only going to get more intensive. If she and Alex were going to stay together, they'd need to make some changes, and neither of them were showing any signs of doing that. Alex certainly wasn't, anyway.

Denise dropped the last bow into the box. 'Oh, I know. It's just tough, that's all.'

Laughter came from the front hall, and Stacy stood up. 'That's Alex and his party now. I'll see you next week sometime.'

The queue for the lift was halfway down the hallway, so Stacy headed for the stairs. Jeez, this had been far and away the most intensive couple of weeks since the hotel had opened last January, even worse than the floods of last summer. She felt as if she hadn't had a day off for weeks – and come to think of it, she hadn't, just the odd couple of hours when she could grab them. At least she wasn't working tonight. Roll on January and some proper time off.

The four flights to the top floor were a bit of a challenge, but at last she was stomping into the flat to be greeted by Rico, a glass of prosecco in each hand and a broad grin on his face.

'Madame.' He handed her a glass and she took it, gaping. What on earth was he looking so cheerful about?

He raised his glass and Stacy clinked and sipped. Cold fizz had never tasted so good. 'What are we celebrating?'

He pulled her into the living room. 'It's more of an apology. I shouldn't have left you for so long today without arranging someone to cover for me. But we can celebrate the most profitable two weeks since we opened, and – I have a surprise for you. Two, actually. Large and small.'

Stacy sipped again. She could get used to a glass of fizz after work every day… 'Okay. Spill.'

'The small surprise is a lovely hot bath waiting for you – or it will be if you give me a minute to run it. And I'll tell you about the second while you're soaking. Don't worry, Dad's gone to the Alpstein for dinner so you have the run of the family bathroom.'

'Is he okay?'

'He'll be fine. It's you I'm worried about. Scram and get ready for your bath.'

Stacy scrammed, not sure Ralph really was going to be okay, but they couldn't deal with that until he came home. Ten minutes later, she was luxuriating in a tub full of aromatic bubbles. By the feel of the water Rico had tipped in at least half of her expensive seaweed and citrus bath foam, but what the heck. She was soaking, she had a glass of prosecco in one hand, and her live-in lover and soon-to-be husband was sitting on the loo seat with his laptop balanced across his knees.

He gave her a cat-got-the-cream look. 'Alan called an hour ago to confirm that he and Emily are arriving on the twenty-sixth. I was telling him how we've almost bitten off more than we can chew with all our festivities, and he gave me a piece of advice.'

'What?' Stacy wiggled her toes in the water, feeling some of the stress of the last few days begin to slide away. Another three hundred bubble baths would have her feeling like a new woman.

'Four words – *book a holiday, Rico.* So I had a look online for some last-minute hols in January – how does a week in the Maldives, followed by three days in Singapore grab you?'

Stacy shot up in the water as he held the laptop where she could see it. Golden sand and palm trees… sunset over the ocean… an exotic cocktail – was it a Singapore Sling?

'Can we afford it?'

'Stop being so sensible and think about all those guests we've had this month. It's ten days, not even a fortnight, of course we can afford it. We'd fly to Male via Dubai, and on the way home we'd go over Singapore. Second week in January, after your parents leave. Bonza plan, or bonza plan?'

Stacy relaxed back in the water. 'Bonza? How much of that prosecco did you drink before I came up?'

'Two sips. Seriously, Stace. Seeing Dad and Carol say goodbye this afternoon made me think. We have to enjoy life now. We're working hard; we deserve something to look forward to. Let's do this.'

Stacy reached for the loofah. 'Book it. And then you can scrub my back.'

Maybe Christmas didn't feel like such a lot of work after all…

***

It was after nine when Ralph arrived home. Stacy was cuddled up to Rico on the sofa with the laptop, planning their time in Singapore, and wow, this was exactly what she'd needed. An evening off and the prospect of a holiday. The whole world looked rosier tonight.

Ralph's sombre face broke into a smile when he saw them. 'You two look like you've won the lottery. What happened?'

'We've booked a holiday next month. Palm trees and cocktails.' Stacy got up and hugged him. 'You okay? Want a coffee?'

'I'll get it. And great news about the holiday. This Christmas stuff is pretty full-on, isn't it? I was wondering if you'd like me to stay on another day or two, give you a hand?'

Rico's reply came almost before Ralph finished speaking. 'That would be great, Dad. Could you stay the week out? In fact, you could maybe stay over Christmas, too?'

Ralph reappeared with his coffee, shaking his head. 'No, I'll get back to Lugano and Guido at the end of next week. He's missing his car. Using my old banger isn't the same, apparently.'

Stacy's heart ached for him. He was joking, but he wasn't feeling it. He'd ignored her question about him being okay, and his eyes were so sad. Just looking at him was bringing a lump to her throat.

Rico passed over the laptop, and Ralph settled down in an armchair to look at the images they'd found of the Maldives and Singapore. He'd been to Singapore, and was in the middle of a story about running away from the aggressive air conditioning in the shopping malls when his phone pinged.

He pulled it out and stared, his cheeks flushing red and then white before he waved his phone at Stacy. 'Guess where Carol is now?'

Stacy thought for a moment. 'Dubai Airport.' But Ralph was staring at his phone again, oblivious to the world as he tapped. Stacy and Rico exchanged glances. Heaven only knew what Ralph was thinking. He'd loved and lost Edie, now he'd loved and possibly lost Carol, and Rico looked as worried as she felt. Stacy gave him a tiny head-shake, and he pulled a face.

She reached out and took his hand. Live the day.

27

Monday, 17th December

Rico clattered down the wooden staircase at ten to seven the following morning, having been woken by a snow plough clearing the main road through Grimsbach. If the road needed clearing, so would the driveway, the car park and the front steps, so he had an intensive bout of exercise in front of him now.

It was something over an hour before he was finished, then he walked around the car park throwing down the crushed gravel that was used here to make sure people didn't skid on the compacted snow. It was more environmentally friendly than salt, of course, but the downside was you had to sweep it all up again when the snow melted and vanished down the drain. Still, the forecast for the next few days was for dry sunshine, so this should last them the week out. He gazed around the driveway and aimed some gravel at the bottom step. Good job, Rico, and all on an empty stomach. Go and get some hot choc, you've earned it. He wiped his hands on his trousers, reflecting wryly that jeans weren't the best gear for this. The bottom ten centimetres of each leg were soaked through and now that he'd stopped moving, it was pretty chilly.

He kicked the snow from his boots on the top step and pushed the door open, to be met by a hum of talk and laughter coming all the way from the restaurant. Rico grinned to himself. The hotel had a different atmosphere every week, depending on the guests, and this lot were a younger, livelier bunch than last week or the week before. Logical, really, all the mums and dads and grandmas and grandads would be busy at home now, getting ready for Christmas with the family. It was the turn of the twenty-somethings to have some fun before Christmas, and the guy in the wheelchair especially was a real live wire.

Alex waved him over to the desk. 'Rico, quite a few guests have been asking about transport to a ski area. I was wondering if it would be an idea to run the minibus up to Wildhaus a couple of times? It's only three-quarters of an hour from here. I could take them after breakfast, come back here, then pick them up at four.' He pushed a list of names across the desk, and Rico's brain whirred. Twelve names... why not?

'Okay. If you can get this many, we could do it say, tomorrow and Thursday. Find out what the price would be on public transport and charge them a few francs less. Great idea, Alex, well done!'

And now to get out of his damp and chilly outfit. He glanced into the spa as he passed, then froze in horror. Margrit had an arm around Stacy and was leading her into the medical room, slowly, slowly, like two old ladies – what was going on? He charged in, only to be stopped very firmly by Sabine, the spa assistant.

'Rico, you can't come in like that.' She waved a hand at his wet trousers and boots. 'Stacy was just dizzy for a moment, that's all. Margrit's got this.'

Oh, good grief. But Sabine obviously wasn't going to budge, and there were no emergency vibes coming from the medical room. Rico charged across the hall and thankfully, the lift was here. He jabbed the fourth-floor button, connecting to Stacy's phone while the lift jerked up. Please, Stace, answer your phone.

She did. 'Sabine said she sent you packing. I'm okay, Rico. Just a touch dizzy for a moment. You know I've got low blood pressure.'

'But why did you get dizzy now?'

She giggled, and lowered her voice. 'If we'd spent more time sleeping last night and less time, ah, you know, it might have been more… restful. But you know what? I don't regret a thing.'

'Ah. I'm guessing Margrit isn't with you now?'

'Correct. I have a cup of tea and a biscuit and instructions to sit tight for half an hour at least. You can come and visit me.'

'With you in five.' He pulled on dry trousers and fresh socks and gave his hair a brush. It was reassuring that Stace was okay, but they were in a sorry state if they couldn't spend an hour or so making love without her passing out all over the place the next day. It was the work, wasn't it? Well, five days to go now and on the sixth, the hotel would empty of guests and they'd be able to relax. And plan how to do things differently next year. Rico set off back to the lift, which had vanished downstairs again. He pressed the button to recall it. Stacy wasn't the only one who'd had too little sleep.

The click of a door closing in one of the attic floor rooms came while he was waiting, and Rico frowned. Theoretically, these rooms were all empty now that Carol had gone; this was probably housekeeping in to clean. He'd investigate later. He had to get to Stacy now.

She was sitting in the medical room looking perfectly normal, and Rico relaxed. He told her about the ski bus plan, and she nodded.

'That's a great idea. We can keep the spa open an hour longer for them on those days, to give them a chance to soak away the ski aches and pains.'

'That would be more work for you in here. Thursday's the Gala Dinner, anyway.'

'And they're all going. I checked and it's a full house for the dinner. Make the ski bus tomorrow and Wednesday instead. I'll get Flavia to cover reception. With Ralph here, that should be enough, as the ski guests won't be around doing things here those days. We'll manage.'

They would, by working even harder than they were now. Rico left Stacy to it. A disturbing thought had come to mind at her mention of Ralph. He hurried back upstairs, taking the stairs this time, and headed straight for the room Carol had occupied. The door was an inch or two ajar, so someone was in there and it wasn't housekeeping, was it?

Ralph was sitting on the bed, his back rounded and a glass of whisky in one hand.

'Oh, Dad.' Rico dropped onto the bed and put an arm around Ralph, sick fear gnawing away at his middle now. Ralph had hit the bottle hard when Mum died. Surely that wasn't going to happen again? He nodded at the whisky. 'Not the best idea, you know.'

Ralph put the glass down on the bedside table. 'I know. I haven't actually drunk any, it was more – a crutch.'

'Have you heard anything from Carol yet?'

'Not since Dubai. I'm not sure when she'll be landing.'

Rico rubbed the thin shoulders under his hand. 'Send her a message. Then she'll have it when she does land.'

'She might not have time for it.'

'It's a text message, Dad, not a spoken convo. If she's busy, she'll wait until she does have time, but she'll answer it. And when you've done that, can you maybe help out downstairs? Stacy had a dizzy spell, so I want to ease her load today.'

Ralph looked startled, then reached for his phone. 'I'll be down in five minutes. You'd better dispose of that for me.' He nodded at the whisky.

Rico clapped his back and left him to it. He poured the whisky back into the bottle in the flat – no reason to waste good Glenmorangie, was there? – and ran downstairs again to tell Stacy to be just a little weak and wobbly today. It would do Ralph the world of good.

***

Twenty more minutes... Those long-haul flights didn't get easier, that was sure. Carol got up for a last walk up and down the aisle before they had to remain in their places for landing. She was stiff all over now, and while she'd had some sleep, a dull headache was tightening across her forehead. She rubbed her eyes. Better do something with her face, too, because right this minute, Barry and Diane and the kids would be driving towards the airport. How excited Emma would be, meeting Grandma's plane. Carol pulled out her phone to look at the photo of Emma and Jonny that Barry'd sent earlier. She'd soon be able to give them all the cuddles they'd missed this past year.

This past week, too. She touched her ear. No problems now, thank goodness.

The plane landed, bounced, then hit the ground again, and the passengers clapped. Carol, by the window, gazed out hungrily. It all looked just as she remembered, a shimmer of heat in the distance and the airport buildings approaching fast. Was Barry here already? But she could turn her phone on properly now. He always messaged when he arrived at the airport.

She tapped around, and oh! Barry had messaged five minutes ago: *In the arrivals lounge now!* And there was one from Ralph too. Carol hesitated, then opened it. *What a long way away you are now! Lakeside feels odd without you. Have a wonderful time with the children, big and small, and send a photo of the sea xx* Longing ached through Carol. If only, if only... She tapped swiftly. *Just landed. Good journey. Can't wait to hold my family. Will send a sea pic in exchange for one of the lake xx* And send, and dear God, how could she have left him?

The next few minutes were a blur as she gathered her things and followed the crowd from the plane, down through security and baggage reclaim and customs into a crowded arrivals hall and oh, oh, there they all were, waiting for her, Barry with a big grin right across his face, and Diane holding the little boy she'd never seen in real life, and an impossibly long-legged little girl who was speeding towards her. Headache gone, Carol dropped everything and gathered the child in her arms. This was why she belonged here. This.

***

'An outdoor aperitif before dinner?' Stacy stared at Ralph. It was a good idea, actually. The moon was shimmering across the garden, and it would be something different. The guests would find it fun.

'I'll organise everything, don't worry. We can put a sign up at reception, and see how many people take us up on it.' Ralph exited the spa, where he'd come to run the idea past her, and stopped for a word with Alex.

Stacy went back to her list. She'd barely been allowed to move from the medical room today, and while she appreciated that Rico was looking out for Ralph as well as her, it did feel as if she wasn't pulling her weight. She waited another ten minutes, then sneaked out. The spa was beginning to empty as guests finished their soak and went upstairs to get ready for the evening, and that was what she was going to do too. If there was an aperitif in the garden, she'd definitely be there.

Rico was already changed and downstairs, she knew that by the scent of his aftershave in the en suite and the absence of the suit he wore to patrol the restaurant in the evening. Stacy had a three-minute shower and pulled on black trousers and a green top, sloshed some minimal make-up over her face, grabbed her jacket and ran back down.

Rico and Ralph were setting up the floodlights on the terrace, and already guests were gathering, glasses in hand and woolly hats pulled firmly over their ears.

'Stace! You can stay at home and blob on the sofa – we'll manage fine without you!' Rico's eyebrows nearly hit the moon when he saw her.

Stacy sniffed. Nice. Lovely to know you were wanted and missed...

Ralph grabbed a glass of Prosecco from a passing waiter and passed it to Stacy. 'Blob on the sofa when she can be standing here sipping bubbles with lovely people like us? She has more sense than that.'

He winked at Stacy and she leaned over to kiss his cheek. Bless him, but all this jollity didn't seem in character. He was hiding his thoughts, which was fair enough down here, but hopefully he'd let them in when it was just the three of them.

Rico glared at his father, then winked the eye that Ralph couldn't see. 'Well, if she falls down flat from being on the go too much, you can carry her back upstairs.'

Stacy laughed, but he was acting too, wasn't he? And how sad it was that they had to.

She was even sadder five minutes later when Rico wound his way round groups of chattering guests on the snowy lawn and came to stand beside her. 'Seriously, Stacy, leave us to it now. Ten more minutes and they'll all go in for dinner, and you need some rest.'

Short of making a scene, there was nothing Stacy could do. And in a way he was right; she was absolutely done in. Nothing a week on a tropical island wouldn't fix, though, and she was going to get that. She made her way to the lift and stood waiting as dribs and drabs of guests passed on their way to the restaurant and their grub. A solitary sandwich was waiting for her upstairs, but the saddest thing of all tonight was that the closeness she and Rico had grabbed so briefly last night was a memory already.

28

TUESDAY, 18TH DECEMBER

Four days and four nights to go, then the first Lakeside advent programme would be over, and it couldn't come soon enough for Rico. He stood at the desk, fielding a couple of queries from guests and waiting for Stacy to arrive and take over. She'd gone into the spa to check something with Margrit, and meanwhile, Flavia was helping in the restaurant because someone was off sick and Alex had taken a minibus full of skiers up to the slopes at Wildhaus.

The front door swung open and an older man came in and strode up to the desk.

'Morning. I bought some stuff from your spa shop on Sunday, and I'd like to leave another couple of orders, please. I'll pick them up tonight.' He plonked an envelope on the desk and turned to go.

'Thank you – are you staying locally?' Rico lifted the envelope. The man had an English – London? – accent.

'At the Alpstein. Just off to spend the day in Zurich.' He tipped his forehead and left.

Rico opened the envelope and gaped. Oh, good grief. There were one, two, three... *nineteen* orders for assorted gift bags here. Either this guy hadn't started his Christmas shopping yet, or half the guests at the Alpstein had ordered more stuff; lovely for the bank balance but less good for the overworked staff. This little lot would keep Flavia even busier than she was now, which might not go down well when she heard about it.

He was right.

'I can't possibly do all this by the end of my shift and still be in the restaurant for lunches and afternoon teas and watch the desk while Alex picks up his skiers this afternoon!'

She glared at Rico, and he tried to look both boss-like and sympathetic.

Alex came in at that moment. 'What, while I pick up the skiers? Which I'm doing at four, by the way. And they all want to go in the tubs when they get back, so I'll tell them in the spa to expect an influx.'

'Presents!' Flavia banged the list down on the desk and Alex picked it up.

'Don't worry. I'll get Ma in, shall I? In fact I could go for her now.'

Rico nodded. Thank goodness Denise was so obliging, but they'd need to think up a way to recompense her. 'Ask her if she wants to come on the staff officially on an informal hourly basis as needed. We can't keep giving her jobs like this and paying her with shampoo.'

Now Alex was glaring at him, and Rico flinched. Jeez, what had happened to respecting the manager?

'Absolutely no way. You know my mother. A suggestion like that is entirely likely to give her forty fits and a major dose of claustrophobia, even if her contract is "informal as needed". Give her vouchers for the supermarket if you want to pay her more. At least she can pass these on if she wants to.'

He strode back out, presumably to fetch Denise. Flavia stuck her chin in the air and went into the spa storeroom with the list, and Rico was left at reception again. And as Dad had gone to pick up a drinks order from the wholesaler, he was stuck here until Stacy was free. So much for doing a stocktake in the bar.

***

'I want Grandma to hold my hand when we're jumping over the waves!'

Emma ran up the beach to where Carol and Diane were sitting under the sun umbrellas with Jonny, who was alternately letting sand trickle through his fingers and throwing handfuls over his dad's feet. Carol smiled and took the little girl's hand. Her legs still felt like so much cotton wool and her headache, which had returned full force in the night, was only just gone, but what did any of that matter? She was with her family and they needed her. Wanted her, too, which was even more important.

They were at City Beach, where there was glorious sand and the bluest sea ever, and plenty of shady grassy areas, though unsurprisingly these were crowded. They'd arrived early and found a spot on the sand near an outcrop of rocks, and Carol was content. It was hot, but all she had to do was sit on her deckchair and recover from her journey and the jet lag. Oh, and make sand pies and go paddling and help with sun cream and buttons and all the million and one things Emma wanted her to do, and it was all wonderful. She went down to the water's edge with the little girl, and they had a lovely time jumping over waves until Diane called them back for more sun cream.

'I want Grandma to cream me!'

'Give Grandma five minutes to get her breath back.' Diane massaged lotion onto Emma's sun-browned shoulders. 'Okay, you're done. You and I can go and choose some ice creams while Grandma helps Daddy watch our things, shall we?'

'Ooh, yes! I'll choose your ice cream for you, Grandma! I know all the good ones!' Emma grasped her mother's hand, and the two of them ran off up the beach.

Carol watched them go, smiling to herself. It was so odd, this Christmas in the southern hemisphere thing. There was a large Christmas tree beside the beach kiosk, tinsel and baubles and everything, and people were standing there in the ice cream queue with their bikinis on. It was a whole different world.

Barry settled Jonny's sun hat more firmly on his head. 'How's the headache, Mum?'

'Ninety-nine per cent gone. It's so lovely to be here, Barry, you can't imagine.' Carol stood up. The afternoon sun had shifted since they arrived; this would be a good time to take a photo of the sea for Ralph. She tapped, then sent it off with: *On City Beach, waiting for my ice cream!* It was late morning in Switzerland, what was Ralph doing? Was he even still at Lakeside, or had he gone back home? Well, she'd soon see if he sent a photo back. Lake Lugano was apparently quite different to Lake Constance. Her phone pinged a moment later. *Give me 5...*

Carol sat back, and smiled at Barry. 'They wanted a pic of the sea at the hotel.'

'Yeah, they don't have one of these in Switzerland, do they?' He stared out over the ocean, an odd expression on his face.

Now might be a good time. If you didn't ask, you didn't get, did you? Carol leaned towards him. 'So what's this surprise you mentioned last week? Something nice?'

He laughed. 'Nice try, Mum, but it's part of your Christmas present. A secret, y'know.'

'Hm. I take it Emma doesn't know?'

'Too right she doesn't, and for reasons that'll become obvious later, she's not to know at Christmas either. This is a grown-up surprise and secret.'

Carol shook her head at him, but it did sound as if an attempt was on the way to get her living over here. That was something Emma shouldn't know until it was definitely sorted.

Diane and Emma came back then, and Emma leaned on Carol's knee, explaining why a Golden Gaytime was the best lolly for Grandmas and why she preferred her Bubble O'Bill. Warmth spread all the way through Carol. Yes, oh yes, she was loved, she was wanted, and that was enough, wasn't it? Her phone pinged, but this wasn't the time to look and see what Ralph had sent. She was here with her family, and she didn't want to be anywhere else.

***

Stacy pointed two guests who were in the spa for the first time in the direction of the changing rooms. 'When you come out, come to the medical room for a quick blood pressure check before you go into the water.'

The couple vanished to get into their swimming gear, and Stacy glanced at the clock on the wall above the door. Ten past twelve, she just had time to–

A shrill scream from somewhere in the hallway had her running to the door. Alex was at the desk with a guest, both rooted to the spot and gaping in the direction of the restaurant.

'That was Flavia,' said Alex, as Stacy sped past.

'Stay here. I'll call you if we need help.' Stacy ran into the restaurant, where around twenty people were having lunch now. There was no sign of Flavia, so she hurried on into the kitchen, hoping fervently that the girl hadn't burned herself. Flavia wasn't the least accident-prone person on the planet; she had already managed to fall through the kitchen floor in the year and a half that Stacy had known her. She burst through the swing door into the kitchen and stood still.

On one side of the room, Rob the chef was plating up for two waiters who were queueing for their orders. On the other, Flavia and one of the sous-chefs were... yes, they really were smearing mashed potato onto a large tray.

Three steps and Stacy was behind them. 'Did you scream, Flavia? And what in the name of anything are you two doing here?'

Flavia was white, apart from two patches of bright red in the middle of her cheeks. She nodded at a ring lying to one side in the middle of the work surface, then added another spoonful of lumpy mashed potato to the tray and spread it out with her fingers, not looking up.

'My great-grandma's ring. I was mashing the potatoes and I was nearly finished when I noticed a diamond had fallen out.'

'How do you know it fell into the mash?' Stacy lifted the ring. It was old white gold with four large diamonds set in a row and a hole in the setting where a fourth should have been. It looked valuable, not at all the kind of thing you'd wear to work, never mind in a kitchen.

'I was looking at it just before I started. I only got it on Sunday. My mum came for a visit. She'd been going through some things of my gran's at home.'

Stacy remembered Flavia's grandmother had died a few weeks ago. She nodded at Berni, the young chef. 'I'll help Flavia, you get back. Do we have enough mash for the guests?'

'Rob's doing more, so I guess so.'

He trailed off, and Stacy grabbed Flavia's arm before she added more mash to the already overflowing tray. 'Stop, stop. Let's put the mash you've already checked into a pan, then we'll see what we're doing. And first things first, we should put the ring somewhere safe before it gets lost too.'

Flavia looked around helplessly, so Stacy pinned the ring into her pocket in the meantime, then started sifting through more mashed potato. And hopefully Sabine was coping in the spa by herself…

'What if someone's swallowed it already?' Flavia was shaking visibly.

'What? You mean some of this went out to the restaurant before you… Help, that's all we need.'

'Two plates went.'

Stacy stared, then carried on with her search. She was emptying the pan onto the tray when Luis, one of the waters, burst through the doors and shoved a half-eaten plate of beef stew and mashed potato into Flavia's hands. There on the side of the plate, nestling between a chunk of carrot and a slither of meat and covered in gravy, was the diamond.

He patted Flavia's shoulder. 'Safely returned, one diamond, and somebody get me another plate for this guy pronto. He wasn't too pleased.'

Rob was plating up already. 'Coming up, but I'll take it out myself, shall I, Stacy? We should tell him there's a reward, maybe?'

Stacy thought swiftly. It was a good idea, but right this minute, Flavia was in no state to think about rewards. She compromised. 'Tell him I'll be out in a moment to speak to him.'

She ran her hands under the tap before going out to join Rob at a window table, where one of the few elderly couples staying that week was sitting. Poor Mr Reynolds looked as if he didn't know what had hit him, but there was a humorous glint in his wife's eye that made Stacy think this wasn't going to be too tricky. By the time Stacy had finished explaining, Mrs Reynolds was all smiles at the situation and her other half was looking mollified, if not exactly delighted.

'Your lunch is on the house, of course,' said Stacy. 'And I think there'll a reward, too. The ring has a great deal of sentimental value for Flavia. She was very upset about losing her great-grandma's diamond.'

Mrs Reynolds patted her arm. 'Oh, bless her, and thank you for lunch, but we don't want a reward at the cost of a young woman like that. The diamond didn't go anywhere near Phillip's mouth, don't worry.'

A few more words, and Stacy left them to finish their meal. She went back into the kitchen, where Flavia was washing the diamond in a small bowl and everyone else was doing what they were paid to do. Panic over and all's well, etcetera, but help, all that excitement had decimated what energy she had left; her legs were like so much jelly now and she still had the afternoon in the spa in front of her, and she should organise some kind of Swiss Christmas treat that three-year-old Lily would enjoy, and...

Stacy trailed back into the spa. Just three working days to go and then came the weekend; the hotel would close for Christmas and she would plant herself on the sofa and blob for a fortnight. Stacy grinned. Who was she kidding? She'd take a few deep breaths, reclaim a good night's sleep or two and party with her family. Oh, yes.

29

Wednesday, 19th December

Rico left his father having breakfast in the kitchen, and hurried downstairs. He'd been running late when he started the non-conversation he'd just had with Dad, and he was running even later now. How was anyone supposed to deal with their only parent who they loved, when that parent was refusing to talk about the issue that was making him miserable? He'd better see Stacy about it; she was downstairs already so she'd missed the breakfast table chat.

She was bending over one of the tubs, talking to a couple he didn't recognise, so they probably weren't hotel guests. Paying visitors, good. He caught her eye, then continued up the side of the spa to the medical room.

She joined him a few moments later. 'Anything up?'

'Dad's talking about going home on Friday. I'm worried about him. He hasn't mentioned Carol since Monday.'

Stacy sat down heavily. 'At least he has Guido and Julia close by in Lugano. You could have a word with them, maybe?'

Rico sniffed. 'You know what these two are like. Watching his brother all cosied up with the love of his life isn't going to cheer Dad up, and it won't distract him, either. He won't even have work to go to, because Guido always closes the boatyard for three weeks at this time of year. Michael and Salome are coming this year too, so they'll be all family together and Dad will be alone. I so wish I'd been more… more encouraging about Carol from the start, then he might confide in me now.'

'I'll have a word. He might open up to me now, you never know. But if Carol's going to make her home in Australia, none of us can be much help to Ralph, unless…' She stared at Rico, and his stomach dropped in very much the same way it would on a rollercoaster.

'Unless we persuade him to go too. Oh, Stace.'

She got up and shut the door, then came back to cuddle him.

A huge lump rose in Rico's throat. Oh, how could he deny Dad a life with the woman he loved? 'Maybe he won't need much persuasion.'

Stacy's phone buzzed. 'Maybe he won't. This is Denise, I'd better take it. We'll talk later.'

Rico glanced round the tub room as he headed back to reception. Most of the guests had gone skiing, so the spa was quiet this week. He stopped for a brief chat with the Reynolds, who'd found Flavia's diamond yesterday – what a nice couple they were. They'd searched Flavia out when they'd finished their lunch yesterday and demanded the whole story about her great-grandma and the diamond ring, which had been great for staff-guest relationships but meant that Flavia had done practically no work all lunchtime. Oh, well.

Alex was busy on reception, having returned from taking his party to the ski slopes, and Rico went into the office to send out the staff rotas for January. It would be a quiet month, but February was filling up now and he would only be working fifty percent after the middle of the month, when his master's degree started in St Gallen.

An email pinged into the hotel account – good, this was from Andi Schmid at the builders. Andi had project-managed the hotel renovation, and this would be about the boathouse rebuild. Yes, the first lot of plans were attached. Rico printed them out and took them upstairs to browse through in peace and quiet.

Ralph was still upstairs, taking some washing out of the dryer. Rico laid the plans on the kitchen table. 'Fancy a coffee? Andi's sent plans for converting the boathouse.'

To his relief, Ralph looked interested. 'Let's have a look, then.'

Heads together, they pored over the plan. The boathouse was on a thin strip of land between the hotel and the border of the neighbouring larger plot, and stretched from the main road down to the lake. Ralph had bought the plot years ago, mainly to stop anyone else buying it and building something unsuitable so close to the hotel. Nowadays, they only used one section of the boathouse for storage, so it made sense to turn the rest into a sauna and fitness room.

'It looks pretty good, doesn't it?' Rico lifted a more detailed plan of the sauna part.

'It does. You should put in hedges when it's done, and separate the part with the boathouse from the part nearest the road. There'd be room for another building there. Something for you and Stacy later, maybe?' He grabbed his washing and left the kitchen.

Startled, Rico, pulled over the plan of both plots and all buildings. Dad was right, there would be plenty of room for another building on the boathouse plot. They could build a little chalet to match the hotel, but only for him and Stacy. It was a plan for later, yes – but an interesting one.

***

Stacy pulled up the last chair and squeezed it round the desk in the office, joining Alex, Denise, Margrit and Flavia, who were already there. 'Okay, people. This is just a quick meeting to discuss how we go forward with the spa shop. It's been more successful than we could ever have dreamt, though it's meant a shedload of work we didn't really have time for, so I want to thank you all for your time and effort. Margrit, you've collated the orders?'

'Yes. I sent the details to you all on an email yesterday. If you look at the first attachment, you'll see what products were ordered in combination with what else. I've made a list of these "sets" of products so that we can always have a few of the most popular combinations on hand. That way, we shouldn't be so rushed again.'

Denise was nodding. 'I think you should sell the individual items as before, obviously, and then have five or six of the most popular sets made up, like Margrit said. If people want a different combination, they can buy the individual items and make their own sets. We could provide the gift wrap for people to do-it-themselves at a small price too.'

'And we should have seasonal wrapping,' said Flavia. 'Something different according to the time of year, like we're doing with the sticky stars and tinsel on the Christmas orders.'

'Good plan.' Stacy shot the girl a smile. 'Can you arrange the gift-wrap, Flavia, as well as the shop brochures for the guests? Which brings me to Alex's part in this.'

Alex sat up straight. 'I was wondering why I'd been invited.'

'Don't look so worried. You're the chauffeur again. We're going to have Denise working from home some of the time. She'll be here too, obviously, but any time that isn't possible she'll be wrapping the sets at home, and you can transport them here.'

Alex hugged his mother. 'That's a great plan. Isn't it, Ma?'

'I think so. I do try not to let the agoraphobia rule my life now, and this way, I don't need to worry about it.' She patted his cheek, and he rolled his eyes.

Stacy beamed around the table. 'Okay, team. We have Flavia on gift wrap and the brochure, Margrit on ordering stock and filling the shop cabinet, Denise on compiling orders, Alex on transport and I'll be floater. Sorted and thank you!'

The team filed out, chatting, and Stacy reorganised the table. Now to get hold of Ralph. She hadn't had an opportunity to have a word about his move back to Lugano. There was still at least an hour before he'd be thinking about lunch, so…

She tapped to connect to Ralph's phone. 'My spa shop meeting's finished – fancy a quick coffee?'

'I'm popular today. Rico grabbed me for coffee too, but you know me, I'm all about coffee. Only if you promise not to try and talk me into staying longer, though.'

'Promise. I don't promise not to mention it, though. Is that all right?'

'Perfectly. I'm upstairs – see you here in five?'

He ended the call before she answered. Eek. Had that gone well, or not? Stacy trailed round to the lift. Gone were the days when she'd run upstairs just for the joy of the exercise…

Ralph was already manning the coffee machine when she arrived in the kitchen. Stacy sat down and lifted the mug he set before her. 'One question, Ralph, then I'll shut up. I know you're torn in two about Carol. Have you considered joining her in Australia?'

The blank look on his face gave her the answer before he did. 'No, Stacy… no. My home is here. It's different for Carol, with her family there. My family's here.' His sigh came all the way from his gut. 'Take away the geography and the family parts and we might have had a chance, Carol and I, but as it is, no.'

'You might feel differently when you've had more time to consider it, you know. And I think you should have another talk with her, now that she's been in Oz for a few days.'

His smile was strangely preoccupied. 'Maybe I will. And now that's enough about me. Tell me about your spa shop meeting.'

Stacy complied, but her mind was still with Carol in sunny Oz. This wasn't finished yet.

***

Stacy shivered in the wind blowing across Rorschach Harbour. It was good to get away from the hotel for an evening, and kind of Ralph to treat her and Rico so spontaneously to a night on the fondue ship, but if she was completely honest, a blob in front of the telly sounded a whole lot more attractive right now.

The boat did look festive, though. Rico put an arm around her as they joined the queue to get onto the ship, and Stacy leaned in for a hug – and to keep warm, too. They moved forward in a general shuffle as people went up the gangway.

'Look – there's David in his wheelchair. I really admire how he deals with his life.' Rico pointed to a little group of hotel guests further ahead.

'I'm not sure he wants admiration, you know. He's trying to live his life normally, and he's succeeding, too.' Stacy led the way into the dining room of the ship. David had been a paraplegic since a skiing accident ten years ago, but it hadn't stopped him completing his training as a lawyer and going on to have a wife and family. She sat down, feeling the thrum beneath her as the ship's engines started. Minutes later, they were moving away from the shore, and Stacy leaned back. Maybe this would be fun after all.

It *was* fun, and it felt good too that they were having a proper 'date night'. The Lakeside guests were at the other end of the room so it really was just the two of them, dipping their forks into the cheese fondue and nibbling. They went on deck after dessert, and Stacy stood gazing out at the German bank, the one they normally only saw at a distance. All too soon the boat turned away to start the journey back to the Swiss side of the lake.

Rico pulled at her arm. 'Let's have coffee in the bar, in the comfy seats.'

The bar was warm, and Stacy shrugged out of her jacket. 'I'll just pop down to the ladies – you can order me an espresso.'

She glanced at her watch on the way back. Ten past ten, they'd be home soon. Tomorrow was the final Gala Dinner, and on Friday the first guests would be leaving. They'd made it through the Advent programme, and–

She stopped beside their place in the bar, a grin spreading across her face. Rico was lounging in his 'comfy seat', his head resting on the wall behind him, eyes closed and snoring gently. She slid in beside him and lifted her coffee cup. At least he'd had time to order, before he nodded off... She'd leave him to snooze until they were back at Rorschach. He deserved it.

30

THURSDAY, 20TH DECEMBER

Carol's hands slid on the handles of Jonny's buggy, and she moved across to the shady side of the street. It was almost thirty degrees already. They stopped to look at a Christmas display in a shoe shop, with little Santas and artificial snow in between the shoes, and Carol gaped at it silently. Somehow, Christmas was more Christmassy when your fingers were freezing and you couldn't feel your feet. Or maybe she was too set in her ways to appreciate this, and for heaven's sake – if that was it, she should learn to be more flexible. Being set in your ways was for old people. Or maybe it was because all her old, happy, nostalgic family Christmases had been in cold weather, and this just didn't feel the same. They strolled on, and she showed Jonny a banner of the three wise men stretching across the street, and now it was his turn to gape silently. Carol grinned, and checked the time. Twenty to six, better get a wiggle on. They were meeting Diane and Emma at six after Emma's visit to the dentist, and having to run in this heat wasn't part of her game plan.

Her phone rang while they were marching along Hay Street Mall, dodging shoppers laden with bags and parcels. Oh, my. It was Ralph. Carol grabbed a bench in the patchy shade of a – was it a plane tree?

Jonny was half asleep now, so she'd have peace of a sort to talk to Ralph.

His voice in her ear didn't sound like half a world away. 'How's sunny Australia?'

'Hot. A little strange. But it's lovely to be with the family.'

A little silence, then: 'How do you feel now about possibly staying permanently?'

Carol gripped the phone. That was the question, wasn't it? Was being with her family worth giving up everything she knew and loved? Giving up on the chance of happiness with Ralph? She cleared her throat. 'It would be different, and a challenge, too. I'm not denying that, but I'd be part of my family again and not just a very occasional visitor. I can't decide yet, though – they haven't told me what the surprise is.'

Another silence before he spoke again.

'Stacy asked me this morning if I would consider moving to Australia.'

'And you said no. You want to stay with Rico and your brother.'

'And Lakeside. And Switzerland, and Stacy and any grandchildren I might have, one day. You see I do understand, Carol. I know it's your decision, and I know I can't ask you to return.'

What would she have done, if he had asked? But he wouldn't; he was a good person. Emotional blackmail wasn't his thing. He'd still be hoping she would come back, but if Barry's surprise was a one-way ticket for all her worldly goods, she'd be relocating as soon as she could. And if it wasn't... Suddenly she knew. If it wasn't, she'd buy that ticket herself.

A clock struck nearby, and Carol stood up. 'I have to go. I'm meeting Diane and Emma. Ralph – please stay in touch?' It was a big ask; she was offering him nothing.

'Don't worry, I will.'

She was left listening to an empty line.

***

Rico wandered around the dining room, which had been set up for tonight's Gala Dinner as soon as they'd finished serving lunch. It all looked amazing; glassware was gleaming, candles were waiting to be lit, and they even had Christmas crackers – not widely used here in Switzerland, but as most of the guests were Brits it seemed festive to include them this week.

In two hours' time, everyone would be sitting waiting for their starters, and this time tomorrow, almost half of this week's guests would have left, and the rest would be having a final soak in the spa or a whizz down the ski slopes. This time on Saturday, the hotel would be closed for Christmas and he and Stacy could relax. Not before time, too.

Stacy appeared and linked arms, and Rico almost jumped. Someone must have slept well... and how very good it would be to sleep well every night, and get their energy and their old life back. He raised an eyebrow at her, and she grinned cheerfully.

'Looks totally fab, doesn't it?'

'It does. And after today, do you know when it'll next look so totally fab?'

Stacy looked blank. 'Someone's birthday? Or do you mean our wedding? That'll be ages away, though. We should have it in the slow season after autumn.'

He shook his head at her. 'Oh sensible Stacy... Why? We can have it in the slightly less slow season before the summer hols. Wouldn't you rather be a June bride?'

A grin spread over her face. 'Perhaps I would. Oh, Mum'll be pleased about that! Good we're talking about it now, because she'll want to fix dates the minute she arrives.'

'Dates for what?' Ralph came though from the kitchen.

Rico winked at Stacy. 'Our June wedding. We'll need to look for a replacement manager for while we're away gadding.'

Ralph slapped Rico's shoulder. 'He's right here. And the room looks wonderful.' He held up his phone to take a photo, then moved away, still tapping.

Rico pressed his lips together. Ten to one that photo was in Australia now. Dad hadn't mentioned Carol today, but then, why should he give his son a running commentary on what was going on, especially when it was nothing good. Heck. Ralph moved away towards reception, and Rico drooped.

'I wish I could see him happy again, and I really wish I hadn't been so negative about Carol at the start. It was just... Mum.'

Stacy slid an arm around his waist. 'Rico, you know he'll never forget your mum. Let's be as supportive as possible until Ralph and Carol sort out whatever they're going to sort out.'

It was all they could do.

Ralph turned at the door. 'Is someone coming to help me turn my Samiclaus outfit into Santa for little Lily?'

'I will. Get into your costume, and I'll join you in ten minutes.' Stacy moved away after him, and Rico grinned. Santa was visiting Lily and her parents – they'd arranged it with Mummy and Daddy first, of course.

Rico followed on to check arrangements for that evening with Alex, whose girlfriend was tonight's star turn.

'What time are you bringing Zoe?'

Stacy was still in front of him. 'Yes – are you sure you don't want to invite her here for dinner, Alex? We have plenty of room for two more.'

There was half a moment's silence with Alex glaring at the reception computer. Then:

'I'm not bringing her. Daniel Marino is. He wants to see her play at a small event, apparently. I'm bringing Mum to hear her, so if the dinner invitation still stands, she'd love to come. I hope.'

'Ask her carefully,' suggested Stacy.

The phone at reception rang, and Alex answered it. Rico pulled Stacy into the massage room, which was empty today. 'I'm not sure I get that about Daniel Marino bringing Zoe?'

Her face was bleak. 'You and me both. Okay, he's the head of the orchestra and her boss, so to speak, but he must have heard her play hundreds of times. Oh dear – I do hope she's not going to let Alex down with a big fat thump. It was always on the cards she'd move on, of course, but he'd be gutted.'

'Someone else to be supportive of.'

'Your dad always talks about the Lakeside family. I guess we can give Alex family support. I'll see what Denise thinks tonight, too.' Stacy pulled out her phone, checked the time, and dived off. 'It's time I was upstairs helping your dad, and we both want to look our best for the final Lakeside Gala Dinner of the year. You can have first shower. Come on.'

***

Stacy glanced across to the other side of the restaurant, where Rico was doing the same as she was, going round the tables, greeting the guests and wishing them a nice meal. It was a very hotel-owner thing to do – who'd have thought when she started her nursing training that this would be where she'd end up? Life was very odd, sometimes, and what they said about you never stopped learning was bang on. This Gala Dinner was dedicated to Christmas and while the guests were certainly enjoying themselves, the Christmas carol and violin-playing sections might well have gone down better with last week's rather older set of guests. On the other hand, Zoe was the same age as most of these people, so she'd go down well anyway.

A little glow of satisfaction warmed through Stacy as she arrived at the table where Ralph was sitting with Alex and Denise. Just a few short months ago, Denise had been housebound by her agoraphobia, and it was partly down to the hotel coming into her life that the older woman had managed to overcome it as well as she had. Denise must bless the day Alex started working here.

Stacy sat down briefly. 'What do you think of the Lakeside cuisine, Denise?'

'Every bit as good as the five-star hotel we worked in, back in the day. You should try for an upgrade for Lakeside, Stacy. Four stars don't do you justice.'

'That's on the list for next year. I'll tell Rob you approve, though. It's always great to have positive feedback from someone who was in the business.'

Stacy hesitated. Alex was listening, but there was a distinctly subdued vibe coming across the table, and she could guess why. He and Zoe had been so close until last summer when she'd gone to work in the famous Zurich Alhambra Orchestra. It was the dream of a lifetime for her, and the end of Alex's dream of them making a home together here by the lake. He could have gone with her, of course, and the fact that he hadn't found a way to do that maybe showed that the relationship wasn't as strong as it might have been. Stacy's heart ached for him, but what could anyone do? In the circumstances, Alex would have to be the one to relocate, and he wasn't doing it.

She moved on down the room as the waiters served the main course, which was the choice of Casimir Rice with chicken, or Malakof, a kind of cheese fritter. Most guests had chosen the Malakof, probably because it wasn't something most of them were familiar with. She watched as people got stuck in; it was going down well, anyway. When everyone was almost finished, she slipped out and joined Rico in reception.

He'd been pulling at his neckline, and Stacy immediately straightened his tie again. 'Stop making yourself all skew-whiff. You look tense – what's up?'

'Skew – what?'

Stacy giggled. Good to know her English vocabulary was still larger than his. 'Squint. It's one of Mum's favourite expressions. Tell me what's wrong.'

'Zoe's due to start playing in fifteen minutes and she hasn't – ah! Here she is!'

The front door swung open and Zoe came in, a tall, thirty-something man with dark hair and eyes hovering protectively around her. Stacy went to hug Zoe and shake hands with Daniel Marino. She'd seen him last October, when she and Rico had gone to a concert in Zurich, but they'd never met.

'Shall I tune up in the office again?' Zoe held up her violin case.

Stacy led the way in. 'Yes. Is this okay? There's water here for you if you want it, and you know where the cloakroom and everything is. I'll come and get you while Rico's doing the introduction, and if you wander down one side of the restaurant going in and up the other on your way out, that would be perfect.' She turned to Daniel to suggest showing him to a table, but he sat down on the desk chair.

'I'll stay with Zoe, then stand at the back to hear her, if that's all right?'

It didn't sound as if he was giving her much choice, but there was no reason he shouldn't do that. Stacy agreed, then she and Rico left the other two to prepare.

'He knows what he wants, doesn't he?' said Rico, his hand wandering up to his collar again.

Stacy slapped it down. 'I suppose when you're the head of a big orchestra you get used to deciding things about your musicians. But I know what you mean.'

Ten minutes later, Rico went up to the dais, and Stacy beckoned to Zoe, now waiting by reception. They stood at the entrance to the restaurant while Rico spoke.

'Ladies and gentlemen, this is the last Gala Dinner before the hotel closes for Christmas, and tonight we have a special guest for you.

Zoe Steinmann is the newest and youngest member of the Zurich Alhambra Orchestra, and she's here tonight to play a selection of Christmas songs for us. Zoe!'

Stacy joined in the spatter of applause, smiling at the little ripple of surprise that went through the room as the guests turned to see Zoe and found themselves looking at a slight figure with long dark hair and a mischievous expression. The first song was *Last Christmas*, and Stacy blinked. That hadn't been on the list of suggestions she'd sent Zoe, but it was going down well with the audience. Had Alex told Zoe the guests were younger this week? *Frosty the Snowman* followed and went down a storm too, and by this time Zoe had reached the dais. The lights in the room dimmed as she started to play *Oh Come, Oh Come Emmanuel*. The audience fell silent, and Stacy was blinking back tears too. Zoe always managed to tug at the heartstrings when she played, the way she immersed herself in the music, swaying slightly up there, a solitary little figure with a moving, passionate face, lost in the wonder of her own music. Stacy glanced over to Alex's table, but Denise and Ralph were alone there now, their eyes fixed on Zoe. Daniel Marino was standing at the back, pride shining from his face as carol after song after carol followed, then Zoe started moving up the other side of the restaurant playing *Silent Night*, which took her out. The audience leapt to its feet, calling for more. She came back all smiles, and played *White Christmas* then *Rudolph the Red-Nosed Reindeer*, which everyone sang along to, after which Rico came out with the bouquet they'd bought for her, and Daniel Marino ushered her out.

'Thank you, Zoe. Are you sure you don't want to stay for some dessert? You've made everyone's evening.' Stacy hugged the girl, who was standing now in her duffel coat looking about sixteen.

'We have to get back. I love it when I can play and people react like that.' Zoe beamed at Daniel Marino.

He took her arm. 'People usually do react like that when you play! Come on. Let's get you home.'

'Are you going back to Zurich?' Stacy was taken aback. Somehow, she'd assumed that Zoe would stay with Alex in the flat they'd once shared.

'Rehearsals tomorrow. Wish us luck for the big tour.'

Another smile all round, and she was gone. Stacy stared at Rico. 'Where's Alex?'

'I'll find him. You say goodnight to the guests.' He strode off, and Stacy trailed back into the restaurant and went to sit with Denise. By the look of the guests, no one was ready for saying goodnight yet. It was going to be another late one.

31

Friday, 21st December

Carol stretched her feet out, then pulled them back as her toes escaped the shade of the tree they were sitting under in Barry and Diane's small garden. Lunch al fresco was the family routine, then Jonny went for a nap while Emma played at something inside. Barry was at work, of course, he wouldn't be back until after six, but Diane was on holiday from her teaching assistant job until January now. Carol reached out and touched Jonny's head. The little boy was nodding over his empty spaghetti bowl. If she lived here, she'd be able to look after the children more, even with a part-time job. Win for her and win for Barry and Diane too.

Diane lifted Jonny and winked at Carol. 'I'll take this monster upstairs. Can you help Grandma, Emma? Show her where everything goes in the kitchen?'

'Yes – show me where the salt and pepper go,' said Carol, lifting the cruet.

Emma was all for it, and Carol loaded the tray with used crocks. How good it was to escape into the coolness of the kitchen after the heat in the garden, and oh, Switzerland and snow felt like a long time ago now. It was twenty-nine degrees here and it still felt odd, with the Christmas tree in the living room and little Emma all excited about Santa – poor Santa, having to wear a red suit and boots in this weather. The good thing was, it was a dry heat, which Barry assured her was more bearable than humid heat.

Carol sent Emma out with a cloth to wipe the table, then loaded the dishwasher. Half past one in Perth, early morning in Switzerland. The hotel would be waking up, people would be leaving today and Ralph would be making the most of his last morning with the family before he went back to Lugano. She wouldn't be able to picture him there. Maybe it wasn't wise to picture him anywhere. Barry hadn't said anything more about the surprise, and she'd told him nothing at all about Ralph. Was there anything to tell, really? They'd exchanged texts and photos of the lake and the ocean, but that was all. There was no way to involve him in her life here, and she wasn't sure he'd want to be involved, if she decided to stay in Australia.

Carol sighed. Four days to go until Christmas morning, when she'd presumably find out what Barry's surprise was. It definitely wasn't another grandchild or grandchildren, anyway, as Diane was diving around in her usual energetic way looking slim as ever and not a hint of morning sickness, which she'd had with both pregnancies before. Carol swallowed. It must be a ticket to Oz...

'What can we do now, Grandma?' Emma came back from the garden, her eyes wide and expectant.

Carol remembered the recipe she'd brought with her, and rummaged round for the flour and sugar.

'You can help me make some lemon and nut Christmas biscuits,' she said. 'Where does Mummy keep her mixing bowl?'

Half an hour later, they both had flour up to their elbows, and Carol was realising this was what she'd wanted from her holiday. Time spent with Emma and baby Jonny was so precious; they were growing up fast. Emma had a real Australian twang, and the sun-browned little face peering into the fridge to see how the biscuit dough was getting on brought a sudden lump to Carol's throat. What was more important to her – seeing her grandchildren regularly, or a second chance at love with Ralph? Because it could be love, and the chance was real...

She pressed shaking fingers to her lips. Whichever she chose, she would be devastated to lose the other.

She saw Emma staring, and reached for her phone and smiled at the child. 'Hold the fridge open and I'll take a photo of the biscuits to send to my friends in Switzerland.' Oh dear – was that really a good thing to do? But she and Ralph *were* friends...

The photo was sent before she thought too hard about it, and apparently Ralph wasn't busy that morning because the answer came back almost immediately, a photo of the forsythia branches they'd cut, tiny yellow flowers growing beside green leaves. That meant luck, didn't it? Carol hesitated, unsure how to reply. Maybe she'd wait until the biscuits were a stage further.

She rolled out the dough when the time was up, and called Emma to help cut it into shapes.

The little girl was intrigued. 'When will they be ready, Grandma?'

Carol pointed to the kitchen clock. 'They have to sit on the tray for a little while before we put them in the oven for ten minutes, then when the big hand's at the top, they'll come out and we'll put on the icing!'

Diane came into the kitchen and inspected the resting biscuits while Carol and Emma were washing the cookie cutters. 'Looking good, ladies!'

'Mummy, can you take a photo of me and Grandma with the biscuits?' Emma ran to pose beside the table.

Carol handed over her phone and joined Emma for the photo. The lump was back in her throat. How adorable her granddaughter was.

'Send it to Switzerland!' Emma jumped up and down beside her as Carol tapped send.

Emma stayed at her elbow to see what the answer would be, and seconds later, a photo arrived from Ralph. The Advent crown at the hotel reception, three candles burning now. Of course. This was the third week of Advent. The fourth candle would be lit on Sunday.

Carol slid the tray of biscuits into the oven and set the timer. Emma stood at the glass oven door for the entire ten minutes, watching the biscuits cook while Carol made the icing.

'I'll do this part – the tray's hot,' she said, removing it when the timer rang and setting it on a cork mat on the table.

'Oh, this is so nice. I've never made Christmas biscuits before.' Emma clapped her hands.

The biscuits were duly cooled and iced, and Emma posed for another photo 'to send to Switzerland'. This time, the return photo was of the snowy hotel garden.

'I wish we could make a snowman.' Emma ran to show the photo to her mother.

'We can't do that, but tomorrow we'll go shopping and see if we can find some silver balls, and hundreds and thousands – I have lots more recipes and some of them need decorations,' promised Carol, and Emma jumped up and down.

'Mummy! Another photo of Grandma and me!'

Carol laughed. 'Last one, then!'

The photo was duly sent to Grimsbach, and the return photo arrived quickly this time too. Ralph and Stacy in front of the Christmas tree in the hallway pinged into Carol's phone.

'Ooh!' said Emma. 'Look, Mummy, a proper Christmas tree in Switzerland! Can we eat the biscuits now?'

''Course we can. You take some plates out to the table, and Grandma and I'll bring the biscuits and some juice.'

Emma vanished, and Carol looked up from the biscuits to find Diane staring at her.

'Carol – is there anything we should know about?'

Carol took a deep breath. She wanted her family within visiting distance, that was crystal clear now. 'No. But I'll show you the rest of my Switzerland holiday photos later, shall I?'

That was all it was, a holiday. If she said it often enough, she might believe it one day.

***

It was the morning after the night before, and four and a half hours' sleep weren't nearly enough, even when you were supposedly young and healthy. Rico trailed downstairs and found Alex draped over the desk at reception. He'd been very non-committal about leaving the restaurant while Zoe was playing last night, saying he had a bit of a cough and hadn't wanted to spoil anyone's enjoyment. Rico didn't believe it for a second, but Alex had about-turned and gone to take his mother home without saying more.

Now, Rico joined him behind the desk and slapped the younger man's shoulder. 'Two days to go. We've nearly made it.'

Alex jerked upright. 'Sorry. Yes. I'm off tomorrow, actually, so this is my last day.'

Rico hesitated. Should he say anything more about Zoe? They were friends as well as boss-employee, weren't they? It would be odd not to… 'Zoe was amazing last night. Will you see her before they go off on tour?'

'No. Wall-to-wall concerts until the twenty-sixth, then she'll be packing, and they leave on the twenty-seventh. I won't see her again until summer, if then. It's over, Rico. I should have told you last night, sorry.'

'Oh hell. I'm sorry too, mate.'

Alex gave him a tight smile, then a couple appeared wanting to check out, and Rico went into the office. The break-up wasn't unexpected and it was probably for the best, but poor Alex. Rico shivered. Imagine if it had been him and Stacy, and she hadn't been able to give up her life in England… and oh, it was exactly the situation Dad and Carol were in now, wasn't it? Carol had the choice of a life with the people who'd always loved her, or a life with Ralph – did she know he loved her? Surely she must, but was it enough? A small cream cloth with something dark beside it was lying under the table, and Rico bent to lift it. The dark something was attached to the cloth and this was Zoe's, the rosin violinists used on their bows. Rico stood for a moment, thinking, then he opened the cupboard for the lost property box, and laid the rosin inside. Ten to one Zoe had another six of these at home, and if she didn't, she'd know where she must have lost it. Leaving it lying around for Alex to find would be cruel. Rico lifted the glasses and bottle of water they'd left for Zoe last night, and slid past Alex to take them to the kitchen. Talk about tidying up after the night before... Back at the desk, another couple had arrived to check out, and Ralph was helping Alex. And he should be out gritting the driveway before the guests all fell flat on their faces on the way out. Rico went for his jacket. The duties of a hotel manager were many and varied.

By half past ten, those guests who were leaving today had gone and most of the rest were in the spa. Rico went upstairs for coffee and found Stacy in the kitchen doing the same thing.

She blinked at him over the rim of her mug. 'Your dad's a bit quiet today. I hope you agree with this, but I practically blackmailed him into staying over Christmas. The forecast's rubbish tomorrow, and it's a long drive back.'

'I'm glad you did. If he's with us, we won't need to worry about him moping around watching Guido and Julia all cosied up and celebrating with Michael and Salome.'

'I know. I think that's the thought that's keeping him here.'

Rico opened the biscuit tin. 'I wish Carol would tell him what she's going to do. It isn't fair, leaving him in limbo like this.'

'I think he'd be the first to know when she decides, so I guess she hasn't decided. You okay? Are *we* okay, now?'

He gripped her hand across the table. 'Nothing the Christmas hols won't sort out, Mrs. One day to go.'

'Yup. And we know now what we won't do next year.'

'We do. We'll have the same kind of programme, but no more do-it-all-ourselves.'

She smiled at him, and Rico's heart leapt. It was going to be all right. For them, anyway.

32

SATURDAY, 22ND DECEMBER

Stacy was checking through the spa kits in the storeroom. Each guest had a bathrobe and two spa towels at any given time, and after a whole year in use, some of them were looking a little well-worn and often-washed. Shabby spa gear didn't go with their image, but the January sales were coming up, so a bit of shopping might be an idea.

Flavia came in with a basket and gathered up a few spa shop items. She rolled her eyes at Stacy. 'Last-minute orders. Mrs Beecham wants stocking-fillers for her grandchildren. Those tiny bottles are awful to wrap because we don't have cellophane bags small enough for them.' She plonked a selection into her basket.

Stacy glanced at her watch. 'Heavens, last-minute's right, she has to check out in just over an hour.' She stared at Flavia's basket. 'However many grandchildren does the woman have?'

'Only four. They're getting three each, but she wants them done individually.'

Stacy's mind was racing. 'D'you know what we could do? Start a line for kids. Just a few bottles, because we don't often have children as guests now, but people could buy them for their families. I'll come and help you wrap those in a moment, don't worry.'

She finished sorting through the clean bathrobes, added another two to the reject pile, then crossed reception. Rico was busy on the reception computer, and he gave her a 'nearly finished' look as she passed by to join Flavia in the office.

To Stacy's surprise, Flavia was sorting through the stationery cupboard. 'You can't have finished all that wrapping already!'

Flavia smiled sweetly. 'But yes. I had an idea. Rob has tiny cellophane bags for sweeties and things from the kitchen, so I, ah, borrowed a few.'

Stacy grinned. Rob wasn't in the building today, as they weren't serving lunches – or dinners, come to that. 'Well done. So you're okay?'

'Yes. Stacy, I was wondering...'

Flavia screwed her face up, and Stacy went in properly, closing the door behind her. By the look on Flavia's face, this was something more personal than present wrapping. Did she know that Alex and Zoe had split up? It was way too soon for her to be thinking any kind of thoughts at all about Alex, though.

Stacy perched on the table. 'Spill. I mean, what is it?' They were speaking English. Flavia's vocabulary was improving daily now, but colloquialisms were a stage too far.

'I was wondering if Denise would like to go to a book sale next week? You know I live near the library. They're selling books they don't need, and people can bring their own unwanted books to sell too, as long as they take any that are unsold away again. They're looking for people to help, and I thought I might go. Denise could come with me. I was going to ask Alex today, but he's not on.'

Stacy thought. At the moment, the hotel was the only 'outside the house' place Denise went to, but she might manage the library too, especially with Flavia there being a bridge between familiar hotel and unfamiliar library. So – a good thought, and if part of Flavia's motivation was to have more personal contact with Alex, well, did that matter?

'I think it's a great idea. Definitely suggest it to Alex. He could do with a boost at the moment, but Flavia – be careful.'

Their eyes met in perfect understanding, and Flavia stood up and put the wrapped bottles into her basket.

'In English you say, slow and steady wins the race. I'll be very slow, don't worry. I'll take these up to Mrs Beecham now. They have to go in her check-in case.'

Stacy stared after her. Only time would tell what would happen there, but she could hope, couldn't she?

By half past ten, the last of the Advent guests had left and the housekeeping staff had started the big clean up. Stacy closed the storeroom door. She wouldn't be able to check the rest of the spa linen until the washing came back from the laundry, which wouldn't be until next week. And reception was deserted, the restaurant too, and only the hum of a floor cleaning machine was coming from the spa. Stacy stuck her head in to see Margrit hurrying up the side of the tub room.

'I'll be off now, Stacy. The tubs are emptied and the medical room's tidy. Have a lovely Christmas – you deserve it!'

'You too! I'll see you next Wednesday, huh?' The staff were having a night out in St Gallen instead of a Christmas party this year.

The front door swung shut behind Margrit, and silence fell. Stacy stood savouring the moment. It was beginning to feel a lot like Christmas... And now to see what her menfolk were up to.

***

Upstairs, a savoury smell was coming from the kitchen, where Ralph was stirring something on the cooker.

'You're making your special spag bol!'

'To celebrate the first Advent in the hotel. Rico's gone for some panettoni for later.'

His eyes were bright, but his manner was downbeat. Stacy leaned on the work surface beside him. Panettone was traditional Italian sweet bread with candied fruit and raisins, and Ralph always had some at Christmas.

'Yum. You okay, Ralph? Have you heard from Carol recently?'

He smiled sadly. 'Lots of pictures, but few words.' He opened his phone and showed her a photo exchange from that morning. Carol was making Christmas biscuits, and no, there weren't many words involved. After the last photo, Ralph had sent: *What are you having for Christmas dinner? It's fondue Chinoise here.* Carol's answer was: *BBQ on the beach* with a cocktail emoji. It seemed a touch abrupt.

Ralph snapped his phone case shut and put it into his pocket. 'I don't think she'll be back, Stacy. I'd like to be... quiet about it, if you don't mind.'

He smiled at her, and all Stacy could do was nod. Poor Ralph. The door banged shut as Rico came in with one enormous panettone and three small ones.

'Enough to last until the new year, guys, even with all our guests.'

Stacy giggled. 'Don't call them guests, that sounds much too much like work. They're visitors. I'm looking forward to seeing Alan and Emily on Tuesday. And Mum and Dad at New Year.'

Ralph fished out a packet of spaghetti. 'Okay, boys and girls, eight-minute warning. Rico, there's a bottle breathing over there. Fill the glasses and get ready to celebrate!'

Stacy took her place at the table, her heart full of happiness and hope, and her head full of tiredness, and regret for Ralph and Carol. All they could do was make the best of it, starting now.

33

SUNDAY, 23RD DECEMBER

Tomorrow was Christmas Eve, and little Emma could hardly speak for the excitement of it all. She'd posted a letter to Santa a few weeks ago, Daddy's largest sock was ready and waiting to be hung up by the Christmas tree, and she was full of the secret presents she'd made at playgroup earlier in the month.

'One for Daddy, and for Mummy, and Jonny, and there's one for you too, Grandma! We're going to put them under the tree tomorrow, and then when Santa's been, we're going to open them all!'

Carol hugged her, a twinge of regret mixing in with another of happiness in her soul. Emma was four, and this was the first Christmas they'd experienced the magic together. What a waste. On the other hand, she was here now, and it would be this and the next few Christmases when the Santa magic was at its height. She wasn't too late.

Barry appeared from the garden. 'Emma, Mummy wants you upstairs to help her with a Christmas secret.'

'Ooh!' Emma vanished, and Carol laughed.

'You didn't have to tell her twice, did you?'

'Nope. Fancy a walk on the beach? We can stick to the shade, and there's something I want to ask you well away from flapping ears.'

'Another Christmas secret? I'll get my sunhat.'

The beach was a five-minute drive away, and Carol gazed out at the crowds of sun-tanned people milling around, enjoying the summer and the special Christmas feeling. Australians. Maybe she'd know some of them soon. It would be nice to meet some of Barry and Diane's friends; so far she'd only met the immediate neighbours, one elderly couple and a family with young children.

Barry pulled into a conveniently shady space by a willow tree and switched off the engine. 'Mum, I want to ask something and there's no easy way to say it, so I'll just ask, okay?'

Taken aback, Carol sat still. What on earth was coming now? It couldn't be the Christmas surprise already. Or maybe it was; he'd said once it wasn't for Emma to know until later.

'Ask away.' Heavens, she sounded quite trembly there.

'Emma was chatting to us yesterday while you and Jonny were upstairs, all about Christmas and Christmas cake and the cookies you were making with her, and she spoke about sending photos to Grandma's "man in Switzerland". Diane's wondering if... I mean...'

Oh, help. She was going to have to come clean about it, exactly what she hadn't wanted, but maybe it was best. Carol took out her phone and showed him the photos she and Ralph had sent on Friday. Barry stared at the exchange, and for the life of her, Carol couldn't think what to say.

'So who's Ralph?' he said quietly, lifting one eyebrow.

'He's the hotel manager's father,' said Carol, feeling ridiculously nervous. 'That's him in the photo with Stacy, the other manager;

she's a nurse as well. This is Rico here.' She swiped to a photo of Rico at the first Gala Dinner.

'And you're friendly with Ralph? Diane saw your face when you were sending these.'

Carol slumped. There was no way she could lie convincingly about this and she didn't want to, anyway. 'Yes. We – it felt as if we belonged together, Barry. And I'm sure he feels the same, but he's been so kind, not pressurising me until I knew if I wanted to move to Australia or not. I don't know what to do.'

Barry put an arm around her and hugged her close. 'Oh, Lord. I wish, I wish you'd told us sooner, and I wish we hadn't decided to keep our news for Christmas. You can certainly move to Australia, Mum, but it wouldn't half complicate things having you on the other side of the world.'

Carol leaned back to see him properly. What on earth did he mean?

Barry continued, the glimmer of a smile on his face. 'It's your Christmas surprise, but I think I'd better tell you now – we're leaving Oz this spring.'

It was the last thing Carol had expected. 'Oh! But – why? – and where are you moving to?'

He was smiling from ear to ear now. 'The company's expanding into Europe next year, and they reckon I'm the right guy to start the new branch – in Munich.'

For a moment Carol was speechless, then she began to sob helplessly.

She could have it all. Her family, Ralph, the hotel... Lugano, which she'd never even seen yet. For Munich and Lakeside were only a couple of car-hours apart.

***

That evening, Carol sat in her room adding the photos they'd made that day to her 'Christmas in Oz' folder on her netbook. The first Australian Christmas all together, and the last. Barry had a selfie stick, and he'd taken one very nice photo of the five of them and the Christmas tree. She would send that to Ralph, with her news. Or – no, she'd do it tomorrow. They exchanged presents on the twenty-fourth in Switzerland, so her news would be his present, and oh, she could send something more personal now without worrying if the sadness of it all was going to drown her. She tapped: *Stand by for a Christmas surprise tomorrow*, then hesitated before adding *x* and sending it off.

It was ten minutes before the reply came, a surprised face smiley and *A nice one, I hope? X* pinged into Carol's phone.

I think so. Wait and see! X went back to Switzerland, and Ralph replied with a finger-drumming GIF. Carol laughed. How amazing, she could laugh now and look forward to seeing him again.

Emma came in and plonked herself down on the bed. 'Daddy said it's Christmas in Switzerland tomorrow. Is it tomorrow in Switzerland yet?'

Carol hid a smile. Emma was fascinated by the thought that time had a different meaning in Switzerland. 'No, tomorrow starts here first. It's after lunch in Switzerland now, and here it's nearly your bedtime.'

'Will they be opening their presents from Santa tomorrow?'

Whoops, thought Carol. Carefully does it... 'Santa doesn't leave presents in Switzerland. He has a helper there, you see, called the Christ Child, and he's the one who brings the presents, after dinner on Christmas Eve. That means Santa has more time for children in Australia, and other places.'

Fortunately, Emma accepted this and ran off to clean her teeth when Barry called her. Carol went back to the netbook. This might be a good time to book her return flight.

34

MONDAY, 24TH DECEMBER

Rico gave a bottle of best fizz a polish and put it in the fridge for later. This was the big day in Switzerland, when families celebrated Christmas together with an evening meal – an early evening meal if you had kids – and then opened the presents that were lying under the Christmas tree. When he and Stacy had children, they'd need to fit in a visit from the Christ Child in between the aperitif and the end of dinner, but that would be a fun bridge to cross when the time came. This year, it was just the three of them. A nice quiet Christmas to contemplate their first Advent season and the plans for next year. Stacy trailed in on a cloud of shower gel and scent, and he sniffed appreciatively.

'Rico, I know I'm thinking this way too late, but it's just the three of us tonight. Alex and Denise are alone together as well, and I know they're having fondue Chinoise too. Maybe we could suggest combining forces?'

'Hm. I guess Alex won't be feeling much of the joy this year.'

'Exactly, and we don't want it to rub off on Denise any more than it will anyway.'

'You could call him and ask. Better coming from you, you can be firm and sympathetic in your usual nursey way.'

'I do not have a usual nursey way... but I'll call him now.' She drifted off into the living room, and Rico assembled mugs for morning coffee. Dad would be back soon; he'd gone for a walk by the lake. And what with Dad in bits about Carol and Alex in bits about Zoe and Denise worrying about the future, it would be down to him and Stacy to provide the Christmas jollity this year.

The flat door banged shut and Ralph came in, red-cheeked from the cold air. 'There's a little crust of ice along the edge of the lake, further along the lake path. We might be able to get our ice skates out in a week or two.'

'Wow. That would be really cool.' Rico went over to the window. The lake did freeze along the banks some years, and sometimes it was firm enough to skate on. It certainly looked cold today, the pale blue sky above and sunshine sparkling on the frosty tree branches in the garden. It was very Christmas card-ish.

Stacy came back in and accepted a milky coffee. 'That's settled. Alex and Denise and their grub will be here at five for fizz followed by dinner. I think he was relieved, and I could hear Denise in the background agreeing immediately.'

Ralph nodded. 'Dinner for five, then? Good plan. It's better when you're with others at Christmas.'

Rico pushed the Christmas biscuits across the table, searching for something to say that wasn't trite. Ralph's phone buzzing saved him from having to say anything, and he watched as Ralph tapped to open the message, his eyes widening as he read.

'Dad? What is it?' Rico stood up. His father was rigid, staring at his phone, his face a complete mask. This must be from Carol, surely she hadn't told him today that she was definitely moving to Perth for good. Not at Christmas. Rico clenched his fists. If she had, he would go personally down there and... he didn't know what he would do.

Stacy glanced at Rico, then put a hand on Ralph's arm and squeezed. 'Tell us, Ralph.'

Ralph handed her the phone and covered his face with both hands. Rico sat down again and slid sideways to see the message.

Merry Christmas! Barry & Co moving to Munich next year!! I return via Zurich 26th January. See you then! Xxx

A huge smile was spreading right across Stacy's face. 'Ralph! This is just the best news ever!' She got up to hug him while Rico leaned across and slapped his father's back.

'You'd better answer that, don't you think?'

Ralph grabbed his phone and tapped. *Merry Christmas! I'll be waiting. This is just the beginning xxx*

A moment or two later he chuckled, though his face was still wet with tears. 'Look.' He held up his phone so that Rico and Stacy could see the photo of Carol on a beach, a toddler in her arms and a small girl by her side. 'Kind of a different Christmas down there, isn't it?'

Rico got up and opened the fridge. That fizz wasn't anything like cold enough yet, but there were a couple of mini bottles in here somewhere too. He fished them out.

'Get the glasses, Stace. If this isn't a good time for the emergency fizz, I don't know what is.'

***

Stacy gave the fifth wine glass a polish and set it on the table. Finished! Their Christmas table was ready and waiting for their guests, no, their friends, to arrive. Rico was in the kitchen making the dip sauces to go with the meat, and Ralph was in his room having the longest Zoom session ever with Carol in Australia. So he was sorted, or he would be. Meanwhile, she and Rico had a week of no work apart from hosting friends and family, and it was going to be so good to see Emily again and catch up with all the news from England.

Ralph's laugh rang out from his room, and Stacy hugged herself. This was the famous first day of the rest of Ralph's life, and who'd have thought a few short weeks ago that Rico would be so happy about it? He'd turned a huge corner too.

Ralph appeared in the doorway. 'Your table's looking good, Stacy. And I heard a car outside just now. Let's start Christmas!'

Stacy ran down to open the front door of the hotel. Hopefully Alex wasn't too dejected, now that they were all enjoying Ralph's good news.

Denise had a bag of food in each hand. 'Merry Christmas, Stacy! This is such a good idea. I'm having my most sociable festive season for a long time. You'll never guess what I'm doing next week!'

Stacy raised her eyebrows. Had Flavia been in touch already? 'I never will. What?'

Alex handed Stacy two bottles and hugged his mother. 'She's only going on the library volunteer team. Flavia needed someone to help, and you know what a great reader Mum is. The best bit is, she'll have a ready-made friend there with Flavia, and I can be chauffeur when needed. It's a great idea.'

Stacy squinted at him. Bless him, he was smiling at his mother, pride shining from his eyes. It would take him a while to get over Zoe, but his feet were on the right path.

Rico and Ralph were waiting at the flat door, and Ralph immediately ushered everyone inside. Stacy put an arm around Rico as they went into the hallway, and he kissed her head.

'Merry Christmas, Mrs soon-to-be-Weber.'

She reached up and touched his cheek. 'Merry Christmas, Rico.'

Acknowledgements

Christmas at the Lakeside Hotel was a fun book to write – all those memories of Swiss Christmases when my children were small, and also the long-ago UK Christmases in Scotland. Children don't appreciate the hoops their parents jump through to create the Christmas magic, so I'll say thank you here to everyone who was ever a part of my childhood Christmases – I really appreciate it now!

Melinda Huber is the pen name I use for my feel-good fiction. In a different life, I write dark psychological suspense novels as Linda Huber. These are all set in the UK, whereas Melinda's books are set in Switzerland, in my home area on the banks of lovely Lake Constance. Most of the towns, villages and tourist attractions in the Escape to Switzerland series exist and are well worth a visit. The village of Grimsbach, however, and the Lakeside Hotel itself are entirely fictional – I wish they weren't! In real life, there's no space for Grimsbach "between Horn and Steinach", but the views enjoyed by Stacy and friends are the same views I see every day from my home a little further down Lake Constance.

I'm grateful to so many people for their help getting these books on the road. As always, love and thanks to my sons, Matthias and Pascal, for help and support in all kinds of ways, especially for their technical and IT know-how.

Thanks also to everyone who gave me help and advice about rewriting my original novellas, with special mentions for Helen Pryke and Mandy James for their editing and proofreading skills and generally for being great people with eagle eyes for mistakes!

More thanks to my writing buddies here in Switzerland, Louise Mangos and Alison Baillie, for help, encouragement and all those glasses of fizz.

Another special mention for James at GoOnWrite for the beautiful cover images.

And to all the writers, book bloggers, friends and others who are so supportive on social media – a huge and heartfelt 'THANK YOU. So often it's the online friends, people I may never have met in real life, who are first port of call when advice and encouragement are needed. I hope I can give back as much as I get from you.

Biggest thanks of all, though, go to the readers – knowing that people are reading my books is a dream come true. If you've enjoyed this book, please do consider leaving a rating or short review on Amazon or Goodreads. Every rating and review counts towards making a book more visible in today's crowded marketplace. Thank you!

(And to anyone who fancies a visit to Switzerland after reading this book – do it! You won't regret it.)

Linda x

ALSO BY MELINDA HUBER

Books in the Escape to Switzerland series:

Saving the Lakeside Hotel
Return to the Lakeside Hotel
Problems at the Lakeside Hotel
Christmas at theLakeside Hotel
Wedding Bells at the Lakeside Hotel

Standalone psychological suspense novels by Linda Huber:

The Paradise Trees
The Cold Cold Sea
The Attic Room
Chosen Child
Ward Zero
Baby Dear
Death Wish
Stolen Sister
The Runaway
Daria's Daughter
Pact of Silence

The Un-Family

Printed in Great Britain
by Amazon